Lydia's Story

The London Blitz Files

Kathleen Heady

NOTE: If you purchased this book without a cover you should be aware that this book is stolen property. It was reported as "unsold and destroyed" to the publisher, and neither the author nor the publisher has received any payment for this "stripped book."

This is a work of fiction. Names, characters, places and events described herein are products of the author's imagination or are used fictitiously. Any resemblance to actual events, locations, organizations, or persons, living or dead, is entirely coincidental.

Lydia's Story

All rights reserved, including the right to reproduce this book, or portions thereof, in any form.

Edited by Jake George (www.sagewordsservices.com)

Cover design by Sage Words Publishing
Printed by Sage Words Publishing,
(www.sagewordspublishing.com)
Copyright © 2012 Kathleen Heady

All rights reserved.
ISBN-13: 978-0-9859185-4-5

ISBN-10: 0985918543

Lydia's Story

DEDICATION

For Tomás, because he is the future.

Contents

DEDICATION ... v
ACKNOWLEDGMENTS ... i
Prologue ... 1
Chapter 1 ... 10
Chapter 2 ... 24
Chapter 3 ... 34
Chapter 4 ... 45
Chapter 5 ... 58
Chapter 6 ... 67
Chapter 7 ... 76
Chapter 8 ... 99
Chapter 9 ... 112
Chapter 10 ... 121
Chapter 11 ... 139
Chapter 12 ... 153
Chapter 13 ... 166
Chapter 14 ... 192
Chapter 15 ... 205
Chapter 16 ... 215
Chapter 17 ... 225
Chapter 18 ... 242
Chapter 19 ... 253

Chapter 20 264
Chapter 21 272
Chapter 22 282
ABOUT THE AUTHOR 287

ACKNOWLEDGMENTS

Thanks to my amazing publisher and editor Jake George, who has believed in me and encouraged me through two books, my husband Larry Brown, my daughter-in-law Catherine Fox, and dear friend Julie Horst, who read early manuscripts and gave me invaluable suggestions, and to my family, who didn't laugh when I said I was writing another book. Also thanks to Peter and Amanda Murphy for organizing two wonderful writing retreats in Wales, which was the inspiration for much of this novel.

Prologue

Henriette Picard rubbed her eyes and pulled the thin blanket around her small shoulders.

"Henriette, wake up!"

"Maman?" The little girl mumbled through the fog of sleep. She smelled the fire burning in the hearth and relaxed a moment listening to its crackling. For a moment Henriette thought it was morning, until she remembered that they slept by day and traveled by night. Her entire world had been turned upside down.

"Non, ma cherie. It's Lydia. Wake up and eat. We must go soon. Tomorrow you will be safe and we can all rest."

She sat up and a shiver passed through her slight body. With her fingertips she touched her ribs beneath her blue wool sweater, knitted by her mother in the last weeks before her departure, and which was still not enough to keep her warm. There had not been much to eat these last few months since the Germans arrived in France. Maman and Papa had grown thin as well, but from worry as well as lack of food. At ten years old, Henriette noted the new lines on their faces and their rare, sad smiles, and knew that that they feared the future. Many Jews had already been sent east, to German work camps. They thought they might be safe in St. Etienne, a small town near the coast of the Bay of Biscay. But the Vichy government seemed out to prove that they were as ruthless as the Germans, and the net was closing in.

Now Henriette and two other children from the village were on their way to Spain – to safety. She sat up on the narrow bed, pushing back the memory of her farewell to her parents two days ago. She did not understand why they could not leave with her. They had business to take care of, they said, and would follow soon. Her brother was in England, and they would all be together there soon. Henriette had seen the hopelessness in their tired eyes, and wondered if they believed their own words.

Lydia called again to the children to hurry. Lydia was an Englishwoman, tall and slender with brown hair, but she spoke French like a native. She told Henriette that she had two little girls at home in England, and they were safe with their grandparents. She had come to France on this dangerous mission because she wanted to help other children find safety. Now she came to Henriette, who had pulled on her shoes and tied the laces. She ran her fingers through her dark curls and felt the familiar tears burning the back of her eyes. With all her body and mind she wanted her mother's hands to comb her hair and tie it back.

"My comb will never get through your curls," Lydia said, as she gently smoothed the top layer of the little girl's thick mane. Her touch was light, but the comb still pulled and Henriette flinched. "Sorry," Lydia said. "My little girls have straight hair. Well, straighter than yours, and they have some waves."

Henriette bit the inside of her bottom lip until it hurt. She did not want to hear about Lydia's daughters right now. She wanted her mother, but if she could not have her, she wanted this kind English woman all to herself. She pulled away from Lydia's touch. "I have to go to the toilet," she said.

Henriette was the last one to run outside to relieve herself, and then she joined the others in the kitchen where Lydia and the farm woman, in whose house they had slept, were handing out fragrant bread and cheese, along with small cups of warm milk. Henriette hated warm milk, and here on the farm she knew it came directly from the cow. She gagged it down because she knew she needed her strength, and watched as the two older children drank their milk down without a qualm. There was a girl named Rose who was eleven, and a boy Michel who was twelve. Rose was several inches taller than Henriette, and had developed small breasts, which meant that she saw herself as a young woman. She barely spoke to the younger girl, and when she did it was to point out some babyish action of Henriette's, such as her inability to walk as fast as the others, or the way she reached for Lydia's hand in difficult sections of the trail. Michel liked to spend his time with the men who led the way up the mountain trail. He made suggestions about when to stop and eat and whether the "women" were getting tired. Jacques and Louis listened to him and considered what he said, but Henriette saw the men exchange glances, and knew they thought of him as a boy.

Lydia was stuffing more bread and cheese and a few apples into her rucksack.

"We need to go, children," she said. "Jacques and Louis are waiting for us."

Lydia made sure the three children were bundled securely in their jackets, scarves, hats and gloves. Since they traveled at night and had begun to climb in the mountains, the air was frigid as soon as the sun disappeared. As the youngest, Henriette received extra attention from Lydia. She tucked the little girl's dark hair behind her ears and pulled the scarf snug so it created a tight bond around her neck. Henriette inhaled the woman's smell as Lydia put her face close to hers. She did not have the same scent as her own mother, but her caring gestures reminded her of her mother just the same. Henriette felt tears in her eyes and blinked. She did not want Lydia to be nice to her! She clenched her fists, wishing she could hit this kind woman who came from England to escort her to safety. The effort to control this mix of anger and helplessness made her want to cry. She couldn't cry. Her mother told her not to cry, and even though she had given in on the first day and sobbed quietly when they left the village, she knew she must not. The older children did not cry, and Henriette did not want to be thought a baby.

There was a quiet knock on the door, and the farm woman, who had introduced herself only as Madame Claude, opened the door to admit Jacques and Louis. A rush of cold air came in with them, and they rubbed their hands together briskly. They were both of average height, with dark hair that looked as if they had not seen a barber in some time. Louis was thin and younger than Jacques. Jacques had broad shoulders and his stomach bulged slightly over his belt, although he told them he had lost considerable weight since the Germans had invaded France. He blamed the loss both on the lack of good food and the exercise he got working with the French Underground. They didn't speak this evening, but accepted the mugs of something hot that the woman gave them, nodded at Lydia, and smiled slightly at the children. Lydia had told the children that they would be in Spain tonight. Then they would be safe and could travel in the daytime. They were all looking forward to a good rest and good food.

"We're ready," Lydia said softly to the two men. Henriette moved to stand close to her. Michel and Rose saw her step near Lydia, and Henriette stepped away again.

"Baby," Michel said in an undertone meant only for the children to hear. "You shouldn't be here. You will get us all killed. You should have stayed with your maman." He glanced at the adults, who stood together in the chill twilight. Their voices were inaudible to the children, but their faces were serious.

Since the adults were otherwise occupied, the two older children moved to stand one on each side of Henriette. "Are you going to cry tonight?" Rose asked. "Like you cry every night?"

"I don't cry every night," Henriette answered, crinkling her face in anger.

"Aha!" Michel said. A quick glance at the adults told him that they were still talking, and he took the opportunity to pinch Henriette's ear. She stifled a cry, which she knew would only bring on more harassment.

Rose smiled in her superior manner. "But you do cry some nights. And I heard you crying in your sleep today. "'Maman! Papa!' you said. You know they will be dead soon."

"No!" Henriette replied, her voice louder than she intended. Lydia turned at looked at her, but said nothing. She was listening intently to Jacques and Louis.

"Never mind," Michel said. "We will probably all be dead soon." He looked around to see who was watching, and then pointed his forefinger at Henriette's chest. "Bang! The Germans will get you. They like killing little children, you know."

The three adults stopped talking and began to pull on gloves and scarves and gather their rucksacks. Jacques moved close to Lydia as they began to break apart and leaned close to whisper in her ear. Her eyes widened. "Of course," She turned to the children. "Remember," she began, her voice just above a whisper, but firm and confident. "Stay together. Walk quickly and quietly. Look out for each other. We will be looking out for all of you."

Rose and Michel exchanged a last smirk and Rose poked Henriette in the side. Even through her sweater, she felt the pain and the beginning of tears. She swallowed and stuck her tongue out at Rose. Louis saw what she did and frowned. He rarely spoke to the children, and Henriette had the impression that he did not like them very much.

Lydia adjusted her own scarf and shouldered her pack. She was dressed in brown – brown wool coat, brown trousers for walking and sturdy brown leather shoes. But her scarf was red. She had never said anything about it, but Henriette thought the English woman wanted a touch of color, of beauty, as she went about her mission. She admired that quality in her. People said the English were drab and boring, and had no appreciation of culture and beauty, but Henriette did not believe that was true. This sense of beauty that Lydia possessed made Henriette's heart reach out to her, but she could never let her know. Letting this woman know how much she admired her would be a betrayal to Henriette's mother, and the little girl could never do that.

Lydia nodded to Jacques and Louis, and Jacques opened the door. The three adults and three children slipped out into the growing darkness.

Jacques and Louis scanned the clearing around the house and turned their heads to indicate that it was clear. It was nearly dark, and a slight breeze had picked up, intensifying the cold. Henriette pulled her scarf more closely around her face. She hated this! They had walked through the forest for three nights, sleeping by day in a farmhouse belonging to a partisan. Last night they had begun to climb a steep path in the mountains, and they would do the same tonight. This was the last night. Before dawn they would cross into Spain, and although there was still a considerable distance before they reached a safe refuge, at least they could walk during the day and sleep in warm beds at night. And they would be safe from the Germans. Henriette had no idea why the Germans hated Jews so, especially Jewish children. She had never heard of anyone who wished harm on children. And although she knew that Jews were different from other people in their beliefs and customs, weren't they human beings like everyone else? She had never felt that anyone wished her harm – until now.

The group crossed the farmyard at a brisk pace and entered the darkness of the forest. The trees were not as thick now that they had reached a higher altitude in the Pyrenees, but Jacques and Louis knew the most hidden footpaths. The two older children stuck close to the men as they entered the wooded area. Henriette walked just behind them and Lydia followed at the rear. Lydia glanced back once at the house, where smoke curled from the chimney, before quickening her steps until she caught up with Henriette and reached for her hand. The little girl accepted her touch and tightened her fingers around Lydia's. Her anger was forgotten, at least for the moment. The dark forest frightened her, and she felt the tension of the group. Even though she could not see them very well, she sensed that Jacques and Louis were watching and listening intently to their surroundings. If they heard the slightest sound, or saw an unexpected light in the blackness, they would stop.

It had happened the previous night. The group had been climbing, just as they were now. They were about an hour into their climb, and Henriette was concentrating on placing one foot in front of the other. She was cold, and one of her stockings had slipped down inside her boot. It was uncomfortable and might create a blister, but she knew they would not stop just so she could pull up her stocking. She focused on lengthening her strides so she could keep pace with the older children and avoid being called a baby. She almost collided with Rose when Jacques and Louis signaled a stop. Everyone froze in place and made their breathing as hushed as possible. Henriette could feel Lydia behind her, and felt protected by the woman's presence. Jacques mouthed the words, "I heard something."

A gunshot blasted the air, but it was far down the hill. Jacques motioned to Lydia and Henriette to take the lead. That was what they did if there was danger. Lydia and Henriette walked ahead, followed by Michel and Rose, and Jacques and Louis at the back of the line. The men listened and guarded the rear, ready to shoot if they needed to. The men would protect the others, and Lydia and the children would run up the mountain and hide if they needed to. Last night they had not needed to hide or to run. They waited in the darkness, and Henriette began to count her breaths. She counted as high as 300 when Louis whispered, "It's nothing. Go on." There were no more gunshots or sounds of any kind that night, only the soft footsteps of the travelers and their steady breathing.

Tonight Henriette listened to the breathing as they climbed. It was more difficult than she expected it to be. The path was rocky and it had grown much darker as soon as they entered the woods. She knew that the faster they climbed, the sooner they would reach Spain and be safe, and she had the shortest legs and the most difficulty keeping up. But Lydia was always with her, urging her along with a smile. It was pitch dark when Jacques stopped and motioned for them to rest for a few moments. They had reached a clearing where a sliver of moonlight allowed them to see the outlines of each other's bodies, although their faces were still obscured.

Louis gathered them all together in a tight circle and whispered, "You may sit and rest, but only for a few minutes. We have about an hour more of hiking before we are close enough to the border that the Spanish patrols can offer us some cover." He smiled at the children, and Henriette recognized kindness in his face, kindness and a deep tiredness. Just like her father. Louis nodded to Lydia. "Water? Maybe a little bread?"

They passed around the canteen that Jacques carried in his pack. Lydia handed them each a chunk of the bread, along with a small slice of cheese that had come from the farmhouse.

The two older children were wide-eyed and quiet. They were almost there, and the tension had built to the point where everyone wanted to move. The adults knew the danger was greater now than the first two nights of their travel. There were not many Nazi patrols in this region, but the risk was great enough that the travelers could not risk a moment of relaxation. Jacques, Louis and Lydia munched quietly on the bread and cheese and took cautious sips of water. They watched the children, who copied the manner of the adults and chewed almost silently, their small jaws working until they were able to swallow.

Louis paused mid-chew and flared his nostrils, tasting the air. He mouthed the word "smoke." Lydia and Jacques met his eyes. They smelled it, too. Louis shoved the last of his food in his mouth and picked up his pack. "Time to go," Lydia said to the children in a barely audible whisper.

The three children swallowed down the last bites of food and looked at Jacques. He nodded and turned, leading the way up the mountain on the path, almost invisible now in the darkness. Lydia turned to look down the mountain. Did she hear footsteps? Her imagination, she decided. She grasped Henriette's hand and hurried after the rest, taking steps as long as she dared without losing the small girl at her side.

The climb grew steeper but Jacques and Louis kept the pace steady. Henriette could tell by the set of their backs that they were worried. The only place near enough for them to be able to smell the smoke was the farmhouse where they slept that day. Henriette looked at Lydia and could tell that she, too, was heartsick that their presence could have brought tragedy on the kind woman who sheltered them, but she pushed away the thought and concentrated on putting one foot ahead of the other and keeping hold of Lydia's hand.

A gunshot blasted the night somewhere down the mountain, but not far enough. The men increased their already grueling pace. Lydia met Henriette's eyes and they followed, lengthening their stride to keep up with the men. They were so close. The sound of danger acted as a burst of energy, an electric shock, to goad them on.

Another shot, and it was closer this time. Jacques turned around but barely slowed his pace. "They won't come up to the border," he said in a barely audible voice. "The Spanish patrols know the area like their own bedrooms. Run!"

Chapter 1

Lydia's Diary – March 1, 1941
London

"I've never been one to write things down. I have only wanted to do my work, care for my family, and enjoy every moment of my life. But the life I have now is one I would never have imagined for myself, and since I am separated from my husband and my children for most of the time now, I feel that I must write done what I think, how I feel, and what is going on in my daily life so that I can share my thoughts with them when all of our lives return to normal.

Normal – what does that word mean now? My children are in Wales, my husband is off on secret missions for British intelligence, and I spend my time here in London going to work every day and returning home to a tiny flat where I sleep alone most nights. That is, I sleep when I am not awakened by air raid sirens and I have to rush to the underground station and set up my little camp in the midst of hundreds of other terrified Londoners.

I have to believe that my family will be together again in the not too distant future. As long as all of us in Britain pull together and stand our ground and do our jobs, we will win this war, with the help of God.

"With the help of God?" I surprised myself as I wrote that, because I have never been a religious woman, and it is so difficult to see the hand of God in this terrible war, but we must believe in some greater plan, mustn't we?

When it is all over, we will talk and love, laugh and cry, and I will read parts of this diary to the people I most care about. I will mostly read it to my dear husband Allan, because he is the one to whom I would be speaking many of these words if he were here. I will share some parts of it with my children, so that they will know that their mother was thinking of them and doing her bit to create a better world for them and all the children of Britain. Some parts I will undoubtedly keep to myself, because they are private thoughts, and when we are all together again, they may not even matter so much. They will only be the words of a lonely wife and mother who misses her family terribly.

But the words will be here; they will be the truth of who I am during this time, and if they mean nothing to me or anyone else in the future, they mean a great deal to me now. This is who I am – Lydia Roberts."

Present Day
Wales

"Maybe we shouldn't have come." Nara turned to her father, Jack Blake, who was devoting all his attention to navigating the narrow road that seemed to wind endlessly around the mountainside in northwest Wales. Although the mountains were not high, and would not even be referred to as such by anyone familiar with the major mountain ranges of the world, Mount Snowdon provided an imposing enough backdrop to give both father and daughter a feeling of awesome respect for the road they were traveling. The rain, which had been coming down in sheets, had diminished now to a soaking downpour. The drop-off on the right side of the road was several hundred feet down a steep green cliff, and there was no room for another vehicle if they should meet one coming from the opposite direction.

"I'm not stopping now, even if I could." Jack's laughing comment was shaky, as he glanced at the steep drop. "I would have to reverse all the way down the mountainside, and I'm not about to do that." He negotiated another hairpin turn, his hands gripping the steering wheel. As they rounded the turn he unclenched his left hand and reached to rub the tense muscles in the back of his neck.

"You okay, Dad?" Nara asked. Jack had undergone chemotherapy just the year before for lung cancer, and although it had been caught early and there were no signs of the cancer now, he still sometimes tired easily.

The two had embarked on this journey as a holiday and a family errand. They were paying a visit to Jack's aunt Rebeca, his mother's sister, who lived in a remote village in northeast Wales. Since Jack's mother had died when he was young, and he spent most of his life on the Caribbean island of St. Clare, he had lost touch with that branch of his family. Only a few weeks before she had contacted Jack to ask him if he wanted a box of clothing and some other items that had belonged to her parents, Jack's grandparents. The boxes dated from World War II, when Allan and Lydia Roberts were killed in London in the Blitz. Rebeca had stored the boxes in her attic for years and never gone through them. It was too painful, she said, and what was past, was past. She had her own problems now.

Nara agreed to accompany her father on the drive from Lincolnshire to Wales to retrieve the boxes and to go through their contents. Nara had begun her studies in art history at the University of London, and was anxious to find out what treasures might have been packed away for sixty-five years. It was also a chance for her to learn more about her father's side of the family, since she had grown up in St. Clare and identified more with her mother's family and the culture of the islands.

"It looks like we've arrived somewhere," Nara said as they entered a cluster of buildings that could be called a village.

"Let's just hope it's where we want to be," Jack replied as he moved his foot to the brake and down-shifted.

A small black and white sign informed them that they had reached the village of Nevin, or Nefyn in Welsh, since all signs were bilingual. Clusters of stone houses lined the main street, which had mercifully widened to two lanes now that they were in town.

"It's the second street and then left." Nara consulted her scribbled notes.

"How far?" Jack asked.

"The edge of the village, it says."

"That could mean anything."

"The village isn't that big."

In the short time the two were talking, they realized that they had reached the opposite edge of the village of Nevin, and the mountain rose straight up in front of them. They slowed to allow a herd of sheep, driven by a border collie and a lone shepherd who strolled after the animals, to pass in front of them. Neither the man nor any of the animals seemed perturbed by the rain as they trudged down the road and passed through a gate into an even more sodden pasture.

"And left again!" Nara shouted.

Jack turned the car into a lane that was barely wide enough for their car, and slowed to a crawl as he tried in vain to avoid the large puddles that made up most of the road. "Are you sure this is right?" Nara asked.

"Yes. It's exactly how Aunt Sue described it."

They drove for another half mile before a stone farmhouse came into view. It was larger than those in the town, and clearly much older. The gray stone was rough and weathered, and a few of the slate roof tiles were missing. The remains of a vegetable garden lay to the left of the house. To the right was an outbuilding, probably at one time used to house chickens or farm equipment, but now it appeared unused. The door was closed but hung on its hinges, and several barrels had been piled in front to keep the door from falling completely off its frame.

Someone had attempted to plant a few flowers in front of the house, but they appeared to be battered by the incessant rain and it looked doubtful that they would survive the season.

"This was where my grandmother grew up?" Nara asked. She had never met her grandmother, her father's mother, who had died before she was born. Catherine Blake had left Wales as a young woman when she married and moved to the island of St. Clare with her husband. She had spent the rest of her life there, except for a few trips back to England and Wales. But she had died in a boating accident when her son Jack was a boy, and he had little acquaintance with this side of his family.

"It's not a working farm anymore," Jack answered. "And I don't think they made much of a living from it when it was."

"How does Aunt Rebeca support herself and her son?" Nara asked.

"I think they own some land down in the valley that they rent out, and of course Evan receives money from the government for his disability."

A border collie who could have been the litter mate to the one they saw herding the sheep down the road emerged from behind the house to greet them. There wasn't room for much more than a dog behind the house, since the mountain rose vertically behind it.

Jack parked the car and rubbed his neck again. His hair had grown back white after the chemo, and his British coloring was a vivid contrast to Nara's dark skin and hair, evidence of her mother's Caribbean blood. Nara was suddenly eager to meet her great-aunt, and reached for her umbrella. The rain had lessened considerably, but she had no intention of meeting relatives looking like she had just taken a shower with all her clothes on. As she opened the car door, the dog barked once, and then stood wagging his tail judgmentally. The front door opened and a slim, gray-haired woman stood in the doorway.

"Barney, easy," she said before calling out to her visitors. "Come on inside. You'll catch your death out there. Don't worry about Barney. He won't hurt you."

The dog remained in the same spot where he had announced their arrival. He shook himself, sending water onto Nara's legs as she passed.

"All right, enough of that," the woman called. "Come on, Barney. You can come in the kitchen and dry off, but only the kitchen." The dog slunk in ahead of Nara and Jack.

Jack held out his hand to his aunt as he climbed the three stone steps to the door. She accepted it briefly and released it. "Welcome, Jack. Last time I saw you, you were a little boy, with curly blond hair like my Evan." She looked them over from head to toe as she stepped aside to allow her nephew and his daughter to enter the house. They stepped into a small entry way and wiped their feet on a woven straw mat. "Don't worry about your shoes. We are in and out all the time here."

Both sides of the small hallway were crowded with both men's and women's boots. The walls were covered with hooks from which hung coats and jackets of all types, from heavy winter parkas to light fleeces to yellow rain slickers. Scarves and gloves filled a basket on the floor, and several large, dark-colored, serviceable umbrellas stood in a metal stand. *It may not be a working farm*, Nara thought, *but the people who live here certainly spend a lot of time outdoors.*

The older woman led them into the kitchen, which was dominated by a huge stone fireplace that sat empty and cold. She saw Nara glance at it and laughed. "We have central heating now. If you were expecting something romantic like a roaring fire in the kitchen and a pot of stew above it, you must be disappointed."

"I'm not disappointed," Nara began, but the woman had turned her attention to Jack.

"Sue told me you haven't been well, so I was a bit surprised when she said you were driving down for these boxes."

"I'm much better now. Good medical care can do wonders. But as you probably know, the treatment for cancer can often be worse than the disease itself."

"Yes. I'm glad to see you in good health. And you have your daughter here to keep you company on the drive." Rebeca graced Nara with a slight smile and nod of her head. "But sit down. You've come all this way." She turned and filled an electric kettle with water from the tap, and switched it on. "We'll have tea in a moment. I'm sure you could use some after the drive up here." Rebeca motioned to a couple of straight-backed chairs at the kitchen table, and Nara and Jack sat. They watched Rebeca as she took out heavy ceramic mugs for tea.

The room was a mixture of old and new. It was obvious that the kitchen had been updated with modern conveniences. An electric range stood against the wall, as well as a refrigerator of relatively recent vintage. But the walls were still rough stone, and no attempt had been made to reconcile the old and new. The room had not been decorated; the furnishings had merely been changed. A few old prints of scenes from Wales in the early twentieth century hung on the wall in identical cheap black plastic frames. One frame held a black and white photograph that showed a group of men in clothing from the early twentieth century. The derricks and machinery in the background indicated that the photo was taken outside a slate mine. Nara and Jack had passed the sites of old mines and quarries on their way through northwest Wales, and Nara knew that some of her family had worked in the mines in the waning days of their operation in the early 1900s. She wondered if the photo included any of her ancestors but was hesitant to ask. Against the far wall stood a rough wooden bench that was piled with newspapers and magazines. An armoire that had once been beautiful, but was now in dire need of polishing, stood at the end of the room. It was clear that the modern end of the kitchen was the one that Aunt Rebeca and her son lived in and used. The table and countertops were spotless, and an inviting wooden bowl filled with apples sat in the middle of the kitchen table.

Rebeca brought them their mugs of tea and one for herself. She set out a matching sugar bowl and a cream pitcher that appeared to be antique Cauldon china from the 1800s, if Nara was not mistaken.

"I have no biscuits, I'm afraid," Rebeca commented as she moved the bowl of apples to the counter. "I'm diabetic. I can't eat sweets anymore."

"I'm sorry," Nara murmured, as she helped herself to cream and sugar for her tea.

"Nothing to be sorry about," Rebeca said. "That's just the way it is." A shadow of something – sadness? regret? resignation? -- seemed to pass across Rebeca's face. Did Rebeca somehow resent the fact that her sister had married and gone off to live on a tropical island while she stayed on the family farm in Wales? Nara knew that Rebeca had been married and had a son; the boy was a toddler when his father was killed in a farming accident. A tractor had tipped over on the man, pinning him to the earth for hours before Rebeca discovered him. By that time he had lost so much blood that before she could summon help, he died in her arms.

Their son was a beautiful curly-haired child, whose mind never developed beyond that of a six-year-old. Jack remembered meeting him a few times when they visited the family on occasional trips back to the UK while he was growing up, but they had lost track over the years. Jack had too much to handle in St. Clare, especially after his own father died, followed by his wife, Nara's mother, to keep in touch with an aunt and a cousin in a remote region in Wales.

Rebeca sat down at the table and stirred her tea. "I appreciate you taking the boxes off my hands, Jack. I told your sister Sue I wanted to get rid of them. I'm cleaning things out. It's either that or I throw them away, and that seems a shame somehow." She stirred the tea again and stared off into space. "Catherine and I hardly knew our Mum and Dad, but I don't want the boxes. There's been too much life gone on since they died. Sue said you like antiques and family history. I'm happy for you to take them."

Jack set down his tea mug. "My mother died young, and my wife, Nara's mother, did as well. It's seems to happen a lot in our family."

Before Rebeca could say anything, the front door opened and then slammed shut.

"That would be Evan." Her facial expression softened. "I named him after my grandfather."

They heard vigorous foot stamping in the hall, and Rebeca called out, "Take your boots off, Evan. No amount of stomping will take the mud off them today."

The stomping stopped, and the only sound was the heavy breathing from exertion as Evan removed his boots. In a moment a tall, handsome man who could have been in his early to mid-forties appeared in the kitchen doorway. At the sight of Nara and Jack he stood still and looked hesitantly to his mother. He ran his hands through curls that once had been blond, but now had darkened to a light brown. He was dressed in brown work pants and a black sweater with a hole in one shoulder where the seam had pulled apart. Since he had removed his boots, he stood in stocking feet, wearing thick wool socks that looked hand-knitted, as did the sweater. Barney the border collie rose from his spot in front of the stove and moved to stand protectively in front of Evan. It was evident that the dog and the man were close companions. Evan reached down and absent-mindedly scratched Barney's head while he stared open-mouthed at the people in the room.

"Evan, these are your cousins, Jack and Nara. They've come to visit us. Isn't that nice?" The pride and love for her son was unmistakable in her voice. "Come sit down and I'll make you some tea."

Evan smiled shyly, but didn't move from his spot in the doorway, nor did the collie move. "It's all right, Evan," his mother coaxed him. "Jack's mother and I were sisters, and I'm giving them some boxes that belonged to the family. They are going to take them to London. You remember when we went to London, don't you?"

Evan's face brightened. "London," he repeated. "We went up in the air."

"We took a trip last summer with some other..." she paused to come up with the appropriate words. "Some other people like Evan and had a special excursion on the London Eye."

"That's wonderful, Evan," Nara commented with what she hoped was an encouraging smile. "That's something I haven't done yet."

"You should go to London and go up in the air on the Eye." This memory seemed to relax Evan somewhat, and he moved into the kitchen and took his seat at the table. His mother placed a mug of tea in front of him. "Warm your hands, Evan. But it's hot so be careful."

"I will, Mum," he answered.

After her son was settled, Rebeca turned back to Jack and Nara. "I know you don't live in London, but that's really they only other place name he would recognize," she said.

"Maybe you could bring him to visit us in Lincolnshire sometime," Nara said. "Although actually I am living in London now. I'm going to school there."

"It's difficult," Rebeca replied, her eyes drifting from Nara to Evan and then to the open window.

Nara's eyes met Jack's across the table. He cleared his throat. He seemed to be having as bad a time as any of them keeping up a conversation.

"I'll have Evan bring the boxes downstairs as soon as he finishes his tea. He doesn't usually take too long," Rebeca said as she turned back. She touched Evan's arm gently and smiled at her guests, but it was obvious that the smile was an effort. She wasn't used to having guests. Her life revolved around her son.

"Actually," Nara began, "we are not going back until tomorrow. We want to visit the University of Bangor to do some research. I'm studying art history, and I'm interested in learning more about the paintings from the National Gallery that were hidden in the slate mines during World War II."

"Yes, I heard about that." Rebeca sat quietly, eyes down and rubbing a thumb against the handle of her tea mug. There was a tiny chip where the handle met the body of the mug, and she rubbed it nervously. "My mother worked there," she answered after a moment. "Well, she worked there for a while when they were settling the paintings in the mines. Mostly she worked in London."

Nara felt distinctly uncomfortable. She was torn between asking the questions that were burning in her mind and politely excusing herself and her father in order to escape from these people and this house. Rebeca Pritchard may be her great-aunt, but she felt no sense of family with her. Nara was aware of a shell around the woman that was not about to be eased by a nephew she had not seen in over forty years and his daughter, who had grown up in a privileged childhood on a tropical island somewhere. True, Rebeca had lost her parents at a young age, and then her husband, and had apparently spent her adult life caring for a developmentally disabled son. Her life on this mountainside farm in a remote corner of Wales could not have been easy. Rebeca's world was closed to them, and their questions would seem not merely idly curious, but intrusive.

Jack spoke first. "But you and Mom lived with your parents in London before the war, didn't you?"

"Yes. Of course." Rebeca's eyes focused off into the distance, as if she were seeing her childhood life in London in the 1930s. "Until the war started, of course. In 1940, when the bombing started, we gave up our house in London and moved here with Nana and Granddad. They raised us." She stopped abruptly.

The tension around the kitchen table was palpable. Evan slurped his tea and stirred it noisily. After a particularly noisy bout of stirring, Rebeca softly placed her hand on her son's forearm, and he stopped the movement of his spoon. He held his head down, never once raising it to look at Nara or Jack.

Nara glanced toward the window, more as a maneuver to switch her eyes from the people at the table than for any other reason. She could see that the rain had stopped, and a glimmer of sunlight shone through the overcast sky. "The rain has stopped."

"Then you will be wanting to be on your way soon," Rebeca said, standing and setting her tea mug on the counter next to the sink. Without looking at her visitors, Rebeca spoke to her son. "Evan, I need you to help me bring those boxes downstairs. Remember the ones I told you about? They're in my bedroom."

"All right." Evan swallowed the rest of his tea and stood. He seemed to sense that retrieving the boxes, as he had been told he would do, would mean the end of the visit from these strangers, and that was something Evan was anxious for.

"We'll be right back," Rebeca said as she stood. Evan followed her from the kitchen and the two of them clattered up the stairs.

Nara looked around. "How did your grandmother go from a Welsh farm up in the mountains to being an art conservation expert at the National Gallery in London?"

"I wish I knew," Jack replied. "But I don't think we can ask Aunt Rebeca any more questions."

"No. Not this time anyway." They stood as they heard footsteps coming back down the stairs.

Under his mother's direction, Evan placed a large cardboard box on the floor near the door. "There's one more," Rebeca said. The two of them disappeared upstairs again, and returned in a moment with another slightly smaller box. "Evan can carry them to your car for you."

Nara and Jack retrieved their jackets from the hooks by the door, and led the way out into the soggy but brighter outdoors. The sunlight cast a golden glow over the mountains, and for a few moments the four of them simply stood, transfixed by the scene. Barney the border collie was the only one oblivious to the evanescent play of light on the hills and valleys, and he pushed ahead of them and went off through a hedge in search of a rabbit to chase or a sheep to herd, as his instinct told him to do. Evan placed the two boxes in the boot of the car and Jack closed it. There was nothing more to say or do. Nara wanted to reach out to her aunt and her shy son, but she knew they would not accept the family affection she was so eager to give. She would not accept it now, and maybe not ever.

"Thank you, Aunt Rebeca." Jack offered his hand again.

Rebeca hesitated a moment before taking her nephew's hand for the briefest of seconds. She laughed a sharp bark of a laugh. "I don't think of myself as much of an aunt. I thank you for taking these old things out of my house. I doubt if there is anything worth much in there, if that's what you're looking for. If there is, you're welcome to it. I don't want to see any of those things. The past is past."

"Thank you for the tea," Nara added. "And it was nice meeting you, Evan." She turned to the tall man who stood by his mother, scuffing his boots in the wet gravel of the driveway. Evan said nothing.

London

"Her boyfriend works at the V&A," Paul announced. "That's even better."

Lisette continued to rub her wet curls with the towel and to glare at her brother. Once again he had forgotten his key. She heard the pounding on the door just as she was stepping out of the shower. The neighbors had complained about his loud voice once before, and she didn't want it to happen again. The less attention they attracted, the better off they would be.

"How about a 'hello, sister. Thanks for getting out of the shower and letting me in,'" she said.

"I don't have time for that," he growled. "I found a report online about an incident last year with an art theft somewhere in the north of England. It mentioned this guy's name and that he worked for the V&A. So I called his office there and said I was trying to find Nara Blake. His secretary wouldn't give me her phone number, but said she would have him call me."

Lisette's eyes opened wide and she was about to speak when Paul interrupted her. "Don't worry. I gave a fake number. But she confirmed without actually saying so that Nara Blake is his girlfriend or fiancée or something."

"Nice going, I guess," Lisette said. "Just be careful with your investigations. Leave it to me. I'm the one who is supposed to be the student doing research."

"You didn't mind that I did the talking when we went to see that old lady in Bordeaux." Paul walked to the sideboard, ignoring his wet footprints on the floor, and poured himself a generous Scotch.

Lisette's eyes tracked his steps, but she said nothing about the footprints. "Have you taken your medication today, Paul?"

"No. Why?" He swallowed down about a third of the Scotch. "Never mind," Lisette said. "The pills and alcohol don't mix. That's all. But you know that."

Chapter 2
Lydia's Diary – March 15, 1941
London

"I bought little dolls for Catherine and Rebeca today – in a little shop near Russell Square. The shopkeeper thinks he will close soon. There is no manufacturing of toys now, and of course there is no importing. I don't know when I will be able to travel to Wales to visit the girls, so it might be best to send the dolls by mail. I keep imagining the girls opening the box and exclaiming over the dolls. One has a blue dress and one pink. Should I specify which doll is for which girl? No, I think I will let them work it out.

My little girls are so different from each other. Catherine is adventurous and will speak to anyone. Rebeca is the shy one. She keeps things in, even though she is only five. I hope this war is over soon. I worry about both of them. What effect will the war and our family's separation have on them?

But who am I fooling? It won't be over soon, or at least not for two or three years."

Present Day
Wales

Nara took her turn at driving as they headed back down the mountain. As they left the small village and began the descent, she heaved a sigh of relief. "That was not what I expected.

I thought country people in most parts of the world were warm and welcoming, especially to family."

"Maybe not when they have been through as much as Rebeca has," Jack answered. "She lost her parents and then her husband, and has had the care of her son all her life."

Nara slowed to allow space for an oncoming lorry on the narrow road. "I wonder what will happen to him when she dies. She must be... what? Late seventies?"

"At least. She was a few years younger than Mom." Jack looked off into the distance while Nara concentrated on the road. A few clouds were blocking the direct sunlight which then emerged from behind the clouds in bright rays that illuminated the hills and valleys. A few pockets of fog remained in the valleys and sat like white cotton wool in the low pockets of land. "Amazing scenery," he commented.

"I can only look at the road," Nara answered. "I don't want to die before I have a chance to see what's in those boxes."

"Then pull over for a few minutes so you can look."

Nara found a turn-off just ahead and pulled off the road. The valley below was a dizzying drop down a steep cliff, but the sunlight had turned the clouds to gold, which reflected off the green of the hills on the opposite side of the valley. A small lake twinkled in the distance as the sunlight passed over it, and then dulled to a shimmer as the clouds shifted.

"I think this is where your great-grandmother got her artistic eye. Just look. No artist could paint those colors."

"It's breathtaking."

"And look at the sheep," Jack added. As their eyes became accustomed to the view, the tiny white dots across the valley revealed themselves to be sheep grazing on the steep hillside, and not the white rocks they originally took them for. "There must be hundreds of them."

"More sheep in this country than people," Nara laughed. She put the car back into gear and turned back onto the road.

"Let's get down to Bangor. I think we have a lot more to learn about Wales and my great-grandparents."

Professor Mark Jones was an expert in twentieth century Welsh history, especially the World War II period. He had grown up in Bangor and gravitated naturally to the history of the region. Both his parents were teachers who instilled in him the necessity of preserving Welsh culture, and they spoke the language almost exclusively in their home. Mark and his two younger sisters were bilingual, but Mark was the only one who had stayed on in Gwynedd, the northwest region of Wales. His marriage of a decade had ended two years ago, and he was pleased with himself that he had accomplished so much in the writing of his latest book now that he was single again.

He was ready to settle down to an afternoon of research when the history department secretary reminded him that the two visitors who had called the previous week were here for their appointment. "Damn," he muttered.

"What's that, Professor Jones?" the secretary asked.

"Nothing, Dana," he answered. "Send them in."

"How can I help you?" Mark asked politely. He really had no idea why they were here. He had supposed they were graduate students from another university; in fact he believed that was what his secretary had told him. But although the young woman looked as if she could be a student, the man with her looked old enough to be her father. He indicated that they should seat themselves in the two chairs facing his desk.

Jack held out his hand. "I'm Jack Blake and this is my daughter Nara." *He not only was old enough to be her father, he <u>was</u> her father. Why would a student bring her father along?*

"I'm trying to find out more about my grandparents, who were killed in the Blitz in 1940," Jack said as he settled himself in his chair.

"She was an art expert, working for the National Gallery," Nara added, "and she was involved in the transport and storage of the paintings that were hidden in the slate mines." She leaned forward as she spoke, energy showing in her eyes and her eager posture.

"Do you know her name?" Mark asked. "That would help, you know."

"Of course we know her name." Nara's eyes flashed, and her chin rose indignantly at his remark. "Her name was Lydia Roberts. And her husband was Allan Roberts. I'm interested because it seems so unusual that a woman would hold a job like that at that time, especially a married woman with children."

"It wasn't that unusual during wartime," he answered. "Where were the children? One of them was your mother or father, I assume." He nodded to Jack. Mark felt that he wanted to have this conversation with the father, who seemed to be allowing his daughter to take the lead.

"They were here in Wales with their grandparents, Lydia's parents," Jack said. "They raised them after Lydia and her husband were killed."

"Again, not that unusual. Many children were sent to the country from London during the Blitz. And the fact that there were grandparents living in a safe area like this." He swept his arm around indicating the Welsh countryside, which was not visible from his window in the city of Bangor. "That is not surprising at all."

"But she went to university, married and had two children, and continued to work in her profession before the war," Nara argued. "A two career household with two growing children does seem out of the ordinary in England in the 1930s, don't you think? And then they just disappeared. Their bodies were not found."

"Again, it wasn't unusual for bodies not to be found when a building or street suffered a direct hit," Mark replied. He felt that the entire conversation was a waste of his time, and wondered again why he had allowed this appointment to be scheduled. One of his teaching assistants could have easily handled this. And there was something about the persistence of Nara's questions that irritated him. He was accustomed to being the professor in charge of his students, and his control of this situation seemed to be slipping.

"It does seem as if the authorities would have found something." Jack spoke up, leaning forward in his chair, and for the first time Mark was aware of the family resemblance, if not in looks, in the persistent attitude. "My mother passed away when I was a teenager, and she rarely spoke about her parents. My aunt, who was their daughter, said that they knew nothing except that the flat had been bombed. Then after the war, they received two boxes from someone in the War Office. Lydia's mother opened them once, went through them quickly, and they have been shut up in the attic in their farmhouse ever since. That is until today when my aunt gave them to us."

"Aren't you an expert on the history of this part of Wales during World War II?" Nara asked, leaning forward as she spoke, and her words conveyed a challenge that Mark did not like.

"Yes. That's my area of concentration. But you are looking for information on someone who died in London."

"But she was from here. She worked here when the paintings from the National Gallery were stored in the slate mines. She had family here. We thought you might have records that would show us something of what she did, when she was last here. Anything." Nara turned to her father as she finished talking, and a look passed between them. The look, the communication without speech, made Mark feel that he was at a decided disadvantage in the discussion. It wasn't even a competition and he felt that he had lost.

Mark fiddled with the letter opener on his desk. He never opened letters with it. Either his secretary opened them, or he ripped off the end of the envelope. He kept the opener for occasions such as this, when he needed something to do with his hands. Now he was methodically pressing the edge of the blade along the flesh of his left index finger. It was just enough pressure to give him a slight sensation of pain, and take away some of the discomfort he was feeling in this conversation. " I'm just trying to get a clear picture of what you are looking for, and why you came to me." *Ouch. That sounded as if I don't want to talk with them. Why can't I just listen? Wasn't that my ex-wife's perennial complaint?*

"All right. Here's what I can do. I'll give you access to our on-line library. You can find out a lot that way. If you find any record of the names you are looking for, you can come back and look for the original documents. You would have to do it that way anyway, and it is time-consuming." He held up his hand when Nara opened her mouth to speak. "I'm not trying to get rid of you." Did he believe that himself? "In the meantime, I'll see what I can find. There are some documents I have easy access to, and if there is something there I'll let you know."

Nara and Jack exchanged glances again. "All right. Can we have your phone number and email so we can contact you?" Jack asked.

"Of course." Mark took two business cards with the requested information and handed one to each of them.

"I'll be in touch as soon as I have something for you." Mark gave his standard closing to a meeting and extended his hand to Nara. She took it and looked him directly in the eye. Her dark eyes seemed to burn with daring and persistence.

"Very nice meeting you," she said. Mark felt once again that he had failed a test, lost a race, or somehow come out the loser.

Jack's cell phone rang as they exited the building. He dug it out of his pants pocket just as they reached the door and could see that it was raining – again. "Hold on, Nara. It's Sue." He flipped open the cover of the phone. "Hi, Sue."

"Hi, Jack. How's everything going?"

"Not bad. We got the boxes. Sue, I have to tell you that Aunt Rebeca is more than a little strange."

"I haven't seen her in years myself, Jack. I hardly remember her."

"And we just talked with the professor at the University of Bangor. He was a little patronizing, but he is going to look some things up for us."

"Good. Anyway, Jack, the reason I called is that Aunt Rebeca called me about a half hour ago. It seems that after you left her house a man called and asked about Lydia and Allan and what they did during the war. She thought it was a little strange to have two people in one day asking about her parents. She didn't tell him anything, or mention that you and Nara were there. She wasn't about to tell a stranger more than she had to, but she thought we should know about it."

"Thanks, Sue. That is strange. Could be a student, but it's odd he would ask about Allan and Lydia by name."

"Rebeca sounded a little perturbed, and thought at first that you and Nara knew the person, but I managed to calm her down."

"We'll keep an eye out for him," Jack said.

"Are you driving back to London today?"

"No. We thought we would stay in Bangor tonight and then get an early start tomorrow."

"Good idea. Be careful, Jack. I do remember those Welsh roads."

"Be careful with myself or with the boxes?"

"Both. But especially with yourself and Nara."

Nara and Jack carried the two boxes into their room at a small guest house on the outskirts of Bangor. "Maybe we can start going through them tonight," Nara said as she stacked one on top of the other next to her bed. The room was small and they had to turn sideways to get around the beds as it was, but it was cozy and attractive. The walls were painted a serene blue, and color photographs of Snowdonia National Park decorated the walls.

Jack gave Nara a tired smile. "You must be kidding. I don't know about you, but I'm exhausted. And we've got a long drive ahead of us tomorrow."

Nara shifted from foot to foot like a petulant child. "I just can't wait to see what's inside."

"You'll just end up tearing everything out willy-nilly and then have to put it back again. And you don't want to risk losing something under the bed, do you?"

"Good point. All right. I'll wait." Nara continued to look longingly at the boxes.

"Let's go get something to eat. I'm starved."

"All right. There's a pub right next door. We can just pop over there."

After a hearty supper of beef stew and salad, and a pint of lager each to relax, father and daughter were ready for a good night's sleep. Jack wasted no time in changing into pajamas and climbing into bed with a book. Nara had just finished brushing her teeth when she noticed her father fast asleep with the book lying open on the pillow beside him. Nara marked the place in the book and turned out the bedside light. She sat cross-legged on her bed in her usual over-sized T-shirt and sweatpants. She was tired, but somehow not quite ready for sleep. She had brought a book to read but was not in the mood. The boxes were there. Surely it wouldn't hurt to take just a peek. She eased herself off the bed quietly so as not to disturb Jack and lifted the top off the larger of the boxes. The contents appeared to be wrapped in tissue paper, and Nara could see a number of small packets filling the box. Dad was right. It was not a good idea to disturb the contents. She would just make a mess and risk losing something. There would be time enough when they returned to her flat in London.

But on top of the parcels lay several notebooks covered in faded cloth. They were about the size of the theme books that students use in school. Nara lifted one out of its nest of tissue paper and let it fall open. The lined pages were covered in a careful, flowing script, and the ink was barely faded. Was this the handwriting of Lydia Roberts? The cotton fabric protecting the thin cardboard cover had been pink at one time, but it was faded now to a dusty rose. Precise whip stitches held the fabric together at the corners of the inside covers. Nara wondered if the book was covered to protect it, or to add some beauty to the ordinariness of the notebook Lydia used to record her thoughts. She must have seen little enough color in the London of 1940. Nara closed the notebook, spreading the fingers of her left hand lovingly across the cover. She looked at the box on the floor in front of her, which held at least a half dozen more notebooks just like the one in her hands. Most of them appeared to be covered in the same manner, with bits of colored fabric.

"She meant for these to be found," Nara whispered. "But I don't believe she intended for them to be hidden for so long."

Nara turned to the first page of the notebook, where she found the date, April 1, 1941, and the name Lydia Roberts. Underneath her name and the date, Lydia had written, "If either of us survives the war, we will tell the truth."

As she read the words, Nara felt the forging of a link between herself and her great-grandmother whom she knew nothing about. All she knew was that Lydia was a strong independent woman who did her job under trying circumstances. Her diaries and the rest of the boxes were her legacy.

She flipped through the pages again, anxious to read Lydia's words, but knowing she would not make much headway tonight, and it would make sense to read them in order. This book began in March, 1941, and the last entry was September of that year, although the last book was only half filled. Was that when she died? Nara gazed out the window at the night. A half-moon shone above the houses across the street, where a few street lights cast soft illumination on the neighborhood. "I thought they died in the blitz," she said quietly. "That ended earlier than September, I'm sure."

Chapter 3

Lydia's Diary - March 10, 1941
London

"It is amazing how I have become accustomed to my routine here in my flat in London. I said 'my flat.' Strange. It is, of course, 'our' flat, mine and Allan's. But he is here so rarely that it seems like it is mine alone. I keep only the barest of essentials here. We have sent our good china and mementoes to my parents' house in Wales for safekeeping. I kept a few inexpensive prints to brighten the walls just a bit, but the flat isn't home; it is a temporary place to sleep and keep a few belongings until this bloody war is over. And the children have never even been here. I have a few of their drawings and letters that they have sent me, but the flat doesn't have the 'feel' of them. Of course I don't want them in London now. As much as I want to see their little faces, they cannot be here now. I know that. I only allow myself a little bit of self-pity every once in a while, and then I pull myself together and get on with my work.

I am fairly contented working in Whitehall now that the National Gallery needs fewer employees. My work at cataloging in the cultural department is important. It may not be something that directly helps the soldiers in combat, but preserving our culture during this time has its own priority. Nevertheless, I am keeping my eyes open for the opportunity to do something that will more directly involve me in the war effort.

I've written enough for now. I need to have something to eat and make sure my bag is ready in the event of an air raid tonight, and the raids have been happening almost every night. I have a couple of eggs and a little cheese, so I might make myself an omelet, although I hear that eggs will be rationed soon. I think I also have a tin of peas. At least I am only cooking for myself, and I am able to eat my main meal at noon in the canteen. I am thankful for small blessings!"

March, 1941
London

Lydia had not grown used to the bombs falling. Each night she obediently picked up her overnight bag when the alarm sounded, put on her brown woolen coat and made her way to the Russell Square Underground station around the corner. If it weren't for the children and Allan – she might have been tempted to stay in her bed, in the flat that she and Allan rented when the war began and they sent the children to live with their grandparents in Wales. Lydia believed that death would come when it was meant to, but Allan made her promise. "I have enough on my mind without worrying about you," he said. "I know the children are out of danger. Let me at least know that you are doing your best to stay safe." He had touched her cheek then, and traced the line of her jaw with his fingers, before going off to meet with the French Resistance again.

Lydia did her best to settle herself in her customary niche under the stairway, just a few feet from the underground rail tracks. It was impossible for her to stretch out her long, slender legs in her chosen nook, but at least she had a bit of privacy. She opened her bag, pulled out her hair brush, and began to give her wavy brown hair one hundred strokes. The rhythm of the nightly ritual always soothed her. Her hair crackled with electricity, and she smoothed it back and tied it with a green silk scarf. Lydia was in her early thirties, but she looked younger. Her fair skin was touched with pink. Her eyes were somewhere between brown and green, and she smiled easily, showing even teeth and a pair of dimples.

As she settled, her thoughts turned to her children, Catherine and Rebeca. Lydia had made the difficult choice to remain in London and use her skills to work for the war effort instead of returning to the safety of her parents' home in northwest Wales. Her loneliness for her two daughters was an unremitting knot in her stomach, but she believed she must work for the greater good. Her parents disapproved of her choice and presented their arguments, both logical and emotional, whenever she returned to Wales for a visit, but Lydia stood firm. And besides, staying in London she could at least see her husband Allan when he returned to London. If she didn't see him and know he was all right, she wasn't sure she could continue to live.

The children were with her parents on the family farm in northwest Wales, as far from the dangers of the escalating war as they could be. She had no worries about their safety. But she could not think of them without an accompanying lump in her throat, and tears threatened in the back of her eyes whenever she let herself think of them.

Lydia rubbed the back of her neck, massaging the muscles at its base with her long slender fingers. The people around Lydia were talking quietly. Many of the women knitted, and the click of the needles provided soothing background music to Lydia's thoughts. Several people pulled out flasks of tea, and an old man who, with his wife, often slept near Lydia's spot, limped over to offer a cup to her. "Thank you," she said as she spread her cold fingers around the brown chipped mug. The tea was strong, hot and sweet, and its warmth spread through her body and temporarily relieved the aches and tension of overwork, too little sleep, and the constant worry about Allan, the children, the future –

if there was to be one. At the same time she wondered how people found time to brew a flask of tea before heading out of their flats and down into the Tube. She tried only to remember to include a sandwich and an apple, if she could find one, in her bag.

"Where is your wife?" she asked, as the man lingered, sipping his own tea.

"Ah." His voice caught. "Stayed above tonight, she did. Her sister in Ealing took ill, so she went to stay with her. Says she'll be all right. I don't know..." His voice trailed off.

"No place is safe; not a hundred percent," Lydia commented. Her voice trailed off, too. There was nothing new to say about these damnable bombs that fell every night. One never knew which block of houses would have been obliterated when the "all clear" sounded and people rose, grateful yet exhausted still from the unremitting tension, from their makeshift beds below ground. And there was always someone who chose to stay at home and did not survive. It was a dangerous game of chance, and even the Underground would not survive a direct hit.

"Your children are safe?" the man asked. He had asked it before, and Lydia had told him, but he seemed to want to stay and talk.

"Yes, they are in Wales with my parents," she answered.

"Oh, yes. I remember you told me." He shifted his weight. He was obviously uncomfortable standing. "You're Welsh then."

"Yes." Lydia wondered if this was an attempt to continue the conversation, or just his way of placing her in a category in his mind. A Welsh woman, married and with children, alone in London during the bombing.

"My mother was Welsh," he added. "She died just before the first war, never lived to see what happened to us, our way of life. They said that was the war to end all wars." He chuckled humorlessly. "And all it did was to kill our best young men, and lead us into this war. I wonder what will happen to us."

There was no answer to his question, and there seemed to be nothing else to say, but the man still stood there. Lydia could not ask him to sit down, because there was nowhere to sit. The hot tea had relaxed her to the point where she just wanted to write in her diary and try to sleep a little. She stifled a yawn. "I'm sure your wife will be all right," she said. "Most of the bombing is in the east end. There isn't so much around Ealing." The walls of the station trembled ever so slightly, as if a train were approaching, and normal traffic was passing through the London Underground system. But there were no trains running these nights; a bomb had fallen somewhere not too distant. Voices quieted for a moment, and the click clack of the knitting needles lost a beat before resuming their rhythm.

"I'll let you rest then," the man said quietly. Lydia looked at his face and became aware of how old and worn he looked. He ran arthritic fingers through his graying hair. "Sleep well." He turned and limped back to his pile of bedding and eased himself down, turning his back to her.

Lydia removed her diary from her satchel; she smoothed the cover and admired the bright pink cotton she had used to cover it. She had used the fabric from an old dress she had worn when the children were toddlers, and they lived in the flat in Finchley. It seemed too gay and bright to wear now, and reminded her sadly of another time in her life. At least in her diary, she could escape her sadness for a bit.

Lydia's Diary – March 11, 1941
London

"Allan has been gone for a week now. Not unusual, but after a week I start missing him more and preparing myself mentally for his return. I begin to look for him on the street near our flat or at the office. I expect every phone call to be him, telling me he is on his way home. I know he is traveling to meet with the French Resistance fighters along the coast, and possibly even to Spain or Portugal, although he only hints at this. I have heard that the French have done the same thing at the Louvre as we at the National Gallery have done – moved our precious works of art out of the museums in the cities to hiding places in the countryside. Not hidden, I suppose, if the Germans were really to search for them, but at least safe from bombing raids. Hitler did not destroy Paris after all, but he does not seem to have the same appreciation for London.

I feel torn sometimes. My job is to protect and preserve the art work of our country, but what about the people? Of what use are paintings if the ordinary folks are killed, families torn apart? But then – what is a country without its history and its culture? Would I want Catherine and Rebeca to live in a post-war world with no beauty? No St. Paul's? No paintings by Gainsborough or Rubens to admire?"

Lydia paused in her writing and absently doodled on the page. Thinking about Catherine and Rebeca could not help but wrench her heart back to the farmhouse in Wales. She drew little circles on the page and as she so did she allowed herself to think of her daughters. She imagined them running together to the village school in the morning. Tall Rebeca, who had her mother's height but her father's light hair and blue eyes. Petite, round little Catherine, who at ten had not yet outgrown her baby fat. She had her mother's dark hair in contrast to fair skin, along with Allan's blue eyes. At this time of year, the winter was over, and the spring rains were bringing out the wild flowers. The girls would be gathering the flowers on their way home from school and bringing them home for their grandmother to arrange and place in a vase. She would caution them to keep their coats buttoned up so they would not catch cold, as she had cautioned Lydia when she was a girl. Tears came to Lydia's eyes and she pulled a handkerchief out of her bag before anyone noticed.

Raising Catherine and Rebeca was <u>her</u> job; she was their mother. But soon, maybe by now even, they would begin to forget her and Allan. They would become wispy memories, the parents in London whom they seldom saw. And Grandma and Grandpa would be the dominating forces in their lives, the people who taught them right from wrong, punished their misdeeds, bandaged their wounds, held them close and nurtured them.

"I've made a promise to Allan. I will keep it. (Her handwriting was clear and firm, written slowly rather than hurriedly to get down the thoughts before they ran away.) It isn't just about our children – God, I love them so!! – It's about all the children on this island.

'Now I lay me down to sleep...'"

The all clear sounded about 6 a.m., and one by one the Londoners sleeping in the Russell Square Underground station roused themselves, packed up their belongings, and climbed the stairs to the surface to find out how their world had changed during the night's bombing raid.

Lydia Roberts was startled awake, amazed to realize that she had been sleeping soundly in her hard little nest near the Underground tracks. She still felt half lost in the dream she was having when she heard the "all clear." She had been dreaming of her daughters and Allan, and her parents. It had been such a joy to be with them, to be home. The peaceful, relaxed feeling faded as she came fully awake. She stretched her legs and sat up. Her watch said 6 a.m. There was time to go back to the flat, wash and change clothes for work. She would even have time for a cup of good tea and some toast before heading to her office at Whitehall. She quickly rolled up her bedding and joined the others trudging up the steps. She exchanged nods and looks of recognition with a few people she knew, but no one spoke much on these mornings, especially when they had heard nearby bombing during the night. No one knew what they would find, or if their home would still be there, and not flattened into rubble.

It was apparent as soon as they reached the surface that there had been heavy damage nearby. The street was filled with police and firemen, working to contain the damage and direct people away from the streets that lay in shambles. As soon as Lydia turned the corner into Tavistock Street, she saw that her block of flats was among those that suffered a direct hit. She felt no sense of urgency as she picked her way through the rubble toward what had been home, or at least the place where she spent her nights and kept her belongings. While the police and emergency workers hurried around her, shouting to the emerging residents to watch their step, Lydia quietly wound her way to what had been her building. The building had sustained a direct hit, and it was clear that there was nothing she would be able to salvage. The emergency workers had cordoned off the area, and a couple of them stood arguing with one of Lydia's former neighbors. Jane Farnsworth was a few years older than Lydia, and worked as a nurse in New End Hospital. Lydia knew that Jane's husband was an engineer who was involved in work for the military somewhere on the coast – Dover, she thought. Lydia didn't know her well, but she walked up to her and put her hand on her shoulder. She felt her thin shoulder bone and the trembling of her body before she spoke. "Jane, Jane, come with me. There's nothing left. Let's go. Come with me."

Jane turned on Lydia as if she were to blame. "I'm not going anywhere!" She spit out her words through clenched teeth. "Everything is gone. My china, my silver, my clothes, my bed." She sank down on the pavement and sobbed. Lydia bent over to comfort her, but Jane would not be consoled; she needed to be angry first. "Get away from me. You with your children tucked away in Wales. That's how you Welsh always are." An aid worker with a badge on her blouse stopped Lydia's hand before she could touch Jane again.

"It's all right," the aid worker said softly. "I'll take care of her." She put her arms around the distraught woman and helped her to her feet, muttering soothing words as she held her upright and began to walk back down the street in the direction from which the women had come just a few minutes before.

Lydia stood for just a moment, trying to get her bearings. She was stunned by Jane's words, but it was not the first time she had heard such things about the Welsh. She had no time to dwell on old hurts now; she needed to deal with the present reality. Her flat was gone. She knew that she would be able to contact Allan through the War Office in order to let him know that she was all right. Her thoughts were far away as she walked, and she stumbled on a large piece of masonry from a neighboring building. "Watch out, miss," a worker called to her. She glanced at him and nodded her thanks. She straightened her back, raised her chin and lengthened her stride. Carrying her bedding and her overnight bag, she descended the 175 steps of the Russell Square underground station and took the train to Westminster and her job in the cultural section of the War Office. It wouldn't be a problem finding somewhere to stay. There were several female co-workers who were looking for someone to share a flat, although she would miss having a place that she and Allan could call their own when he was in London. But it couldn't be helped. There were definitely people who were much worse off than they were. Their children were safe with their grandparents, not shunted off to some stranger's home like so many London children had been. And their belongings that held sentimental value – a few pieces of furniture, the girls' baby pictures and their wedding photos – all were safe in Wales.

Lydia came up out of the Tube at Westminster, trudging along with the crowds heading for work in the government offices down Whitehall. It was only then that she became aware of the fact that she was walking to work in the clothes she had slept in, and carrying a suitcase and bedroll. A few people glanced at her as she paused on the sidewalk to adjust the load she carried, but most took no notice or averted their eyes. War had a strange effect on people. It created friendships in unlikely situations and circumstances, like the man who offered her tea when they slept in the Russell Square station. War also produced a wall of privacy around the individual sufferings in people's lives. No one was untouched, so it was better to respect actions and behaviors that might seem strange in more normal times. One never knew what fresh tragedy or pain might befall any person.

When Lydia reached the door of her office building, she saw her friend and coworker Maggie Turnbull approaching from the other direction. Maggie's blue eyes widened when she saw Lydia. "What happened?" Her eyes shifted to the suitcase. "Where are you going?"

Lydia laughed shakily. "Besides to work, I'm not quite sure where I'm going." She paused for a beat. "My flat was bombed last night. A direct hit. There's nothing left."

"Oh, Lydia, how awful!" The younger woman took the suitcase from Lydia's hand and put her arm around her shoulders. "Let's go inside. We've got to find you a place to stay." She stopped halfway through the door, blocking a middle aged man in a suit and bowler hat who was entering the building just behind them. "Where's Allan?"

"Allan is fine as far as I know," Lydia answered, as Maggie led her across the lobby and down a side corridor to the ladies' room. "He is away from London right now. I'm not sure where. I'll have to see if I can get a message to him somehow."

"We'll talk to Major Dexter. He can surely find out where he is and get a message to him."

"Yes, I'm sure he can." Lydia was not sure how much Maggie knew about the clandestine operations of the cultural department. She knew that everyone in her department had clearances, but that didn't mean that everyone knew everything, or should know everything.

Once inside the ladies' room, Maggie went to work on Lydia. She sponged the dirt smudges off her dress and brushed it and tidied the cuffs and collar. Once it had been one of Lydia's best dresses. Now the dark blue showed signs of wear, and Lydia wore a white tatted lace collar to cover the worn spots on the dress's own collar. When Maggie began to dab at Lydia's face with a flannel, Lydia came to herself and took the cloth from her friend. "I can wash my own face," she said, laughing a little. She cleaned the grime from her face, reapplied face cream from her suitcase, and added lipstick. She brushed her hair and pinned back the sides with plain bobby pins. "That will have to do," she said, closing her case. "I'm not the first person to be bombed out of my flat with nothing, and I won't be the last. We've got work to do."

Lydia's Story

Chapter 4

Lydia's Diary – March 18, 1941
London

Allan is back in London. He came to Whitehall first and found me there, so I was able to tell him about the bombing. At least he didn't have to go back to Tavistock Street and find the flat gone and think that I had gone with it. We are staying with Major Dexter and his wife in Pimlico now. It's much closer to work – I only have to go from Victoria Station to Westminster, and it's only one train -- but I don't feel comfortable in their house. The Dexters are very kind to share their home, but I feel as if we are imposing. Amelia Dexter is quite frightened staying in London, but she doesn't want to leave her husband. They have a family home in Derbyshire but she refuses to go there alone. She hinted that maybe I could go there with her, but of course that is impossible. I have my work here. If I went anywhere it would be to Wales, but I am not even considering that.

Allan is quite disturbed about the situation in France. He says that what is happening with the Jewish people is much worse than we realize here. We hear so little of what is really occurring on the Continent. We are so absorbed in our own lives and fighting this war for our own country, that we don't remember that people in Europe are much worse off. What would it be like if the Germans occupied Britain? I can't even bear to think about it. But it has happened all over Europe. There are families just like ours who have been torn apart forever. And God forbid -- Why doesn't God forbid it? What does that expression mean these days? —God forbid if you belong to a group such as the Jews who are targeted by the Nazis. Apparently they are being asked to give up their valuables -- paintings, jewelry --and the next step could be to concentration camps. Allan is trying to see that some of the art works are secretly transported to England so they can be returned to the rightful owners after the war.

After the war? I wonder when that will be? I just can't believe the Germans will conquer England. That just can't happen. And will I be here to see if it does or does not?

I am going to ask Allan if it is possible for me to travel with him to Spain. At least we will be together, and I will be of more use helping him there than sitting in an office typing up lists. I have too much time to think here.

March, 1941
London

"It's too risky, Lydia." Allan Roberts lit a cigarette and inhaled. He looked through the smoke at his wife's face. Her dark eyes brimmed with unshed tears, and the heightened color in her cheeks clearly showed the tension she felt, but would not openly discuss. Allan and Lydia knew few people in London. They had not been part of any social scene before the war, and the neighbors they knew during the few years they spent in Finchley with the children were gone from London now. The children had mostly been evacuated to the countryside; the men, of course, had joined the military, and the women were working somewhere for the war effort.

"There will be opportunities for you to be more directly involved in the war effort in the future, but things are so unstable on the Continent right now…

"Allan, listen to me." Lydia wiped away her tears with the back of her hand. "I'm as much of an art expert as you are. I did my thesis on Degas. I know what to look for. I know how to identify, label and pack paintings for shipment. I'm going crazy sitting in the office typing, even if my work is valuable because I have top secret clearance. I'm not comfortable here with the Dexters. Mrs. Dexter is afraid of her own shadow and..." Lydia stopped to pull an embroidered white handkerchief out of her bag to wipe her face and blow her nose. "And I think about the girls all the time. I wonder sometimes if I can do this."

Allan took a sip from the mug of ale that the barmaid had set before him minutes ago. The Bag o' Nails was a cozy pub near Soho that had been one of their favorites before the war; it was a good place for them to talk privately away from the Dexters' home. Lydia played with the rim of her glass; she had been nursing her drink since they arrived. Since the bombing of their flat two weeks ago, she had been wound up as tight as a top. She slept poorly and ate little. The tension showed in the set of her shoulders and the thinness of her face, and her eyes focused off in the distance most of the time. Lydia was a brave woman; Allan had seen that quality in her as they said goodbye to the girls, and in the days and weeks that he had left her to cross the Channel with the Free French fighters and other British undercover operatives. He crushed out his cigarette and took her hand in his. "Maybe you are right," he said. "You need more important work to do. We agreed to work together and then I've left you here typing in an office." He took a large swallow of his drink and picked up his pack of cigarettes. *No*, he thought, *I just put one out*. "Let me talk to Dexter, and some of the others. If you feel like you are doing something for the war effort you will feel better." Allan smoothed his brown hair back from his brow and adjusted his glasses. "I know what you mean about Mrs. Dexter. She drives me a bit batty, too. But I can avoid spending time with her. You can't."

"Thank you, Allan. That's all I ask." Lydia took a tiny sip of ale and then replaced her glass on the table. A soldier in an RAF uniform at the end of the bar began to sing, and his buddies and the girls they were with laughed and then sang along. Lydia watched them, a sorrowful expression on her face. "We've got to do it, don't we?" she asked, still facing the singers. "We have to do what we can to give them something to be happy about."

Allan's blue eyes softened. His eyes were a pale, almost incandescent blue that shone golden in the dim light. He raised her hand to his lips and kissed it tenderly. "Nothing lasts forever, my love. We've only got this moment, just like them." He indicated the group at the end of the bar who were struggling with a rendition of "Chattanooga Choo Choo." "All we can do is the best we can." He was about to say something else when the air raid siren squalled.

The owner of the pub came out from the back room yelling to everyone to take refuge in the cellar below the bar where he kept supplies. Lydia looked a question at Allan. He stood up, took her by the hand and followed the others in the direction the barman indicated. "We're better off here," he said quietly in her ear as they descended the steep staircase into the gloom of the Bag o' Nails storeroom. "It's foolhardy to risk going somewhere else when you hear the siren." Lydia nodded. She always felt so much braver when Allan was with her.

The barman opened a couple of bottles of his best whiskey for his guests as soon as they were settled below ground. "On the house," he declared, "or under the house." Everyone roared with laughter; the tensions along with the alcohol had a strange effect on one's sense of humor. Someone began to sing again, and the others joined in with enthusiasm at first. One of the young women took her partner's hand and they began to dance. Then the cellar walls trembled and a few pieces of masonry fell from the ceiling. The singing tapered off and the dancers returned to their drinks. The barman made the rounds again, refilling glasses. Allan allowed his glass to be refilled, but Lydia shook her head no. She liked to at least have some control over her faculties, even if the world around her was out of control. She moved closer into the circle of Allan's arm and remembered all the nights she had spent below ground in the Russell Square Underground station, with only strangers and her diary for company. She closed her eyes. No more masonry fell from the ceiling, and the trembling of the earth seemed to move farther away from them. Eventually Lydia slept.

She awoke when Allan shook her gently. "Lydia. Lydia. The all clear has sounded. Let's go see what damage was done."

They joined the rest of the group, subdued and quiet now, climbing up the stone steps to the main floor of the Bag o' Nails. The barman led the way. He inched the heavy wooden door open, fearful of what he might see. Then he pushed it wide. "No damage," he said, "other than some dust on the floor." A collective sigh of relief coursed through the group; they felt it more than they heard it. It was as if a breeze blew from the front of the group to the back and everyone exhaled at the same time.

They walked to the front door of the pub, still remaining in their group formation, as if they were clinging to each other until everyone knew what truth they would have to contend with. The barman opened the front door to a scene of carnage. The bomb had hit the block of stores just on the other side of the street. Police and firemen were already rushing about, doing what they could to put out the fires and rescue the injured. A couple of bodies lay in the street, already covered, but the sheets that hid them were soaked with blood. Allan strode to the nearest fireman. "Is there anything we can do?" The man wiped the sweat off his face with a dirty sleeve. "It was a direct hit. Few survivors. But you can help shift some of these timbers just to be sure." He seemed to be rationing his words, saving his energy for what was important.

"Jack! Over here!" Another fireman shouted to the one Allan was speaking with. Without a word, he turned and dashed to a spot where several large beams had fallen in the street. The two men began to attempt to lift one of the beams, but it was too much for the two of them. Allan and the barman took in the situation immediately, and ran to help. They were followed immediately by another of the men who had been in the bar.

Lydia was unable to see who was beneath the beam, and with the men working together, she stepped back into the shelter of the pub door. Finally she saw them lift the beam up and move it aside, and then unbelievably, she heard the cry of an infant. One of the firemen rushed toward Lydia, apparently thinking that a woman would know to better know how to deal with an infant. Lydia's stomach clenched. She did not want a baby, anyone's baby, to die in her arms. But she took the child and with the fireman's help, gently moved aside the pale blue blanket, filthy now, to find that the child appeared to be unharmed. It was a little boy, and he kicked his tiny legs in vigorous protest of his treatment. Except for a small scratch on his cheek, he was fine. The fireman wrapped the child again. "We need to get him to a hospital, just in case," he said. "His mother's dead," he added bluntly. "There's a hospital just over in the next street and down a block. Could you take him there? There will be family members asking questions, I'm sure. Just tell them what you know. If we find any identification, we'll notify the hospital."

"Of course." Lydia was glad to have something to do, and called to Allan. He was still helping the firemen move beams, searching for those who survived and those who did not. He stopped his work and walked toward her. "I need to take this little one to the hospital. Mercy is just in the next street."

"Do you want me to go with you?"

"Not if you are needed here. I'll be okay." The child had stopped crying, but turned his head in the unmistakable manner of an infant searching for food.

"I'll see you back at the Dexters'." Allan kissed Lydia gently on the cheek. He smelled like smoke, grime and sweat, and something else. Fear maybe? Lydia turned quickly and walked along the undamaged side of the street, holding the baby close. His soft weight in her arms reminded her painfully of her two girls when they were infants. So small and helpless, and so light. She shifted the baby into a more comfortable, secure grip as she walked, and the infant reacted to the movement by turning his head to her breast. "Poor little one, you need your mama." Lydia could not contain the flood of tears that emerged from some deep place inside and almost blinded her. She stumbled and someone grabbed her elbow. "Careful there, ma'am." Lydia blinked rapidly to clear her vision. Mercy Hospital was just ahead. She walked in the front door, avoiding the emergency entrance which was swarming with ambulances and injured people who had walked in off the street since the bombing.

The receptionist looked up at her inquiringly. "Hello," Lydia said. "This baby is not injured, at least not noticeably. But his mother was killed just over in Sedgwick Street. The fire captain asked me to bring him over here to be checked."

The receptionist looked at Lydia as if she didn't believe her. "No name?"

"Not yet," Lydia answered. "The fireman said they would send identification over here if they found something." Lydia bit her lip to control her tears. The poor little thing would never know his mother.

"All right. I'll see what I can do." The receptionist stood up, and Lydia could see the woman's badly swollen ankles as she walked away. She was probably on her feet all day and helped out at the reception desk to give herself a respite from standing. She returned a moment later with a young student nurse, all blond curls, starched striped uniform and big blue eyes, eager to do some real work for the war effort.

The older receptionist led the young girl around to the side of the counter where Lydia stood with the baby, who was beginning to fuss with his need for food. "This infant was found over in the bombing just now. His mother is dead." She took the baby from Lydia and placed the little one gently in the student nurse's arms. "Take him and see if you can find some milk for him. Up to the nursery, I imagine. Maybe they can check him over. ID Baby John Doe for now. That is if we don't already have a Baby John Doe. If we do, just be creative." The young woman cradled the baby in her arms and walked away while the receptionist's tired eyes met Lydia's. "Thank you," she said, and then turned to speak to a nurse who was waiting at her desk.

Lydia's Diary
March 19, 1941

I was able to find a taxi easily from the hospital back to the Dexters' house. I briefly considered going back to the bombed-out street to look for Allan, but I knew I would only be in the way, and might not be able to find him. The firemen and police would have things in hand, I would only be one more person looking for someone, and it was entirely possible that Allan had already gone home.

As I stared out the taxi window at the darkened city, I continued to wipe away stray tears. I try to tell myself that my work at the Special Branch, the undercover agency of the War Office, typing and organizing lists of art work both in Britain and in Europe, is important work. My efforts to preserve the culture are important as well as saving our lives from the Germans. But somehow I feel useless and miss the children terribly. I don't have enough to occupy my mind.

The dimmed headlights of the cars as one drives around the city only add to the gloom. I have always loved London.

It has always seemed to be such a vibrant city. But not now. Not during wartime. All the things that I love -- the art work, the history, the parks -- everything has either been moved away and hidden, protected with barriers of sandbags and scaffolding like Nelson's statue in Trafalgar Square, or turned to more utilitarian uses.

I arrived back at the Dexters' home to find a panic-stricken Amelia Dexter alone in the house. Her husband had not arrived home yet either, and she was beside herself with worry. She was sure we were all dead. I was able to assure her that at least Allan and I were fine, and Mr. Dexter often worked late.

I think I hear Allan's voice.

March, 1941
London

"I can't go on like this!" Amelia Dexter screamed at her husband as soon as he and Allan Roberts walked in the door. The two men had shared a taxi from the site of the most recent bombing in London just on the edge of Soho. Allan's face and clothing were caked with dirt and soot from the fires, and his pants legs and shoes were soaked where he had waded in water from the fire hoses. John Dexter was in somewhat better shape. He had arrived on the scene shortly after the bombing, and had at least managed to stay dry, but his left jacket sleeve had sustained a long rip, and his shoes were covered with mud. A long, grimy scratch extended down his left cheek, and it was this injury that elicited a second scream from Amelia.

"John! You're hurt!" She flung herself toward him, mindless of her dressing gown whose tie belt loosened as she moved. She leapt towards him, throwing her arms around him and plastering herself against his bulk, as if the substance of him could be more real if her body touched as much of his as possible.

John looked over his wife's head in embarrassment as Lydia Roberts paused in her quiet descent of the stairs to greet her own husband. Lydia smiled tentatively. She knew that she looked exhausted, but her quiet demeanor belied the strain that she felt. Lydia continued down the steps toward her husband, placing each foot securely on each step as she touched it. "Allan." Her voice was clear but soft. Allan's ears were attuned to the nuances of her speech after twelve years of marriage.

"I'm all right, Lydia. You got the baby to the hospital?"

"Yes. They are taking care of him."

"Baby? What baby?" Somehow the word "baby" had penetrated Amelia Dexter's emotional fury and she lifted her head from her husband's chest. John attempted to pull her dressing gown together to cover her breasts. "Why do they have to kill the babies?" Her shriek tore from her throat, and threw her into a paroxysm of coughing.

"Amelia, Amelia," John held her by her shoulders as she bent over trying to catch her breath. "You can't let yourself fall apart like this. Amelia. Come. Sit down."

"No," she gasped. "No. That's enough. I don't want to know anymore. I don't want to know what time you get home and what shape you are in. I don't want to know about babies and bombs and Churchill and Hitler and all the rest." She straightened herself and removed John's hands from her shoulders with a precise movement and stepped back from him. She tightened and retied her silky gown around her slim waist. "I'm going to Derbyshire. Call me when the war's over, John. I don't want to see you until then."

Allan Roberts maneuvered his way around the Dexters and their problems to reach his wife, who stood frozen on the stairway three steps from the bottom. He glanced at the other couple but continued on to the stairs.

"Let's go upstairs, Allan," Lydia said. He took her hand and they went up together to the guest bedroom that had been theirs for the past week. After they closed the door, Allan began to remove his filthy clothing. He shivered with the cold as he pulled off his wet socks and shoes. Lydia waited until he had rubbed his feet briskly with a towel and dressed again in warm clothing – a pair of navy blue pants and a gray sweater he had owned since the early days of their marriage. She rose from her seat on the bed and slipped into his arms, which he wrapped around her.

"Like a hand in a glove," he whispered as he kissed her soft hair, which still smelled of smoke. She nestled deeper into his embrace.

"I hope we always fit like this, Allan. I hope we don't become like the Dexters."

"I don't think it's likely." He tipped her chin up and kissed her lips. "You are smart and sensible. She's... I don't know what she is. She doesn't have a purpose. You do."

"Do I, Allan?" She moved back just enough that she could look up into his eyes. "What is my purpose?"

Allan shifted his eyes from hers and then back and tightened his arms around her. "You are a talented art historian and cataloger. You are the mother of two wonderful little girls..."

"Whom I never see," Lydia interrupted.

"Lydia," Allan pushed her hair back from her face and regarded her. "You can return to Wales whenever you want. You know that."

"You know that's not the answer, Allan. I have my job to do just like you do. But I want to do more."

"You are going to Wales next week, aren't you? To the storage facilities in the slate mines?"

"Yes, I am. And I'll stop and see the girls and Mom and Dad." She wiped a few tears from her eyes. "It's so heart-wrenching to visit for a few days and then leave. I would almost rather not see them."

"Why do you think I don't go?" Allan said. "The war will be over one day, and we will be together again." He walked to the desk and opened his briefcase and extracted a brown envelope from which he pulled a single sheet of paper. "There is something you can do, Lydia, when you return from Wales."

She had taken off her shoes and had begun to carefully remove her stockings. It wouldn't do to ruin them. New ones were almost impossible to find these days. "What is that?" She paused with one stocking rolled half way down and looked up at him.

"Go visit this boy." He handed her the paper with the name and address of an exclusive school just outside of Cambridge.

"He's French?"

"And Jewish. I've been in contact with his family. They sent him here to school at the beginning of the war for safety. They have a younger daughter, but they felt she was too young to send away. I don't know how long they will be safe where they are. He is a somewhat reckless boy, prone to taking risks, opening his mouth when he shouldn't. I think they thought he would be better off in England."

"How did you come in contact with the family?" He turned to look at her, his eyes penetrating and his lips a firm line. "I know. I shouldn't have asked."

Allan removed his glasses and rubbed his eyes and Lydia could see how tired he was.

"It's not that. It's just such a sad situation. The family has lost their home already, and they own several beautiful pieces of art. There are some paintings and jewelry that they are holding onto for now. It's not a huge collection and the Resistance seems reluctant to help them. It would be risky for me to do anything on my own, but I hate to see them lose their treasures. Some of the items have been in their family for generations. And of course it is clear that several of the townspeople would like to get their hands on whatever the Jews own."

"So why do you want me to visit the boy?"

"Just so I can let the family know he is all right, and you can convey their love to him. But he's difficult. They warned me and now I'm warning you. So don't expect him to show any gratitude to you, or anyone."

Chapter 5

Lydia's Diary – March 26, 1941
On the Train from Wales to London

Allan and I had one more day together before he returned to Dover to prepare for his next assignment, and I left for Wales to visit the slate mines – and my family. The train was crowded most of the way to Bangor, and I was forced to stand, swaying with the motion of the train and thinking about my life. I spent two days at the slate mines going through the lists of smaller paintings that had just been organized in one of the storage rooms. It is sad to see those beautiful works of art hidden from view underground, but we are fortunate to have this location. It would be tragic to lose them to German bombs. At least those old slate mines are serving a purpose, and a noble one at that.

I spent two days with the family, and it was as heart-wrenching as I expected to be there for such a short time, and then to say good-bye. It was difficult explaining to the children and my parents that once again Allan was not with me.

Mom and Dad still don't appreciate that I am doing vital work for the country and our future. They want me there on the farm with them and the girls. And of course they lose no opportunity to remind me that that is where I belong. They were so proud of me when I went to University, and then to

London to work at the National Gallery, but ever since we had the girls, they just have not understood that I need to keep working. And it's not for the money, it's for me. It's who I am. And it is so difficult for the girls to be caught in the middle. What are they supposed to say when Grandma asks them: Wouldn't you like your mother to stay here with you? Of course they would. But the girls understand that there is a war on, and they know that plenty of other children have been evacuated from London, and not all are lucky enough to have grandparents to stay with.

The train is stopping in Chester now, and I need to get some tea. The trains aren't heated as well as they used to be. A few more hours and I will be back in London.

I will go visit the French boy at his school on Saturday. Allan will appreciate it. And maybe it will lead to some further involvement in the work in France.

Present Day
Driving from Wales to London

Nara read another diary entry and then looked at her father, who was taking his turn at driving. Nara had been talking nonstop since they woke up and she admitted that she had begun reading the diaries the night before. "If they didn't die in the Blitz in 1940 or '41, when and how did they die? And why was it kept a secret?" She looked again at the small stack of notebooks, all covered in faded pink cotton, which she had piled on the back seat of the small car. "Do you think we should read the last ones first, and find out?"

"That might not tell us anything," Jack answered. "I think we should read them in order."

"Even then, we might not find out what happened to them. She might not have written everything down. And it certainly wouldn't tell us how they died."

"No, but it will tell us what they were doing between 1940 and 1942."

"We need to go through the rest of the boxes, too."

Jack sighed and smiled at his daughter. "And I need to stop and stretch my legs. It's your turn to drive."

Fifteen minutes later they were back in the car with paper cups of coffee in hand. Nara took her seat behind the wheel and adjusted the rear view mirror.

"It's just unbelievable," Nara said. "Lydia and Allan sent their children to their grandparents in Wales. 'Not unusual during that time' as our friend at the University of Bangor told us." She adopted a sarcastic tone of voice in order to imitate Professor Mark Jones, who they agreed had been needlessly superior and unhelpful. "And then they stayed on in London and were never heard from again. The children, Aunt Rebeca and Grandmother Blake, were simply told that their parents' flat suffered a direct hit, and they were gone. And the boxes were put away in the attic and never opened."

Jack took a sip of his coffee and opened the first diary again. He read the words that Lydia had written on the first page: "If either of us survives the war, we will tell the truth."

"Will we recognize the truth when we find it?" he asked softly.

"They didn't die in the Blitz, Dad, they couldn't have. The diaries go up to late 1941. The Blitz ended in May." Nara spoke as she pulled out into the traffic of the M6 toward London. Once again Nara stated the one incontrovertible fact that she had gleaned from her reading of her great-grandmother's diaries during her sleepless night in the guest house in Bangor.

"Then why did we believe all these years that they did?" Jack answered. "It makes no sense. Surely they, or one of them, would have visited their children during that time." Nara slowed down to allow another car to merge in front of them.

"It almost seems as if she expected to die. I think she had some doubt that they would survive."

"I know. But so far she writes about Allan going to Spain

while she is in London doing cataloging, that doesn't sound like very dangerous work."

"Just being in London at that time was dangerous. That's why they sent the children to the country, remember?"

"I suppose." Nara was quiet for a moment. "I suppose everyone felt that way, not knowing if they would survive. I cannot imagine living through something like that, can you? Not knowing if your family, if your way of life would be destroyed? How did people get by day to day?"

"Just by getting by day to day," Jack answered. "That's it right there. That's how I survived after your mother died."

They were both silent. Jack rarely spoke of the death of Nara's mother, who had died of meningitis when Nara was just three years old.

"I wish I remembered her better, Dad." Nara's voice was barely audible.

"I know, Nara," he said. "But there's a lot of her in you." He patted her hand on the steering wheel.

They left off the serious topics of conversation as they entered London traffic, and Nara needed to concentrate on her driving.

"You could stay the night, Dad," Nara said as they unloaded the boxes at the flat Nara shared with her half-sister Lily. "Lily won't mind, and the sofa is comfortable. I've taken several satisfying naps on it."

"Thanks, Nara, but it's only a couple of hours drive back to Springfield, and I promised Sue I would take care of a few chores at the bed and breakfast tomorrow."

After Nara and her sister Lily shared a pizza for dinner, Nara made a quick call to Alex, the man she had begun dating the previous year. An expert on British religious art employed at the Victoria and Albert Museum, he had returned only that afternoon from an extensive trip to the

United States. He had visited several museums, evaluating nineteenth century British paintings and decorative pieces in American museums, and generally promoting goodwill between the institutions. It was not Alex's favorite type of work, Nara knew, but he did it when he was asked. He much preferred studying the art in the small village churches throughout England. That was how Nara and Alex had met a year ago, when he was working on an investigation of a theft in the church in the small town in Lincolnshire where Nara was living with her father and aunt.

With their hands cleaned of tomato sauce and grease, Nara and Lily settled themselves on the floor with the first of the two boxes from in Wales. Nara removed the six diaries; all covered in faded pink cotton, from the box and set them gently on the floor next to her.

Beneath the notebooks, wrapped in tissue paper which was crumbling now with age, was a crepe dress that once must have been bright green, faded now to a metallic greenish black. Lily ran the clingy fabric through her hands. "This is beautiful. Imagine having the figure to wear something like this, and she had two children."

"Look at this." Nara had unwrapped a small bundle of photographs. The first was larger than the rest and had the engraved mark of a professional photographer.

"A wedding picture?"

The black and white photo showed an attractive couple standing together under a gnarled tree whose branches must have shaded generations. The woman was almost as tall as the man, and although no one else was in the photo to lend comparison, they had the appearance of both being taller than average. The woman was dressed in a calf-length light-colored dress with long gathered sleeves. She wore a small hat with a short veil that was pushed back over her head, and in her hands she held a bouquet of what looked like lilies. But the most striking thing about the photo was the way the woman looked at the man, clearly her new husband, instead of at the camera. Her face held such light that the passage of more than seventy years had not dimmed the picture of her joy. The man stood straight, looking directly at the camera, with a broad smile showing even teeth. It must have been a breezy day, because his dark hair stood up at the crown, and a lock had fallen across his forehead.

"She was in love with him," Lily said.

Nara turned the photo over and read, "Allan and Lydia Roberts, June 4, 1933."

"She's beautiful," Nara added.

There were more photos of the couple, some in albums, labeled with white ink on the thick black pages, some in envelopes with notations such as "children," "friends," or "travel." Some photos showed older people who must have been relatives, friends the couple's own age on picnic outings, and a few in front of the Eiffel Tower on a trip to Paris. One album showed the beaming new parents with a small bundle wrapped in white lace. There was a little girl celebrating her first birthday, complete with a cake with one fat candle, and Lydia proudly hovering next to her child, who would have been Catherine. Farther on in the album there appeared another white bundle, and then more birthdays as the two girls grew into toddlers and then young children on the first day of school. All the photos were labeled in the same meticulous handwriting as the wedding photo. "Catherine and Rebeca, 1936...1937...1938..." The last photo in the pile was not labeled. It showed the two little girls with school bags, standing in front of the Welsh farmhouse with an older couple. One of the grandparents stood behind each of the girls, with a hand resting possessively on a small shoulder. No one smiled. The older couple squinted at the camera as if the sun was in their eyes. They were dressed for farm work -- the man in rough trousers and a long-sleeved work shirt, the woman in a print house dress and apron that covered her body from her chest to her calves.

"The grandparents must have sent this to Lydia and Allan

in London." Nara placed the photo on top of the pile.

"I can't imagine that it made them very happy," Lily commented. "The girls look like they want to run away, and the grandparents are holding onto them."

"No wonder Rebeca is bitter, and Dad said his mother never wanted to talk about her childhood," Nara added.

The contents of the two boxes were much the same. Nara lifted out another dress. This one was an elegant navy blue with a long flared skirt, a wide white collar, and short sleeves. She stood and held the dress in front of her own slight body and laughed as the skirt dragged the floor. "It's beautiful," Lily commented. "Styles of that time were so soft and feminine, even in the midst of the war."

"But later on skirts became shorter, in order to preserve fabric."

"I wonder if that's the real reason," Nara added, "or if the women just decided that shorter skirts were more comfortable."

Nara rewrapped the dress in its tissue paper. They found a pair of silk stockings that looked brand new. There were a few toys: a well-worn teddy bear, a few child-size cups and saucers, remembrances of a little girls' tea party. "At some point we are going to have to find out how to preserve these things. I can't think that folding them up in tissue paper and putting them in a box is the best way to accomplish that."

"It should be easy enough to find out. There are plenty of museums in London that do that sort of thing."

In the bottom of the second box they found a doll, lovingly enfolded in a hand-quilted blanket inside several layers of white tissue paper. The doll was almost the size of a newborn baby, but resembled a little girl more than an infant. Her head, arms and legs were porcelain while the rest of her body was a pink fabric. The cheeks and pouted lips showed a pale blush. Her long blonde curls were flattened at the back of her head from the years sitting against the flat side of a box, but she was in remarkably good condition. Lily lifted her, examining the lacy pink dress and matching underskirt. "This was someone's treasure. I wonder if it was Lydia's, or if she bought it for one of her daughters and never had a chance to give it to her. And I wonder why only one? She had two daughters."

"Maybe it was for the two of them to share. It must have been difficult to find a doll like this during war time, and even more so to find two of them," Nara answered. She examined the doll, turning it over, and undid the tiny buttons on the back to loosen the dress. "Look at this," she said. She showed Lily a row of tiny stitches running down the front of the doll's chest from just below the neck. The stitches were meticulously spaced and perfectly straight, and ran for about three inches.

"It might not have been new. She might have found it somewhere and mended it," Lily said, running her fingers over the stitching. "She was very good with a needle. The stitches are beautiful."

Nara buttoned the doll's dress and rewrapped her in the blanket. "No, wait," Lily said. "Why don't we let her sit out and breathe for a while. Let her hair and dress have some air."

"Good idea." Nara removed the blanket and carried the doll and blanket to a chair in the corner by the window. She folded the blanket to make a cushion and seated the doll on it, propped against the back of the chair. "She's pretty." Nara cocked her head to study the effect. "I think she likes it here."

"I think so, too," Lily answered with a tired smile.

"Lily," Nara said, as she stood looking out the window behind where the doll was seated on the chair. The street below was quiet, with only an occasional car passing. A bus pulled away from the stop across the street from their building, and a man and a woman stood together for a moment before going their separate ways. "Do you think the boxes and diaries are safe here?" she asked.

"What?" Lily answered. "Why wouldn't they be? What is

in them that anyone would want?"

"I don't know." Nara began to pick up the plates and glasses from their dinner. The pizza box held one remaining slice. "There was that man that Dad told me about, who called Aunt Rebeca after we were there."

"But there's nothing valuable in these boxes," Lily said. "They are historically interesting, and the doll may be worth a little bit, but I don't think there is much monetary value." She stood and stretched. "And interesting as the diaries are, I don't think they hold any deep, dark secrets that anyone would care about. And no one even knows that the diaries exist except us."

"I don't know. It's just a feeling," Nara said. "Maybe I'll take them up to Springfield and have Dad take care of them."

"Well, I'm sure he would like to see them. It's up to you. I'm going to bed." Lily picked up the shoes she had kicked off earlier and headed into her bedroom.

Nara straightened the kitchen and turned off the light and then stood at the window for a few more minutes. The London street was dark and quiet. That was one of the reasons she and Lily had chosen this flat. But now for some reason the silence felt sinister. The boxes, the diaries and their mysteries sat in silent testimony to the man and woman who had owned them. The doll sat in her chair, and seemed to yearn for someone to love her. "There are secrets here," Nara said softly. "More secrets than we realize."

Chapter 6

Lydia's Diary – April 1, 1941
London

One advantage to living with the Dexters is the food! I actually think I have put on a few pounds! It isn't that they have any more food, since the rations are the same, but they have a cook who prepares the food, and it is certainly tastier and more substantial than the boiled eggs and tinned fruit that I was living on in the flat. We even had trifle for dessert tonight. I don't know where she found the cream. I suppose professional cooks have their ways and their connections for locating scarce items. Amelia Dexter doesn't seem to think anything about it. She just eats what is placed in front of her and barely comments on the meal. I have added my ration coupons to theirs, and I think the cook appreciates it.

Amelia mentions Derbyshire once in a while, but she has not made any preparations to go. I don't mean to be unkind, but the woman can't seem to make a decision on her own. I would never want to be so dependent on my husband that I couldn't make a decision for myself. Even my mother, who is so traditional in many ways, will stand up to my dad when she has a strong opinion. We Welsh women are made of strong stuff, and I want my daughters to grow up the same way.

There I go, thinking about the girls again as I always do.

And why not? I am their mother. I must get to sleep, so I can get up again and do what I can in my small way to bring this war to an end and go back to my job of being a mother.

Good night, little girls. Sleep tight in your beds in grandma and grandpa's house. Mummy loves you.

Present Day
London

Alex Collier intended to go to bed early that night, after his exhausting day traveling from Los Angeles to London. If he went out at all, it would be to see Nara. He had missed her while he had been away. They had been together for a year now, and her exuberant, feisty presence in his life gave him an eagerness for living that he had not felt in a long time, if ever. He had renewed energy for his work at the Victoria and Albert Museum, where he specialized in British religious art, mostly from the medieval period. He had been doing an increased amount of traveling in the past few months, which took him away from Nara for extended periods, but she was back in school studying for a Master's in art history, and she shared a flat with her half-sister Lily. Alex knew that Nara had experienced an extraordinary number or changes in her life, and was willing to stand by her until they were ready to make their relationship permanent. They had occasionally spoken of marriage, but it didn't feel right for either of them just yet. Alex had already had one marriage that ended in divorce, and he was willing to bide his time before making another commitment, however much he loved Nara. And he did love her.

All of Alex's good intentions for the evening were spoiled by a message from his friend and co-worker Andy McCormick. Andy was often given to wild schemes and far-fetched plans that never seemed to work out, like the time he planned to take his girlfriend, along with Alex and Nara, to a play at the Globe Theater. Andy arrived dressed as a typical

Elizabethan groundling, complete with a bag of plastic fruit he planned to lob onto the stage if the acting was bad. But he left the bag of fruit on the Tube, and a sudden downpour soaked all the groundlings and they ended up warming themselves in a nearby pub. But Andy was intelligent and a loyal friend who had stuck with Alex through his divorce several years ago, and Nara thought he was funny. It took a lot to have a girlfriend and a best mate who got on well, and he could never imagine any attraction between the two of them so jealousy was not an issue.

Andy's phone message was cryptic and mystifying. "Alex. I have a question. Do you know anything about a Cézanne painting that went missing during World War II? It showed up here at some point and then disappeared again. Call me."

Andy's specialty wasn't French post-impressionists any more than Alex's was, and Alex was at a loss as to why he would be calling him with a question about a Cézanne. There were, to be sure, many works of art that were lost, stolen by the Nazis, or destroyed during the World War II years, and there could have been a Cézanne or even more than one that disappeared during that time, but Alex had no knowledge of it. He began to unpack his suitcase, and progressed as far as pulling out the dirty clothes and piling them in the laundry basket, when he gave in and phoned Andy.

Andy heard Alex's voice on the phone and wasted no time. "Can you meet me at the Red Lion in half an hour?"

"I'm exhausted, Andy," Alex answered. "What's this all about?"

"I'll tell you over a pint. It's very strange."

"I know nothing about Cézanne, Andy."

"Neither do I. Half hour at the Red Lion."

Alex reached the pub -- which was just around the corner from his flat near Regent Square -- before Andy, and was sipping a pint of lager when Andy walked in. Andy ordered a pint for himself and joined Alex. "Good trip?" he asked after a long pull on his mug.

"Good enough. I satisfied the boss. Shook hands and made connections with a few American museums. Not my favorite part of the job, but I seem to be good at it."

"That's because you look so intelligently British."

"Intelligently British?" Alex nearly choked on his drink. "Where did you pick that and up and what on earth does it mean?"

"You know. You've got the glasses, the accent, all this knowledge about stained glass and rood screens. Americans love that stuff."

"Maybe," Alex answered. "But I would much rather stay here."

"With Nara." Andy's intonation made it a statement rather than a question, and he waggled his eyebrows up and down for effect.

"With Nara," Alex agreed with a smile. "And I like my work here better. I'm not a schmoozer." He finished his drink and shook his head when Andy started to gesture for a refill. "So what's this about a Cézanne?" The long day with little sleep was catching up to him, and he stifled a yawn.

"Oh, right." Andy signaled to the barman for another drink for himself. "A graduate student from the University was asking about it."

"At the V & A? He'd be better off at the Tate. They have the impressionists. That's not our area."

"I know. I told him. But he seemed to have heard of you. He mentioned your name."

"Probably saw those TV programs I did for the BBC years ago. They still pop up in the middle of the night now and again. They're embarrassing at this point." Alex removed his glasses and rubbed his eyes in an effort to stay awake and reasonably alert.

"Anyway, what made me call you was that he mentioned that he heard this Cézanne ended up in Wales, and I told him about Nara and her relatives in Wales..."

"You told him Nara was in Wales? Are you an idiot? She doesn't need some nut case bothering her or showing up on her aunt's doorstep." Alex interrupted. He was losing patience with the conversation, and wanted nothing more than to sleep. "And why is he asking?"

"He is writing a paper on art that was stolen from Jews during the war and never recovered. And before you yell at me again, Alex, he's a descendent of the family it was stolen from, and he's willing to share the profits with whoever can help him find it."

Alex slammed his mug down on the table, causing several people at nearby tables to look up. He stood, pulling on his jacket. "Call me tomorrow, Andy." He was aware his voice was louder than was appropriate and lowered it. "I can't deal with this craziness tonight. I'm not getting involved in some wild goose chase for a painting that probably doesn't exist. How do you know this guy is telling the truth? It sounds like a scam to me. And he had better stay away from Nara and her family."

Andy looked crestfallen, but he often looked crestfallen when Alex shot down one of his ideas. Alex knew his friend would get over it. "Good night, Alex. Get some sleep."

"Good night." Alex turned and walked out the door. As he headed toward home, the fresh air woke him up just enough that his brain begun to function again, and he stopped suddenly, nearly causing a couple of teenagers to run into him. "You drunk?" one of them asked as they moved around him. "No," Alex muttered, and continued walking slowly. Hadn't Nara mentioned that someone had phoned her aunt in Wales after she and Jack left? Could it have been the person Andy was talking about? Inside his flat once again, he put his hand on the phone to call Nara, but he was just too exhausted for a conversation. Surely she would understand. Within ten minutes he was asleep.

"Paul, it may be gone -- destroyed -- or it may still be in France."

"What? The Cézanne or the necklace?"

"Either one. I'm not sure I even believe the story of that necklace. That sounds like something Grandmère imagined. You know she was, especially toward the end." Lisette slipped off her shoes and tucked her stocking feet under herself on the sofa in the rented flat she shared with her brother.

"Grandmère knew what she was talking about. She told me about that necklace when I was five years old. There was nothing wrong with her mind then. And she had the names of those British spies who stole our valuables, Allan and Lydia Roberts, in her papers."

Lisette groaned and collapsed on the sofa next to him. It was going to be a long night, with another of these fruitless, frustrating conversations with her brother. "Paul, did you ever think that Grandmère didn't want you to know? Even when you were fourteen, when she died, you were obsessed with this stuff."

"Grandmère didn't understand. Or maybe..." Paul's eyes took on a glow, like he could imagine the thoughts of his great-grandmother. "Maybe she wanted me to find out the names after she died, when we went through her papers. Maybe she wanted me to work to find my heritage, to be worthy of the Grassin name."

"Maybe she wanted *us* to be proud of the person she was, not go wasting our lives searching for treasure."

Paul took a noisy slurp of coffee and continued to glare at his sister. "Have it your way, Lisette. All I know is that Jewish woman who was rescued because of *our fortune* should have been the one to die."

"You should never have visited her, Paul. You had no right."

"I was respectful and polite, dear Lisette. I know how to

behave when something this important is at stake." Paul held out his empty coffee cup, but Lisette ignored him. He went to the kitchen and poured himself another cup. "It doesn't really matter now. Grandmère did some of the work for us. She had the address in Wales for that bitch and her idiot son, and the company on St. Clare. That family is full of idiots – they just gave me the names and address in Springfield without even asking who I was." Paul swallowed a mouthful of coffee, grimaced at the hot liquid, and set his cup on the table next to his chair.

"Use a coaster, Paul," Lisette told him. "We'll have to pay if we damage the furniture."

Paul picked up his cup, but instead of moving it to the coaster, he upended his coffee onto the surface of the wooden table.

"Paul, are you out of your mind?" Lisette shrieked. "We don't have the money to pay for damages! This is not our furniture!" She leapt off her seat to find a rag to clean the mess, but as she passed his chair, Paul grabbed her wrist with his left hand. Stopped short, she pulled against his grip. "Paul, please." She pulled again but he only laughed and tightened his hold on her.

"You see what you've become, Lisette?" His voice was shrill and maniacal. "You've become a servant, a maid!" He twisted her arm and stared at her.

"Paul, that hurts." She bit her lip to stifle the pain and he laughed again.

"You are an a-ris-to-crat, Lisette." He pronounced each syllable distinctly, as if she might not comprehend the word. "Hire a maid to clean it up. Hire a cook. Hire a chauffeur. Once we have what belongs to us, we can live the way we want to live and not worry about spilled coffee."

"The way you want to live, Paul. That's not me."

"Then why are you here with me, Lisette? Tell me that." He twisted her arm again.

"Paul, please. Let me go."

"Tell me why you are here with me." His voice had changed to a wheedling, childless sing-song. "Why is Lisette here with her little brother?" He grinned at her.

"To protect you from yourself, Paul," she said quietly. She took a deep breath. "Now let me go and we can talk."

He released her this time with a push that sent her stumbling a few steps before she regained her balance.

"I don't need you, Lisette. But I can't hurt you because you and I are all that is left of our family. The Grassins were one of the wealthiest families in France. We survived the Revolution. We lived through Napoleon and his nephew the other Napoleon. Grandmère's parents lost it all when they tried to *modernize* after the First World War. And then Grandmère's father made friends with those Jews. That when the trouble really started. People are not created equal, Lisette. Haven't you learned anything? We have nothing left, but I intend to get back what is ours. Once I do that, I will let you go."

"I'm going to bed, Paul. I'm not leaving you yet. But just be aware that I'm only doing this for the same reason you are. You are the only family I have."

Lisette's hands were trembling as she removed her earrings and replaced them in her jewelry case. She believed that she could handle Paul, but this trip to London was beginning to feel like a huge mistake. Unfortunately, she had committed herself to finishing her degree here at the University College of London. She had the money to cover her tuition and living expenses in London, but she would lose most of it if she returned to France. She changed into her nightgown and washed her face. Could she threaten him with returning to France if he didn't behave himself? Would he believe her, or recognize it for the idle threat that it was? Maybe she could find someone at the university who would listen to him. If he had someone else to talk to about his crazy schemes, maybe he would leave her alone. And if he turned out to be right, and some of their family's treasures could be reclaimed, it would be good news for both of them.

She climbed into bed and sat a minute before turning out the light. She could hear Paul talking to himself and pacing around in the living room. She hoped she had remembered to lock her bedroom door. She always locked the door, or he would barge in at any time of night for one of his semi-sane conversations. Each time was the same. "The Jews took our wealth. We are aristocrats. We deserve what is ours." Lisette was weary of it all. Her best hope was that she could one day earn enough to hire someone to care for him and she could have a life of her own. His footsteps stopped outside her door, and she quickly turned off the light. She had taught him that one thing, if nothing else: If my bedroom is dark, don't even knock. I won't answer.

Chapter 7

Train from Cambridge to London
Lydia's Diary - April 9, 1941

The boy frightened me. He was only fifteen years old and I should feel sympathy because of the difficulties of his family, and all the Jews in Europe, but there is something strange and disturbing about that boy.

I took the train to Cambridge and then another train to Compton. It was a bit of a walk out to the school but the day was fine so I didn't mind it. The people at the school were nice enough. I had to wait quite a while for the boy to arrive to talk with me. I suspect he did not want to come. Fortunately my government credentials helped smooth the way in being allowed to see him, and I am sure the headmaster of the school thought I was on some official business.

But the boy! He is nothing like what Allan thought he would be. He walked into the visitors' room and stood with his hands on his hips. He was small for his age with curly dark hair. I have never seen such an arrogant look on a child's face. He glowered at me. There was no hello. "You have news from my parents?" he asked.

"Not much," I answered. "But I know they are well, and they send you their love."

"That's a useless message." He paced around the room,

never once sitting and facing me directly. "They need to increase my allowance," he said.

I was shocked. I tried to tactfully explain their circumstances and the danger his family was in, but my words didn't seem to mean anything to him.

Apparently his parents set up an account at a bank in London when he started school here, and now he wants more money. I don't know what for. Surely he has enough for his school expenses and a bit of spending money.

I have to say that I don't like it, but there is nothing I can do. I'll talk to Allan when he gets back.

The atmosphere at the Dexters' seems to have mellowed into a sort of truce now. After Mrs. Dexter's outburst the night of the bombing, I thought she would leave immediately for their house in Derbyshire, but she is still in London and still complaining. I was worried, with Allan gone so much, that I would need to find another place to live, and that would have been difficult. The bombings have created an extreme housing shortage. I could not have stayed alone in the house with Mr. Dexter, even though they do have a housekeeper. I suppose Maggie and her boyfriend might let me stay with them for a while, but that would be uncomfortable, too, and crowded. Their flat is small, and there wouldn't be room for Allan when he is in London.

I just have to hang on day by day, as everyone is; I'm not the only person with these kinds of dilemmas. I need to be grateful that my family is safe and I have a roof over my head and deal with tomorrow when tomorrow comes.

We are almost back to King's Cross so I need to close this and get ready to fight the crowd through the station. Shall I take a taxi or the Tube? Probably the Tube would be quicker at this hour, even with the walk from Victoria Station.

April 11, 1941
London

Lydia was at her desk in the War Office the next morning when Major John Dexter approached her. "Lydia, could I see you in my office for a moment?" His face was serious and her first thought was that something had happened to Allan. She replaced the papers she had been working on and locked them in the bottom drawer of her desk before following him down the corridor to his office, her heart pounding. "Have a seat, Lydia," he said. Another gentleman whom Lydia had not seen before sat in a chair facing Dexter's desk, and she took the second chair. When she sat she realized her hands were shaking. *Allan. Please don't let this have anything to do with Allan.*

"Lydia, we are considering a new job for you, if you are interested. Your husband mentioned that you might be ready for something more challenging." He paused. "Your children are well cared for in Wales, I believe."

"Yes, they are with my parents. They are fine." She was more relaxed now. It wasn't anything to do with Allan.

"Good." Dexter looked at some papers on his desk and then back at Lydia, with a glance at the man seated next to her. "This is Captain Roland. He is our liaison with the French Resistance. As you know, besides fighting the Germans to preserve our lives and our countries, we are fighting to preserve our way of life. And our way of life includes the valuable, no the priceless, works of art in all the countries of Europe. The Nazis have stolen a great number from France, but many more are hidden, just as ours are, as you know."

"You speak French, do you not, Mrs. Roberts?" Captain Roland asked.

"Yes, I do," Lydia answered, wondering where this was going.

"And you are knowledgeable about French art." Captain Roland's pale blue eyes bore into hers.

"Yes. I did my Master's on nineteenth century French

painters."

"I know."

What else did he know? she wondered.

"Come with me tonight," Roland continued. "I want you to meet some of the French Resistance contingent. Their headquarters is in Pimlico, not far from where you are staying with the Dexters." He glanced at Dexter, whose face remained expressionless. "We want you to work with some of them on identifying and cataloging some of the lost paintings. Some have been identified only by description, and we want to see if you can recognize them."

"It will help us," Dexter added, "when this bloody war is over, to have some idea of what we are looking for. And there may be more serious work for you later, Lydia."

"More serious work?" she asked.

"Yes." Again his eyes met Roland's, but neither of them altered his facial expression. "Possibly more risky work."

"There's more to it than Dexter said, I'm afraid," Captain Roland told Lydia as they settled at a table in a pub a few blocks from their destination in Pimlico. He had asked her to meet him so he could brief her on the people she would be introduced to that night.

"What do you mean?" Lydia asked as she sipped a glass of wine which she didn't want, but Captain Roland insisted she accept.

"There are some actual paintings from France here in London, as well as the ones we are trying to identify from description," he said.

"What do you mean? Paintings that were smuggled out of France?"

His blue eyes sparkled and he flashed a smile. She had wondered if he were capable of a smile. "Dexter said you were quick." He took a swallow of wine and lit a cigarette.

He offered her one and she took it, grateful for something to do with her hands. "Yes. They smuggled some smaller pieces from individual collections out of the country. It was dangerous. They could have been caught, or the paintings lost on the crossing to England." He took a drag on his cigarette. "But they are here, nonetheless."

"And the owners?" she asked.

"What owners?" Captain Roland looked blank.

"The owners of the paintings. The people they belong to."

"Oh. I get it." He lit another cigarette and offered Lydia one but she shook her head. "You mean the Jews who owned the paintings."

"Are they all Jews?"

"Most of them. They are the ones who are desperate, and they are the ones who have the wealth to own paintings and jewelry."

"And so you protect their belongings for them until the war is over? Will they get them back?"

"If they are still alive."

Lydia felt cold. This man was a member of the SOE, the British Special Operations Executive, a covert military operation. He was trusted, apparently, by both the British government and the French Resistance. "Where are these paintings kept?" she asked.

"They are stored at the Resistance headquarters in Pimlico right now."

"That's not safe. They could be bombed at any time."

"True. That's where you come in. You are going to help us evaluate and catalog what we have, and then we can store them properly in a safe place."

"And you have a list of the owners?"

He laughed, and several people nearby turned to look at them. With a smile still creasing his face, Captain Roland reached across the table and took both of Lydia's hands in his. It happened so quickly Lydia had no time to resist.

"Lydia, trust me." His hands were warm and strong and he held hers firmly. She tried to pull away but it would have taken a conspicuous effort, so she let it be for the moment. "You are smart but too skeptical. I wouldn't have expected that from a beautiful woman like you."

"What does that mean?" Now she did pull her hand out of his grasp.

"You are implying that we are doing something illegal. Nothing could be further from the truth. Just like our government, the French Resistance is fighting a battle to preserve their culture and national heritage. If something is given to us in trust we will preserve it for them -- or their heirs. If they *sell* it to us, that's another story."

"And how many people sell their valuables to you?"

"More than you might imagine. They don't want the Germans to get their hands on their possessions, for one thing. So they would rather sell them to us. And they need the cash. They think if they are arrested or forced to leave the country, they can use the cash to grease the right palms to ease their way, or buy their way out of trouble."

"And can they?"

"Maybe. It depends." He drained his glass and looked at her for a long moment. "Lydia, we are all doing our jobs the best way we can. We can't stop all the unscrupulous operators out there. We are saving priceless art treasures from falling into the hands of people who will use it for their own purposes." He played with his glass, and turned to motion to the barman for a refill. "We want you to help us, Lydia. You come highly recommended, both in your professional and art credentials and your security clearance. And you speak French." He accepted a fresh drink and sipped. "And you are married. You are probably less likely to get distracted. Probably."

Lydia's mind was spinning. She knew she would do the job. It was the challenge she had been waiting for. And there might be opportunities for more active involvement once she had proven her worth. She sincerely wished she had time to discuss all of this with Allan, but she was already committed. If she refused this offer, it was unlikely that her name would be put forward for more responsibilities in the future. Captain Roland seemed to walk a fine line between respectability and the edge of unethical behavior. He was obviously trusted by the War Office, and held all the proper clearances and credentials of his own, although she was in no position to ask for them. His manner was disconcerting, and Lydia wasn't sure if he was coming on to her, or just exercising his male prerogative to flirt with any woman he met.

"I'll do whatever I can to help, Captain Roland," she said.

"Thank you. I know you will. And please call me Edward."

"Edward," she repeated.

He looked at his watch. "We'd better go. They will be waiting for us." He dropped some money on the table and nodded at the barman.

They left the pub and didn't speak as they walked down Belgrave Road. Halfway down the block he placed his right arm on her right shoulder, effectively encircling her. He pulled her a little closer to him and lowered his head. "Just listen tonight, Lydia," he said. "Don't say too much. They will trust you because you are with me, and they know I have the highest security clearance – and of course they know me well."

Lydia pulled away and stopped. The street was empty except for the two of them. "What do you take me for, *Captain* Roland?" she asked. "A child? A country girl just off the farm? Do you think I don't know how to handle myself in a sensitive situation? Why do you think I was chosen for this job?"

He smiled. "Because you are beautiful?"

Lydia took a deep breath. She wanted to walk away, but the job was too important. This was her chance to make a difference, and she wasn't going to allow one fool to ruin her chance. "No, Captain Roland. I was chosen because I am an expert in my field. I am an art historian and cataloger. I have an advanced degree in that area and worked at the National Gallery before the war. Because of my work and my reputation, I, too, have high security clearance. Don't condescend to me, Captain Roland."

"Sorry, sorry." He raised his hands, palms outward, in an apologetic gesture. "I am sorry, Lydia. Believe me. I'm not questioning your qualifications, but most women..."

"Most women what?" Her blue eyes sparkled in the evening light. Lydia was probably two inches taller than Captain Roland, a fact that had not been obvious when they were seated in the pub. She had the advantage of looking down at him.

"Most women... " He rocked nervously from foot to foot, as if the motion might create a perception of height. "Most women clearly are not as competent as you, Lydia. I apologize."

"Thank you." Lydia did not expect him to concede so quickly, and she felt a slight surge of disappointment. She would have enjoyed a good fight, but it would not have been constructive. "Let's do our job." She began to walk again and he quickly caught up with her.

"I'll introduce you to a few people. They know you are coming. They won't question your ability. They just want to meet you."

As they climbed the steps at 122 Belgrave Road he added, "I can see you home if you like. I believe we go in the same direction."

"Thank you. I would appreciate that." Lydia was thinking about the dark streets during the black-out and the paucity of taxicabs when she accepted his offer. It was only a few blocks to the Dexters' house – she could make it alone. But it was too late now.

Lydia's Diary – April 9, 1941
London

I have to work tomorrow, but I can't sleep. Starting tomorrow I will no longer be sitting at a typewriter in Whitehall. I will be working at the French Resistance headquarters three blocks from here in Pimlico. I am so anxious – yes, anxious is the right word – to see the paintings they have smuggled out of France. It frightens me to think that some of them were taken unscrupulously from people who are in desperate situations. I guess that is a euphemism for saying "stolen." I am making a promise to myself to do everything I can to keep accurate records of the works of art that I handle, and, if possible, to see that they are returned to the hands of their rightful owners.

Finally – *finally* – I have a job in this war that is important. I am doing something to make the world a better place – because where would we be without art and beauty in the world? I still miss my children, and my husband whom I worry about constantly and see not nearly often enough, but I think the ache will not be as sharp, now that I have work to do.

April, 1941
London

Lydia did, indeed, have work to do. She was amazed at the quantity of paintings, jewelry, and small objets d'art that had come into the hands of the French Resistance. "How do you manage to bring these things out with you?" she asked. "It must be terribly dangerous, and the extra weight..."

"Much of it was smuggled out before the war," Suzanne Valbert, the Resistance fighter who was working with Lydia, told her. "Some was carried out by the owners, or friends of the owners, and was either turned over to us for safekeeping, or sold to us. And the items are small enough to fit into knapsacks. We do what we can." She went to a filing cabinet at the other end of the large sunlit room on the second floor of 122 Belgrave Road, and pulled out a large folder that overflowed with loose papers. "These are sketches, and descriptions, of other works that have been seen but that we have not been able to remove."

"Seen where?" Lydia asked.

"Various places," Suzanne answered. "Houses, churches, even bars and hospitals." She walked to a large rectangular table in the middle of the room. Suzanne was almost as tall as Lydia, willowy thin and with flashing dark eyes. Lydia felt that she had to be on her guard with every word she uttered. Suzanne considered her a threat; that much was clear. She knew that Lydia's expertise was vital, but she was not about to allow Lydia anymore control than was absolutely necessary.

"What are you going to do with them?"

"With these papers? *You*," Suzanne replied, "are going to identify them from the sketches, if possible, and if not, transcribe the notes so we have clear descriptions for after the war. This is the art of France we are talking about here." Suzanne stood as if at attention, waiting for Lydia to thoroughly absorb the monumental importance of her task. Lydia thought she looked as if she might break into a rendition of "The Marseillaise."

"You understand?" Suzanne asked after a suitable pause.

"Yes, I do," Lydia answered. "Where would you like me to begin?"

Suzanne dropped the folder on the table in front of Lydia. "Just see if you can sort this out, to begin with."

Lydia's heart sank as papers spilled out of the folder. Sorting scraps of paper seemed more like a file clerk's job. "Wouldn't it be better to go through the paintings and actual objects that you have stored here first? Those are tangible items. If I can identify and catalog those, then they can be stored properly and safely. They aren't safe here. There is the danger of bombing, of course. But also the temperature and humidity have to be just so for proper storage of art work, depending on the type of work it is – oil, pastel, water color, and the age of the work. And of course the condition it is in. Are the pieces in frames? Are any of them rolled? Have they been damaged by water or mold? If you want to preserve these works of art, you need to take these things into consideration, or they will lose value."

Suzanne stared at her. "I don't know about any of that. They told me to get you started, and these papers are in such a mess, I thought that would be the place to start." Some of Suzanne's self-assurance seemed to have evaporated. Perhaps she had not been told that Lydia was an art historian. "I've never even seen the paintings they brought here. I know they are stored in the attic…"

"In the *attic*?" Lydia eyes opened wide in horror. "That is the worst possible place in this house! First there is the possibility of bomb damage. Even if it weren't a direct hit, if this building collapsed, the paintings would all fall down to the lowest level. Anything stored in an attic is vulnerable to shaking if bombs are falling nearby. The vibration isn't good for the paintings. *And* the attic has the greatest variation in temperature and humidity. Do you know how high the moisture content is in the air during one of our rainy periods?"

"I'll be back in a moment."

Suzanne walked out of the room and closed the door, leaving Lydia alone. The early spring sun shone through the window, and the hopeful chirping of birds outside in the garden was the only sound. Lydia opened the bulging file in front of her and picked up the first sheet of paper. The writing was in French, which Lydia read easily, but the words had been hurriedly written in pencil. The words described a tapestry in a small church in the village of St. Remy near Bordeaux. The church history claimed that the tapestry dated to the 1200s. It was described as being about fifty centimeters by sixty centimeters, and the picture woven into the tapestry showed the birth of Christ, with several saints, including the patron of the town, in attendance. Lydia had never heard of such a tapestry, but she knew there were treasures like this in villages all over Europe, probably all over the world. There might be another record of it somewhere to corroborate with this penciled description. On the same piece of paper, she read a description of a jeweled crucifix. It was about twenty centimeters in height, and purportedly studded with rubies. It was from the sixteenth century, or so it was thought.

Lydia wondered how much use these hurried descriptions really were, or would be after the war. But they might at least help to reinforce ownership in some cases. Clearly a great deal of effort had been put into collecting the notes of many people. She paged through the file and found handwriting done by many different people. Some were painstakingly done in fine ink, and others scribbled in pencil like the first one she read. They didn't seem to be in any particular order, so she pulled a sheet at random out of the center of the pile. This one was written neatly in blue ink, and read:

To whoever finds this letter:

I am entrusting two small paintings done by the artist Claude Monet, and purchased by my father, Josué Caen, from the artist himself around the year 1900. One of them is a small study of tulips, in yellow and white, and the other shows the bridge across the stream behind my father's house outside St. Remy in winter. These are my legal possessions and I intend to claim them when circumstances permit.

The letter was signed by David Caen, and agreed to by Laurent St. Gervain of the French Resistance forces.

Lydia put the letter back into the folder and stared in space. She was disturbed by what she had read. If the letters and descriptions on these papers were to be believed, there must be hundreds of priceless treasures documented here. And many of them were in this building. Would their rightful owners ever see them again, she wondered? It would be so simple to say, at the end of the war, that the paintings and jewels had simply disappeared. Who could prove otherwise? And if, as some said, Hitler was on his way to systematically killing the Jews, who would there be to reclaim lost property? It would be extremely difficult for heirs to prove ownership, especially if they were children. Lydia had the feeling that she had fallen into a rat's nest of double dealing French patriots. They were saving French art, as Suzanne Valbert had so dramatically pointed out, but saving it for whom?

Just then Suzanne returned to the room, followed by a uniformed dark-haired man whom Lydia had met briefly the night before. He was of medium height, with wavy hair that needed a trim. He wore dark rimmed glasses and reminded Lydia slightly of Allan, except this man was shorter and more heavily built. He smiled and held out his hand to Lydia. She thought he might intend to kiss it, in true Gallic fashion, but he only held it for a moment and released it.

"I'm Jean Bertrand, the chief of cultural operations here. Suzanne tells me that you think the paintings we have stored here could be in some danger." He pulled out a chair and sat down next to Lydia. Suzanne stood behind him, ramrod straight as usual, her face expressionless.

"I do," Lydia answered, and repeated her assessment of the peril of storing fragile works of art in an attic in war-ravaged London.

"I see your point," Jean answered. "You worked at the National Gallery here in London before the war, correct?"

"Yes. My area of specialty is art history and cataloging. I study paintings, help to authenticate the time period and artist, and use a system devised by the National Gallery to keep of record of any particular collection. There are private collectors who use a similar system."

"I see. Clearly you know what you are doing." He tapped his fingers on the table, glancing around the room as if seeing for the first time. Then he turned back to Lydia and leaned forward slightly, looking at her directly. "What would you suggest?"

"I would suggest that you allow me to go through whatever you have stored. The paintings are the most delicate so they should be the priority. I would like to go through them, catalog them, assess them for any damage so far, establish provenance, pack them properly and then store them in a safe place. But first and foremost, we need to remove them from the attic."

Suzanne seemed about to say something but Jean spoke before she had a chance. "Certainly. We will start moving them down to this room immediately. I'll find some men to do the work. It won't take long." He stood to leave, flashing a friendly smile at Lydia.

"But I thought..." Suzanne began.

"It doesn't matter," Jean answered her. It was clear he was her superior, and he wanted her to know it. "We will do it the way Lydia wants."

He left the room, oblivious to the look of hatred Suzanne gave to Lydia. Lydia knew she had made an enemy, but the protection of the paintings came first. She would deal with the personal conflicts later, but now time was crucial in evaluating the paintings stored in the attic.

Within the hour, several young men had climbed the stairs to the attic and carried down crate after crate and bundle after bundle of paintings and other objects whose identity Lydia could only guess, to the second floor room where she had been assigned to work. Jean told Suzanne to give Lydia any assistance she needed, and even asked her to bring coffee for them as they began their work, an instruction that Suzanne resented with a flash of dark eyes and a rattle of cups and saucers as she set out the coffee. The coffee was weak and undoubtedly mixed with ground barley in order to stretch it, but it was a treat Lydia had not enjoyed in a long time. She thanked Suzanne, hoping to placate her after her resentment against both Lydia and Jean, but she said nothing and avoided meeting Lydia's eyes. She gave instructions to the men carrying the crates from the attic, and she seemed to enjoy that role as the men obeyed her orders without question.

When everything had been moved from the attic, the lower room was half filled. Suzanne looked at all the crates and wrapped paintings, and then at Lydia with something like triumph, as if to say, *You wanted them. Now you've got them.* The file folder of notes and descriptions of art works still in France remained on the table. Lydia picked it up. "I think we can put this away for the time being. The notes are obviously valuable and should be kept safe, but we aren't ready to deal with them yet."

"Très bien," replied Suzanne, who swooped the file up and returned it to the cabinet it came from. "What would you like me to do?" Suzanne asked in accented English.

Lydia was walking around, surveying the various packages, boxes and individual paintings. She ignored Suzanne's attitude for the moment. "Let's start with the packaging that looks loose or damaged, because that may be a clue to the condition of the paintings inside." She paused and bent down to examine a parcel wrapped in brown paper that was torn at one side. "We'll start with this one." She carried the parcel to the table and gently removed the paper wrapping. She laid the three small paintings in a row. "Good frames. They have protected the paintings. Oils. Looks like nineteenth century." She picked up a magnifying glass and examined one of the paintings. "There is a tiny bit of mold in the corner here. See?" She offered the magnifying glass to Suzanne, who took it from her like an obedient child. "It's not serious. It can be easily removed, but let's hope that's the worst that we see."

"What about the others?" Suzanne asked.

"Let's take a look." Lydia studied each of the other two paintings. "About the same as far as the mold goes. They should be fine once they are stored properly." She turned over the last painting and studied the back. "A name. I assume that's the owner?"

"Probably," Suzanne answered. "There should be a tag or a label on one of the paintings in the group." She picked up the first painting. "Yes. Here is it." She pointed to a paper label that had been typed with a name and town and glued to the back of the painting.

"All right," Lydia answered. "At least some attempt is being made to preserve provenance."

"We do what we can," Suzanne retorted in her haughty voice.

Lydia continued to study the paintings. "No artist's signature. It could be hidden by the frame, of course. It might be a student of Delacroix. It is similar to his style." She turned to Suzanne. "Would you mind beginning a list? Let's write down everything we know about these paintings. Approximate size, what is written on the label, brief description of subject matter, even the type of wrapping and the fact that they have slight mold damage. We need to keep meticulous records, and then repair the damage if possible, repack the paintings and move them to safety. I'll make some contacts this afternoon and see if I can find a place for storage. Outside of London, preferably, but we don't have time to move them too far, at least not yet."

Suzanne began the lists without saying another word. The two women worked side by side for several hours. Lydia was engrossed in her work, and meticulously organized the pieces according to type of painting, extent of damage and estimation of value. It was impossible, of course, for her to make any kind of accurate estimate of the value. All she could do was to record works that were clearly signed by Picasso, Monet or some other well-known artist. There were other unsigned pieces that were labeled as those of a prominent name, but Lydia couldn't be sure. Several of the paintings showed slight mold damage as the first three had, and a number of them had small scratches that could be repaired at some later time. Lydia did not have time to deal with those now, as it would take a restoration expert to handle it, and they were not likely to worsen if they were stored correctly.

By mid-afternoon, the two women were exhausted. Suzanne leaned back in her chair and rubbed her neck. Her earlier animosity seemed to have evaporated. "We've made a start," she commented. They had, in fact, cataloged approximately half of the art works in the room. "Shall we have some lunch?"

Lydia was aware that the offer of lunch was a definite thawing in Suzanne's attitude, and she wanted to accept. She did, after all, have to work with her for the foreseeable future. But she was desperate to find a safe location to store the paintings. She had a friend at the National Gallery who could remove the mold, but time was crucial. "Yes. I'm starving. But I need to make some contacts about the storage of the paintings and the removal of the mold. Is there a telephone here?"

"Yes, of course." Suzanne stood and left Lydia to follow her down the stairs into a small office. One of the young men who had helped carry the paintings down from the attic sat at a desk with some papers. "Lydia needs to use the phone, Henri," she said. He gathered the papers and stood and scurried out of the room. "Don't be too long, Lydia," Suzanne said, wagging her finger as if reprimanding a child. "I'm starving, too," she said in English and laughed. Then she left Lydia alone. Lydia was unable to determine if Suzanne was still angry, if she was trying to be funny, or both. She decided to let it go for the moment. At least the Frenchwoman wasn't glaring at her anymore.

She reached her friend at the National Gallery, who promised to come the next day to assess the mold damage, and possibly clean some of the paintings. Now that all the National Gallery's collections had been moved into storage, there was not much call for repairing paintings, and he was glad to have something to do. Lydia tried to reach an associate at Special Branch who might have suggestions for a safe storage facility, but she was unable to contact him. She had some ideas herself. There were hundreds of churches throughout England that were built with crypts beneath. It was possible there might be one not too far outside of London that they could use, if the temperature and humidity were constant as they were in the slate mines in Wales. She even considered finding out if they could be taken to Wales. Surely the mines had room for a few more paintings. But the transport would be expensive and time-consuming, and she doubted they could acquire enough vehicles and petrol to make the journey. The National Gallery's works had been taken to Wales before the war shortages had begun in earnest.

Suzanne was waiting for her in the front office when Lydia finished her phone calls. "Success?" she asked.

"Success on the mold removal. He will come tomorrow. No success with my contact for storage, but I have some ideas of my own."

"Good. You can tell us at lunch."

"Us?" Lydia asked.

"Jean is meeting us," Suzanne said as she opened the door to the sunshine. "There is a little place just down the street, although we will have to eat English food." She gave Lydia a look that made it clear exactly what this French woman thought of English food.

Lunch was a strange affair. The pub was the same one where Lydia and Captain Roland had met just the night before, and appeared to be a gathering place for the French Resistance. The three of them ordered the ploughman's lunch, a traditional British pub lunch which Lydia thoroughly enjoyed, although the bread and cheese were of poorer quality than what one would have found before the war, and the slice of beef was small. The pickles were crisp and juicy, however. Suzanne criticized every aspect of the lunch, from the table setting, to the service by the flustered young barmaid, to the food itself. Jean repeatedly tried to silence her. She did not respond to his looks, or his quiet requests as he repeated, "Please, Suzanne, let it go. It's wartime."

To which she responded, "English food was bad before the war, now it's only worse."

Finally he ignored her and changed the conversation. "I see that you made good progress today, Lydia."

"Yes," she answered. "Suzanne and I were able to go through about half of the paintings that were in the attic. I have a friend from the National Gallery coming tomorrow to look at the mold damage. But I want to move all of them to a safer location as soon as possible, and I haven't found a suitable place yet."

"Ask Captain Roland," he said between bites of bread and cheese. The "poor quality" British food did not seem to discourage his appetite. "He always seems to know someone. He can probably find petrol for you as well because you will need transport."

"I'll call him after lunch," Lydia answered.

"He won't be in," Suzanne interjected.

Both Lydia and Jean turned to look at her. Suzanne had cleaned her plate and sat sipping the ersatz coffee served at the pub. "He won't be in," she repeated. "He called this morning with a message for you, Lydia. He said he will be away for a few days and will be in contact with you on Friday. He didn't think you would need anything." She finished her sentence with a lift of her chin that seemed to say, *So there!*

Lydia stared at her. "And you waited until now to tell me?"

"I forgot," Suzanne answered, her face a mask of innocence.

"Captain Roland is my superior. If he has a message for me it is important," Lydia replied.

"It was just a message. I told him you were busy with the paintings."

"Did he ask to speak to me?" Lydia struggled to maintain a calm voice, aware at how silly this must sound to Jean.

"I don't remember." Suzanne pushed her coffee cup to one side, as if dismissing it and Lydia at the same time.

"Suzanne, please," Lydia began. "In the future, if there is a phone call for me, or someone to see me, will you notify me immediately? Let me determine if it is important or not."

"If you want." Suzanne rummaged in her bag and pulled out a silver compact and powdered her nose. She finished, closed the bag with a snap and stood. "Shall we get back to work?"

That night Lydia dreamt of Captain Edward Roland, Jean Bertrand, and Suzanne Valbert. Captain Roland wanted to send Lydia back to Wales, and Suzanne agreed with him. "She's only fit to be a mother, can't you see?" Suzanne said in her French accent. "She needs to be with her children." Jean seemed to be trying to stick up for her, but his voice was so indistinct that none of them could hear his words, although Lydia was the only one who was making an attempt to listen to him. The other two ignored him and continued to argue about her in shrill voices. Lydia tossed and turned as she tried to make herself heard. Then another voice intruded in her dream. "Lydia. Lydia. Wake up. I'm home. Wake up."

She struggled to open her eyes when someone sat on the bed. She rolled over and collided with the bulk of her husband, Allan. "Oh, Allan," she said with relief. He bent over and kissed her lips.

"You must have been dreaming, love. You kept saying, 'Listen to me. Listen to me.' Who did you want to listen? Me? The girls?"

The dream was fading but Lydia knew it was not about Allan and the girls. "No. I think it was about work." Her words were thick with sleep, and Allan kissed her again.

"You will have to tell me about it in the morning." He stood and began to remove his clothing. He must have just gotten in, Lydia thought. He was still wearing his jacket.

"What time is it?" she asked.

He looked at his watch. "Five a.m."

"I have to get up in two hours," she moaned.

"Then we've got two hours, and you might even get a little bit more sleep." He slid into the bed beside her and pulled her toward him. She was aware of his strength and the warmth of his body, even though she had been in the soft nest of blankets for most of the night and felt deliciously warm and cozy. He kissed her again, a more lingering kiss this time, and rubbed his fingers up and down her spine, sending shivers along its length. She smiled to herself and thought how lucky she was as she moved closer to him. "Did you miss me?" he whispered as he nuzzled her neck, and moved his hand from her back to the feel of her breast beneath her cotton nightgown.

"Oh, God, Allan!" she said somewhere between a moan and a giggle.

"Is that a yes?" he asked. He put his hand under the bottom of her nightgown and ran it up the length of her thigh. "I love your long legs." He pushed the nightgown up to her hips and continued to explore with his hands. When he reached between her legs, she parted them instinctively and his fingers moved inside her. He caressed her gently, and she moved in response to his caresses. He moved on top of her; at the same time, he pushed the nightgown up so he could reach her bare breasts. He fingered her nipples as he moved inside her, sensitive to her growing response. They moved together rhythmically and reached climaxes at almost the same time. He relaxed and rubbed his cheek against her neck. "I love you, Lydia."

"I love you, Allan. You have no idea how I love you."
"Maybe someday you can tell me."
"I thought I just did!"
"Oh, that's what all those funny noises were about." He moved off of her and settled against her outstretched body. A moment later he was asleep.

Lydia thought she only dozed, but it seemed just a moment later that her alarm went off. It was 7 a.m. Allan slept on. *He must be exhausted*, she thought. He probably got no sleep last night until he arrived here, and who knows how much sleep he got when he was away. She so wanted to stay home and spend the day with him so they could both catch up on events of the past two weeks, but it was impossible. Even in her old job at Whitehall, she would never take a day off just to spend time with her husband, and he would not have done it to spend time with her. The war effort was too important. It just wasn't something that was done.

He didn't even know she was working with the French Resistance now, unless Major Dexter told him. She wondered how long Allan would be home. She smiled to herself as she wrapped up in a dressing gown and slipped down the hall to the bathroom. Home? Where was home? She passed the Dexters' bedroom. There was no fear of disturbing them. Amelia Dexter would not be up for hours, and her husband was already downstairs and about to leave for the War Office. Lydia shivered in the chilly air as she bathed. She thought of last night's, or rather this morning's, lovemaking. She and Allan were together so rarely that last night had the quality of a dream or a miracle. She returned to the bedroom and quietly took a dress from a hanger. Mrs. Dexter had given her a few dresses after the flat had been bombed. They had been a little big around the waist and a little short for Lydia's lanky frame, but she had done some quick alterations. Her sewing ability was not what her mother had hoped it would be. Sewing was not something that Lydia was interested in at any point in her life. She could sit for hours studying a painting with a magnifying glass, but handling a needle and thread bored and frustrated her. She pulled on a precious pair of silk stockings and the black pumps she wore every day. They had been in her bag the night the flat was bombed. At least her hair was no problem. She brushed it and pushed the waves into place, securing them with a few bobby pins. She put on lipstick and slipped the tube into her bag. She would have a bite of breakfast and be ready to go.

She bent over Allan and kissed him gently on the cheek. "See you later, love," she whispered. He took a deep breath and slept on.

Chapter 8

Lydia's Diary – April 11, 1941
London

I am alone at breakfast this morning so I will use the time to write a few words. I can't express how happy I felt when Allan came in early this morning! At least one of the pieces of my world is back in place! I do, however, have a niggling worry in the back of my mind that he is not going to be happy that I am working with the French Resistance, even though it is just in a house in Pimlico. I don't know. As close as we are, I have a fear that he won't be happy that I made the decision without him. But what could I do?

April, 1941
London

The French Resistance office was dead quiet when she arrived. The young man who had been in the office with the telephone the day before sat in the same place, and he appeared to be perusing the same sheaf of papers. "Bonjour, Madame," he greeted her.

"Bonjour. Where is everyone?" Lydia asked.

He waved his hand in dismissal of the entire situation. "Some have gone." He did not say where they had gone.

"Some have not arrived yet. I think there was a celebration last night."

"A celebration?"

"I don't know. I was not invited." He stood up the stack of papers and tapped them on the desk to straighten them. The celebration, and his lack of an invitation, did not seem to bother him too much.

"I'll just go ahead and get started then." Lydia moved toward the door to the room where she had worked the day before.

"You can't go in there," the young man answered around a mouthful of something chewy.

"Why not?" Lydia asked. Her hand was already reaching for the door.

"Because it's locked, and I'm not allowed to open it."

"What? Do you have the key?" Lydia experimentally turned the doorknob and confirmed that it was, indeed, locked.

"I have it," he answered. "But only approved personnel are allowed to open it."

"And I'm not approved personnel?"

He looked at her, trying to decide if she was or was not "approved personnel." She stared back at him intently, waiting for an answer. She wasn't his superior, but she wasn't *not* his superior either. Lydia was at the end of her patience. "Are you going to unlock the door for me or not?"

"No." He did not sound sure of himself. "I can't."

"Listen." Lydia pulled a wooden folding chair next to the young man and sat down. "What is your name?"

"Henri."

"Henri, I understand your reluctance to open the door for me, since you don't know me. But time is crucial. The sooner we catalog and repair these paintings, the sooner we can move them to a safer place." Lydia noticed a glimmer of apprehension in the boy's eyes. How old was he? Nineteen? Twenty? And why was he here in London instead of fighting in France? "It's not my fault, or your fault, that everyone else is late today. But the work still needs to be done. And I have an official from the National Gallery coming in an hour to see if the damaged paintings can be cleaned." This wasn't exactly true, but Lydia thought that calling Robert Clay an "official" was a small lie considering what was at stake.

Henri looked a little frightened, and then seemed to come to a decision. He tossed the ring of keys across the desk. "It's the one with the red mark on it."

Lydia located the correct key and inserted it into the lock. As she began to turn it, Henri said, "I'll tell them you took the keys out of the desk."

"What?" Lydia turned around.

"You can handle Suzanne better than I can. I've seen you do it."

"Do you take orders from Suzanne?" she asked. Lydia was more confused than ever about who actually ran this office.

"I'd better. She's my sister," he said.

Lydia decided that he was undoubtedly right, and that she *could* handle Suzanne better than he could. She felt more than a little sorry for him, having to deal with Suzanne as an older sister. And why were they here – together? She unlocked the door and tossed the keys back across the room to him. "All right, Henri. I'll take responsibility."

Everything in the room appeared just as she had left it the afternoon before, which was a profound relief to Lydia. But since the staff had been celebrating the night before, there would not have been time to disturb any of her work. She opened her notebook, which she had carried home with her, and skimmed over what she had completed the day before.

She picked up Suzanne's notebook to verify the information, since Suzanne had been taking the bulk of the notes while Lydia examined the paintings. As she opened the book, a small sheet of pale blue note paper fluttered to the floor. Lydia picked it up and automatically read what was written there. In French, the note read:

Chère Suzanne,

It is not yet safe for either you or Henri to return, especially not Henri. Talk has died down, but I know he would be questioned, and worse, if he returned. Don't be foolish, Suzanne. I know you have your dreams, but right now you *must* put your safety first.

Your maman send her greetings and love, as do I.
Papa

Lydia replaced the note and put Suzanne's notebook back where she found it. She did not want to even think about what Suzanne would say, or do, if she found out that Lydia read her note. She spread out her own notes and focused on identifying and recording the details of more paintings. But one part of her mind continued to mull over Suzanne and Henri, and what the note meant. What had Henri done that he might be questioned about, and by whom? Most likely Lydia would never know. As soon as the art work here at the French Resistance headquarters was packed and stored again in a more secure location, she would not see these people again.

The sunlight, along with the noises in the street, woke Allan. He rolled over to the soft impression Lydia left on her side of the bed. It was no longer warm, as he foolishly hoped. She had gone to work and left him to sleep. He needed the sleep, no doubt about it. He had averaged about three hours a night for the last two weeks. And as usual when he returned to London, his elation at being back on home soil and with Lydia was soon marred by the knowledge that he would have to leave again. Sometimes he was home as long as a week, and sometimes he would be called the next day and given orders to return to Spain where he worked with the French Resistance against the Nazis. Once he had parachuted in to France, but most often he was transported by boat and dropped off on a deserted beach near the Spanish border. Either way, he knew he put his life in peril every time he made the crossing. Crossing the Channel was more dangerous than the actual work he did, where he lived in a safe house in a village near the coast. His clandestine assignments were exciting the first few times. The work was such a drastic change from his steady, conservative life before the war, when he and Lydia and the girls lived in their attractive little house in north London. He and Lydia had commuted into central London each day, and they had the money to send the girls to an excellent primary school. Now he sometimes had difficulty believing that had been his life. He had not seen his daughters in six months, and although he missed them terribly when he thought about them for any length of time, or when he looked at the small photo of them that he kept in his wallet, most days he did not think of them at all.

This fact disturbed him, so he threw himself even harder into his work. He adored his wife, and the time he spent with her on his brief trips to London were like a renewal of their courtship and the early days of their marriage before the children were born. He knew that many men in his situation became involved with women in France, but he had no intention of being unfaithful to Lydia.

Allan forced himself to get out of bed. He knew the Dexters understood how exhausted he was, but he still felt ill at ease if he slept too late in the morning. He found the bathrobe Lydia had bought for him after their flat was bombed and prepared to slip down the hall to the bathroom. He opened the door a crack, and all was quiet.

After bathing and dressing in clean clothes, Allan was famished. The Dexters' housekeeper was kind enough to make him a simple breakfast of scrambled eggs on toast and strong tea, but she made it clear that she did not normally prepare meals at unorthodox times like 10 a.m.

He left the house for the walk to Whitehall. It would take him twenty minutes on foot, but he was ready for it on this warm spring morning, and he wanted to see what London was like, if it had changed since the last time he was here. He crossed Vauxhaul Road and then decided to angle over toward the Thames and walk through the Victoria Tower Gardens. It should be beautiful this time of year. Daffodils and tulips bloomed even in wartime if they were given half a chance. He was not disappointed, and his steps slowed as he inhaled the fragrance of springtime. Normally on a warm spring morning the park would be filled with mothers pushing prams, but it was rare to see children in London at all these days. He passed the Houses of Parliament on his right and Westminster Abbey on his left, and felt the swell of pride he always felt when in the center of his London. With the Abbey looming over his shoulder, he whispered a prayer to whatever God might be listening, that his country and his way of life would be preserved. Life was too precious and too fragile. He could not bear the thought that his and his family's lives could change, but he knew it was unavoidable.

He stepped inside the dim interior of Whitehall and allowed his eyes to be accustomed to the low light before entering the office where Lydia worked.

"She's not here?" he said when her co-worker Maggie answered question about her whereabouts.

"No. She's on a special assignment."

"Where? Doing what?"

"I don't know. I haven't heard, but then I might not, mightn't I?" Maggie smiled sweetly at Allan. She had always rubbed his nerves the wrong way, and he realized it even more so when Lydia was not present to act as a buffer. Her hair was a little too blonde, and her skirt a little too short. She was pretty in a childish sort of way.

"I suppose not. Who knows then?"

"Dexter probably. You could ask him." She was chewing gum, a habit that Allan detested.

Major Dexter – he wanted to correct her, but he knew it would be pointless. "I'll go ask him. Thanks."

"Wait." Maggie put out her hand and he turned back. "Buy me lunch? I'm off in half an hour." She cocked her head to the side and grinned at him.

"I was hoping to have lunch with Lydia."

"You mean she didn't tell you she had a new job."

"I got in very late last night, and she left early this morning." Allan had no wish to explain himself to Maggie Rhodes. "I'd better catch Major Dexter before he goes out to lunch. Goodbye, Maggie. I'll talk to Lydia tonight and find out all the details of her new job, but thanks for telling me." He left the room and headed down the corridor to John Dexter's office. As Allan reached the office, Dexter himself emerged with a younger man whom Allan did not recognize.

"Allan! Welcome home! Or welcome home for now, I suppose I should say." The older man laughed heartily. "Do you know Captain Roland?" He indicated the blond uniformed man, about Allan's age, who stood at his side.

"Allan Roberts." Allan held out his hand.

The two men shook hands, but John Dexter seemed in a hurry and not inclined to pleasantries. "Wish I could invite you to lunch, old boy," he said to Allan. "But Roland and I have an errand that can't wait, I'm afraid."

"Actually I stopped by to ask you a question, Dexter," Allan said. "Where is Lydia working these days?"

Dexter's eyes shifted uneasily to Roland's, and back again to meet Allan's gaze. "You mean she hasn't told you?"

"I only got in late last night. And she was gone when I woke up this morning."

"Taking advantage of the time off to catch up on your sleep, what?"

"I get bloody little of it when I'm working," Allan answered. He was feeling annoyed with Dexter, and inexplicably with Roland as well. *Why didn't he just answer the question?*

"Of course. Of course. On second thought...." He glanced at Roland again. "Walk with us for a few minutes and I'll explain."

They moved out into the bright spring morning and joined the crowds moving up and down Whitehall. Everyone was in a hurry. There were men and some women in uniform; people out for a quick lunch from the government offices that lined the street; taxicabs and buses moving in the traffic.

John Dexter maneuvered to walk between Allan and Captain Roland as they made their way down Whitehall toward Trafalgar Square. "She's helping us out at the French Resistance headquarters."

This was not what Allan expected. "Doing what?" he asked.

"Nothing dangerous." Dexter laughed. "At least not at the moment." The men slowed momentarily as a group of military officers emerged from a gated area that led to Churchill's War Cabinet rooms. "She's cataloging some of the art they managed to spirit out of the country. It's her area of expertise, but you already know that. Captain Roland here introduced her to the appropriate people over there."

Captain Roland said nothing, and Allan again wondered why the man made him feel so uncomfortable.

"How long do you think it will take?" he asked, directing his question to Dexter.

"No idea," Dexter replied. He turned to Captain Roland. "Do you have an answer to that, Roland?"

"No, I don't. I know several people there, but I have never seen the paintings. I believe they have them stored in the attic, but I don't know how many they have. I think they have other things as well – jewelry, maybe a few small decorative items. Whatever they have been able to smuggle out."

"Paintings stored in an attic in London with bombings every other night." Allan shook his head. "Lydia must be beside herself. No wonder she left early for work."

"Must leave you here, old boy," Dexter said as he paused in front of an archway that led through to the Admiralty Building. "Roland and I have some business."

The men shook hands again, and Allan had the distinct impression that Roland was sizing him up, for what reason, he had no idea. But he felt as he had as a young boy when a competitor in childhood games sized him to determine how hard a fight he would put up, or a classmate with whom he competed for academic honors. Whatever it was, Allan was ready. He was no longer just the intellectual academic, armed with his knowledge of art. His work with Special Branch had made him tough, both physically and emotionally, and he was sensitive to any nuances of body language that might necessitate swift action. Whatever Roland was up to, he would find a formidable opponent.

Although Allan was quite familiar with the work of the French Resistance headquarters in Pimlico, he had never actually been there. All of his work with the Resistance had been carried out under the auspices of the Special Branch. He was not going to go there now and look for Lydia. It would be inappropriate from a professional standpoint. Additionally, he was not at all sure how he felt about his wife working with the Resistance arm of a foreign government, even in times such as these.

He and Lydia had always had individual professional lives, but they had worked in tandem, as they were both in the field of art history and preservation. Their jobs had seemed to balance each other, and they discussed the work that each was doing and made suggestions to each other. All that changed when war broke out. At thirty-seven, Allan was too old to serve in regular capacity in the military. He volunteered to do whatever he could, and was eventually recruited by Special Branch as a liaison between members of the French Resistance in Spain and southern France. It had shocked Allan that he had been asked to become what amounted to being a British spy. John Dexter, who had recruited him, told him that he had the ideal qualifications. He spoke French fluently and had spent time in southern France during his university years, and his knowledge of art gave him a cover. He had begun by simply meeting with French representatives to relay information to the British government, but eventually he was asked to travel to the border of Spain and France high in the Pyrenees Mountains along with French agents. He found that he was good at presenting himself as a Frenchman, and was able to glean valuable information on the actions of the Vichy government and the German troops in the region. The French accepted his knowledge of art and he was instrumental in smuggling out the valuables of a number of people, especially Jews.

As he walked on toward Trafalgar Square and its statue of Lord Nelson clothed in its wartime protective scaffolding, his thoughts were not on his work; he was thinking about Lydia. Although they had discussed her dissatisfaction with her office job at the War Office, he was worried about her taking on a more active role in the war effort. What had Dexter been thinking? And she had simply gone and done it while he had been away, without discussing it with him first. Of course, what could she have said when she was asked, *I have to ask my husband?* Lydia was too much a professional and modern woman to do that. But nonetheless, it disturbed Allan. What if something happened to both of them? Who would take care of the children? The answer to that was easy, of course. Their grandparents would take care of them, as they were doing now.

Allan crossed Trafalgar Square and passed the National Gallery and thought of Lydia's work there before the war. She had been invaluable in resettling precious works of art in the depths of the slate mines in Wales. He had not worried about her then. So why was he worried now? He was deeply committed to his work, and on some level he could not wait to get back to the Continent and the people he worked with there. But Lydia was a constant. She was always here in London waiting for him. If she changed too, what would happen to them?

Allan turned back and entered the National Gallery. He was surprised to see a crowd of people entering the main hall, but then he remembered. Although the bulk of the museum's art collection had been moved out of London for safekeeping, the directors did not want it to lose its importance as a center of art. The museum had begun with exhibits showing works of new artists and soon added daily lunch time concerts. A canteen staffed by volunteers served lunch to concert-goers. Allan joined the queue and purchased a ham sandwich and coffee. He stood in the lobby and listened to the music; someone with a beautiful soprano voice was singing an operatic aria. It was something Lydia would enjoy, although Allan was not a big opera fan. He wondered if she had been to any of the concerts.

He finished his sandwich and left the museum. He would walk back to Whitehall and see if Dexter had returned. But on the spur of the moment he turned and walked down the Mall toward St. James Park. He needed some time to walk and think before going back to Whitehall. Lydia was everything to him, and he realized that he was more terrified of her changing and becoming more independent than he was of losing her. Loss of someone you loved was always a possibility in wartime, but one rarely thought about the way in which war changed the people who survived.

Lydia had chosen to remain in London and work during the war. But Allan knew that although he didn't think twice about putting himself in danger, he drew a hard line at the same thing for his wife. He didn't know if he could bear the knowledge that she was involved in any type of risky activity. But how did *she* feel when he was gone? She knew he was taking risks, although he never told her in so many words. Was it because he was a man and she was a woman?

Lydia twisted a lock of hair around her fingers as she sat at her work table in the French Resistance headquarters. The confrontation with Suzanne about the key to the room where they were working with the paintings had been worse than she expected. Suzanne had screamed at both Lydia and Henri, although the brunt of her outburst had fallen on Henri. Lydia did not know whether to be relieved or troubled that he had borne the greater portion of his sister's anger. He said little, but simply sat at his desk and waited for the storm to pass. Lydia suspected that he had endured that sort of thing before and knew how best to handle it. Lydia followed his example, and after a few attempts to put forth reasonable arguments, she gave up and waited as well. The screaming finally ended with Suzanne bursting into tears. She sobbed into a man's white handkerchief that she pulled from a pocket, but Lydia noticed that while the tears were genuine, at the same time Suzanne looked over the handkerchief to judge the reaction of her audience, which consisted solely of her brother and Lydia, since everyone else was steering clear of the room. Neither Henri nor Lydia gave her the attention she wanted, so the sobbing soon subsided into sniffles.

"Bien. Bien. You have what you want, both of you. I have other work to do. You don't need me. I'm going to the other office to write some letters."

"Do you need your notebook, Suzanne?" Lydia asked. "The one you were using yesterday when we were working?" Lydia was thinking of the blue note paper with the mysterious message from Suzanne and Henri's father.

"Mais non, I don't," she answered. "You need those notes. Keep it. I have other notebooks." She waved her hand in dismissal and left the room, apparently forgetting about the note tucked in the back of her notebook.

Lydia did not want to risk Suzanne's anger when she remembered the note, as she surely would. And since she had told Lydia to use the notebook, it would be reasonable to assume that she would see the note at some point. Lydia went into the room and retrieved the note, and without looking at its contents again, she folded it neatly in half with the writing on the inside. Perhaps Suzanne would not remember that it was not folded originally. Lydia took it to Henri and handed it to him.

"What's this?" he asked.

"It was in the back of your sister's notebook. It looked like a personal note so I thought perhaps you could give it to her when she calms down."

Henri opened the note and glanced at the contents. He looked up and met Lydia's eyes. "You read it."

"Yes," she said. "I couldn't avoid it. I didn't know what it was. It simply fell out of the book."

"It doesn't really matter if you did," he said. "Everyone has done something these days. Something that would not be right in normal times, but now..." He shrugged.

"I know," Lydia answered. "It doesn't matter to me. But it might to Suzanne."

"Yes. It will. I'll think of something." He toyed with the note, sharpening the edge of the crease with his fingernail.

"I think I can work at least another hour before I break for lunch," Lydia said, when the silence had grown uncomfortably long. "You know where I am if anyone needs me."

"Oui," Henri answered. He took a deep breath. "Suzanne has always been like that. I apologize for her."

"It's not your fault, Henri," Lydia said. "As you said, everyone has something to be on edge about these days."

Chapter 9

Lydia's Diary – April 15, 1941
London

It's not that I am afraid, but I am ill at ease with the people I have been assigned to work with. I was under the impression that I was sent to help them because of my special experience and skills in the art world, but I am being treated like an intruder. I am not a confrontational person, but the more time I spend with Suzanne, her brother Henri and the other French Resistance workers in the office in Pimlico, the more I feel as if open conflict is about to break out right there in the office. And it isn't just the historic rivalry between the British and French; there is something more. They don't want me there, but I have been forced upon them. Did they want someone else? Had they expected a man to be sent to do the job that I am doing? I just don't know. I am making good progress with identifying and cataloging the paintings I have been given, and I am working with the SOE to find a place to more permanently store the pieces.

The only person who has seemed the slightest bit friendly is Henri. Ever since the incident with the keys, he and I have formed a sort of silent alliance. We provide buffers for each other against Suzanne's tirades and unreasonable demands.

I had hoped to be able to discuss the entire matter with Allan, but there just has not been any time. He was only home for three days this time, and he seemed reluctant to listen to what I had to say about my work. It is almost as if he doesn't want me working there at all. And he was unwilling to listen to my reasons for working there and the difficulties I have encountered. This seems to be a test of our relationship, and I pray we get through it. The pressures and strains that we are experiencing are more than either of us expected. It is as if we are on the brink of some stupendous change in our lives – our lives together and our individual lives. All I can do is try to muddle through day by day.

April, 1941
London

It was the day that the first of the paintings were to be moved out of London that the situation with Suzanne became untenable. With the help of her own contacts, Lydia had been able to find a small village church in Berkshire, less than fifty miles from London, that contained an undercroft of sufficient size to accommodate the paintings. The vicar had been reluctant at first because it was not strictly a British operation, but he had finally come round with the argument that art did not belong to any one particular country, but ultimately to the world. It wasn't just French and British art that was being protected, but that of Western civilization. The paintings had been carefully wrapped and packed the day before, and were ready when the lorry arrived at nine the next morning. As Lydia began to direct the loading of the transport, and both French and British workers carried the cargo out the door, Suzanne became hysterical.

"What are you doing? YOU." She aimed the anger at Lydia. "You have no right to order us about. Just because we are in your country, you have no right to treat us this way!"

The French workers continued to carry the paintings out the door. They were used to Suzanne's emotional outbursts. The British workers stopped in their tracks and stared at her.

Henri froze, and then he did something that Lydia had not expected. She had only seen him in the subservient younger brother position with his sister, but clearly there was another aspect to their relationship.

He stood and took her arm, guiding her into another room. "Suzanne. It's all right. You have to let them help. You can't do it all yourself." He closed the door and Lydia heard him continue to speak calmly to her, although the words were muffled. Lydia nodded to the British workers, who resumed their task. After a few moments, Lydia thought she heard sobbing from behind the closed door.

The transportation, unloading and storage of the paintings in the undercroft of St. Anselm's Church in Swallowfield took the better part of the day. Lydia affixed thermometers and humidity gauges to various spots throughout the storage area and promised that someone would return periodically to check on the condition of the paintings. The vicar also came around to the idea that he could contribute to the war effort by occasionally checking himself to see if all was well with the paintings, although Lydia felt considerably better just knowing that they were no longer in an attic in London.

It was almost dark when they arrived back in London, and Lydia decided to go straight home to the Dexters' house. She felt dirty, tired and in no mood for another confrontation with Suzanne. She planned to take a bath and write some letters. She had been so busy lately that she was behind on her correspondence with the girls and her parents. She was surprised, therefore, to find an officer from Scotland Yard waiting for her in the Dexters' drawing room, while Amelia Dexter sat nervously in a chair facing him. She had just served tea, and was attempting to carry on a conversation with someone whom she could only associate with bad news.

When Lydia walked in, Amelia Dexter's relief was evident. "Lydia, I'm so glad you are here. This man is from Scotland Yard and he wants to talk to you. I told him I wasn't sure when you would be home, but he insisted on waiting. I'm so glad you are here. John isn't here yet, of course."

"It's all right, Mrs. Dexter," Lydia said, her voice as exhausted as the rest of her. "I'll talk to him and see what it's all about."

Amelia Dexter looked around as if seeing her own house for the first time. "I'll leave you then." She looked from one to the other, unsure of what to do next, and finally resolved her indecision by simply leaving and closing the door behind her.

A short, balding man of about fifty with intelligent blue eyes and a pleasant face, he stood and introduced himself as Inspector Walsh of the homicide division. His face was sympathetic as Lydia registered shock on hearing the word homicide. She was more than shocked. Her blood ran cold as she imagined something awful had happened to one of her parents, or, God forbid, one of the children.

"My family?" she questioned in a breathless voice, as the blood drained from her cheeks.

"It's nothing to do with your family, Mrs. Roberts," he said. "Please sit down."

"Oh, thank God." She collapsed gratefully into the nearest chair, a blue overstuffed one that was John Dexter's favorite.

"Have some tea." The inspector motioned to the tea service on the table between them. "You must have had a rough day. You work for the War Office, I understand."

"Yes." Lydia poured herself a cup of tea and added a generous spoonful of sugar. She saw no need to elaborate further on her job, and that she was connected with the Special Branch. "You are from homicide, so this must be in connection with someone's death."

"Yes," he answered. "A young man named Samuel Picard, a student at Compton School, was killed last weekend."

Instinctively Lydia covered her mouth with her hand. "My God! What happened?"

"You knew him." His words were a statement, not a question.

"I met him once," she replied. "But a young boy! What happened? Who would do such a thing?"

Inspector Walsh allowed himself a small smile. "Indeed. It is my job to find out exactly who did do such a thing."

"But why are you here? I only met him once, very briefly."

"And what were the circumstances of that meeting, Mrs. Roberts?" His voice sounded official and cold.

"My – my husband asked me to visit him," she replied. Lydia was thinking quickly. Some of her knowledge of Samuel Picard's circumstances could be classified information, but with a homicide involved... Sure Scotland Yard would know most of the information she had learned from Allan.

"Why did your husband – Allan, I believe his name is – ask you to visit this boy?"

Lydia took a deep breath. "The boy is – was – alone here. His family is in France. In some danger, I understand."

"How do you know his family is in danger, Mrs. Roberts?" He was taking notes in a small notebook.

"Everyone in France is in danger, I would think," she blurted out.

He answered for her. "The boy and his family are Jewish," he stated.

"Yes," Lydia agreed.

Inspector Walsh seemed to come to some sort of a decision, because he looked Lydia directly in the eye. "Samuel Picard was found on the ground outside his dormitory. He had been hit on the head and then apparently pushed out the window of his second floor room."

Lydia winced.

"The blow to the head was certainly enough to kill him," Inspector Walsh added. "Your husband visited him last Friday evening and was one of the last people to see him alive. You visited him. Now your husband has disappeared, supposedly on some secret mission for the government. I need to speak to your husband, and I need to find out who killed this boy and why."

Lydia chose her words carefully, although her mind was spinning. "My husband has a classified job for the government. I don't know where he is at the moment."

"Is there someone who does know?" Inspector Walsh continued to take notes, and the scratch of his pencil was the only sound in the room.

"Of course there is," she answered. She supposed there was no harm in giving Dexter's name. Not everyone who worked for him was involved in clandestine operations.

"Can you give me a name, Mrs. Roberts?" Why *was this man so suspicious? How could he suspect that either she or Allan could have anything to do with the boy's death?*

"Major John Dexter. His office is in Whitehall."

Walsh looked up at her sharply, and she wondered if the name was familiar to him. "And he is the man who owns this house."

"Yes. My husband and I have been staying here since our flat was bombed in April."

"I see. I will need to speak with Major Dexter. I would like to corroborate the information you have given me and find out when I can question your husband."

He turned a page in his notebook. "Why did you visit Samuel Picard, Mrs. Roberts?"

"I told you. My husband asked me to. My husband travels constantly for his work, and he felt sympathy for the boy, and asked me to convey a message…"

"A message? From whom? What was the message?"

Lydia felt that she had almost given too much away. She was sure she should not reveal that British agents were traveling across the Channel and working with the French Resistance. Even though the two countries were allies, the exact movement of agents was not generally known. And Lydia did not know how much knowledge Scotland Yard possessed relating to these activities. She was out of her depth in this discussion, and she glanced toward the front door, wishing that John Dexter would return home and help her out. "I'm sorry," she said. "I can't say anymore without clearance from Major Dexter. I work for him as a cultural liaison. I'm an art historian."

Walsh continued to write without looking up, and then he took another tack. "Were you aware that your husband visited the Picard boy last Friday night?"

This was the question Lydia was dreading, but she had no choice but to answer. "No. I had no idea." Her voice was soft. The fact of Allan's visit had been preying on her mind since Inspector Walsh had first mentioned it. Why had Allan visited the boy? And why had he not told her? She had just been there, and Allan knew it. She had told him how unpleasant she found the boy. Perhaps Allan had gone to reiterate the fact that his parents were not able to increase his allowance and tell him again about the danger they faced. Or was there something else?

"Where were you Friday night, Mrs. Roberts?"

"I was working," she answered.

Inspector Walsh closed his notebook. "I'll contact this Dexter tomorrow. And if you see your husband, please tell him that we want to question him." He stood and began to walk toward the door. "He could be in serious trouble." Lydia stood, too, but felt unable to move. "I'll see myself out," he added.

Lydia hoped to escape up to her room without further conversation with Amelia Dexter, but it was not to be. Amelia opened the door from the kitchen as soon as the front door closed. "What was that all about?" she asked.

Lydia considered lying for about half a second, but couldn't come up with a plausible story so she blurted out the truth. "A boy at Compton School was killed, and they want to question Allan because he visited him."

Amelia Dexter stared, and while she looked shocked with disbelief, the slight twinkle in her eye gave away the fact that she had just heard juicy gossip. "They certainly don't think Allan killed the boy, do they?"

Lydia was horrified to hear the idea put into words, although it had been floating on the periphery of the conversation between her and Inspector Walsh. "No, of course not. Allan visited him because he had a message from the boy's parents. That's all."

"Wait a minute," Amelia said. "Didn't you go up to Compton last week? It seems like I remember you saying..."

Again, thought Lydia, there was no point in lying. "Yes, I did. I had to visit the school in connection with my work." *Okay. That part wasn't exactly true.* "And I did see the boy because Allan had mentioned him." Lydia sighed deeply as she realized how dead tired she really was. "Mrs. Dexter – Amelia, I'm sure it will turn out to be nothing. And now if you don't mind, I am exhausted and famished. Would you mind terribly if I go up and bathe, and then come down and make myself a sandwich? I haven't eaten anything since lunch, and I can't even remember what I ate then."

"Of course, dear." This was a role that Amelia played well and enjoyed. "Go make yourself comfortable. You look as if you worked hard today." She looked Lydia up and down, taking in the mud on her shoes and the streaks of dirt on her skirt. "There is some sliced beef left over. I would be happy to make you a sandwich. Tabitha has gone home, I'm afraid."

"Oh, don't bother. I can make my own sandwich."

"Please. It's no bother."

Lydia gave in. She did not feel like arguing about a sandwich. "Thank you," she said, and tried to smile. "I'll be right down."

Chapter 10

Lydia's Diary – May 1, 1941

Major Dexter refuses to tell me where Allan is, or why he visited Samuel Picard. I'm not even sure if he knew about the visit, but at any rate he isn't telling me anything. I don't think Dexter realizes that Allan discusses his work with me as much as he does. I'm sure he doesn't discuss his work with his wife! It's been a week now since Inspector Walsh came round, and he hasn't returned. I don't know if he has talked with Dexter or not. Probably, but no one is telling me anything. I am frantic with worry about Allan, even more than I usually am. He *couldn't* have killed the boy. That is just unthinkable. Why is he even suspected? Or maybe he isn't now. Why won't anyone tell me what is going on?

I have been sorting and cataloging other things brought over from France – jewelry, silver pieces, even some books -- and making a supreme effort to label each one with the owner's name if at all possible. Henri is more or less friendly, and everyone else stays away from me as much as possible, including Suzanne. There have been no more emotional outbursts, or at least none that I am aware of.

I can't see that there will be work on this particular assignment that much longer. I do so hope that I do not have to go back to my boring office job when I am finished with this cataloging work. I think I will talk with Dexter tomorrow and ask him what I can do. Maybe I can convince him that not only am I capable, but because I am already somewhat involved in what Allan is doing, I could be of help. There must be someplace else I can be of use. There are plenty of women performing important jobs during this war.

It's time to go to sleep. At least here at the Dexters' home we only need to go to the lowest level in the house if there is an air raid, although there has not been one in a few weeks. They seem to think the house is strong enough to survive anything but a direct hit. And I suppose if there were a direct hit, we would never know what happened anyway, would we?

Goodnight, my husband, wherever you are. And goodnight, my daughters, safe and sound with your grandparents. How I wish this war were over.

May, 1941
The English Channel

Allan dozed in the motor launch. It was a smooth crossing, or as smooth as one could expect crossing this turbulent stretch of water between England and France. He had been dreaming of Lydia. He came awake when the sound of the motor altered as they approached the beach. All was dark, except for three momentary glimmers of light up past the beach -- three momentary glimmers that just as quickly were extinguished. The boatman eased the launch as close to the beach as he dared and whispered, "Good luck, men." Allan and the other two British agents climbed out and trudged through the wet sand toward the spot where the lights had shown just moments before. They were met by three members of the French Resistance – two men and a woman, who reminded Allan somewhat of Lydia, tall and lanky with light brown hair. The woman was called Annette. She and one of the men, Adrian, were frequent contacts whom Allan knew well. The second man, little more than a teenager, was a newcomer.

"Bienvenue," Annette said, and although it was dark there was just enough light to see the flash of her teeth as she smiled.

"Merci," Allan whispered.

The six of them walked single file through the scrub above the beach, and then separated. Each of the British agents was assigned a partner. Allan followed Annette along a path through the woods in order to approach the village from the back. Neither of them spoke until they had entered the small house where she lived with her father. The older man sat at the kitchen table in the darkness and lit a candle when the two entered. "I have bad news," he said. He sat with a bottle of wine and a glass in front of him. He motioned to his daughter to get glasses for herself and Allan.

"It won't be much longer," he said. "Many of the townspeople blame the Jews, or if they don't outright blame them, they believe we would be better off and that the Germans would leave our town alone if the Jews left. If that means turning them over to the Germans, they will do it."

"Can we get them into Spain?" Allan asked. He was hungry, and the wine was only exacerbating his hunger pangs. But he knew the father and daughter had very little food themselves.

"It's very dangerous, Allan," Annette answered. She did not sit down, but stood at the darkened window sipping her wine, and staring out into the night.

They sat in silence for a few moments. "The boy is getting to be a problem," Allan said.

"What boy?" asked Annette.

"Samuel Picard. I'm not sure what's going on, but he wants his parents to send him more money. My wife visited him. I asked her to," he added at the surprised look from Annette and her father. "He refuses to accept the fact that his family is in serious danger for their lives, and are in no position to increase his spending money." Allan took another sip of wine. The hunger pangs seemed to have eased somewhat. "So I went to see him before I left London. His reaction was the same. I tried to persuade him to tell me why he needs more money, but met with no success. He's an angry young man, but money isn't going to help. He seems to think the war was started purely to spoil his life as a rich school boy."

"In a way it was," Monsieur Tunet answered. "He is a Jew. Hitler wants to kill him."

Annette finished her glass of wine. She returned it to the kitchen counter with a bang. "We can't solve it tonight. Let's get some sleep while we can. Allan, you know where your bed is." She left the kitchen, and they could hear her close the door to her bedroom.

"Samuel Picard isn't the only one who is angry," Monsieur Tunet said quietly as he finished his glass and pushed the cork back into the bottle.

"We are all angry, André," Allan responded. He stifled a yawn.

"It's more than that. This town is a powder keg. I'm worried about the Picard family. There has always been resentment against the Jews. Old prejudices die hard and the old families are the worst. They have long memories. And even if their wealth disappeared at the time of the Revolution, they still believe they have a right to it."

"What can we do?"

"Nothing." The old man rose from the table and placed the bottle of wine on an upper shelf. "You can't change the evil of centuries just because you want to. Maybe this war will change it, if any of us live through it. And maybe not. Annette is right, Allan. We can't solve it tonight. Get some sleep."

Exhausted as he was, from tension, the journey across the Channel and his worry about the Picard family, Allan was unable to sleep. He was disturbed about Samuel Picard's attitude. It was probably best if he said nothing to his parents. He didn't want to call attention to himself or to them by paying them a visit. Samuel was in no immediate physical danger, while they and their young daughter Henriette were. He thought of Lydia and how distant he had felt from her on the last visit. He had hardly seen her, and he was not sure how he felt about her working with the French Resistance. She was still in London, following a regular routine as she had been in her job at Whitehall, but the job seemed to create an independence in her that rocked his foundation. He had always known about her work, and before the war it had been very similar to his own. It was one thing for him to take on a wartime job that permitted him to take risks he would never have dreamed of in peaceful times. But not his wife – it wasn't right for her.

Allan finally dropped off to sleep a couple of hours before dawn and only woke when the rising sun shone into his room, and he smelled something that might be coffee, but couldn't be. His stomach began to growl again, and he rose quickly and dressed. The aroma did not prove to be coffee, but the barley and acorn substitute that most people used these days, if they even had that. But it was hot and gave Allan the feeling that he was drinking coffee. There was bread and cheese, which Allan ate eagerly. Annette ate nothing, but stood drinking the hot beverage and looking out the window as she had the night before.

"What are you looking for?" Allan asked her.

"Anything or anyone who doesn't belong," she answered.

"Has there been trouble here?"

"No more than usual."

"Which means...?"

"It means no more than usual," she snapped. She set her empty cup in the sink and faced Allan. "Occasionally we see a few Germans in town. They come through, ask a few questions, demand everyone's IDs, throw their weight around and leave. At least that's all they've done so far." She pulled on a red sweater over her dress. She was ready to go... somewhere. "I don't want them here at all. I'm afraid of them, all right? If they find out we are Resistance, they will shoot us. At any time they could decide to take away the Picards and the other Jewish families. They have done it in other towns not far from here." She looked at Allan, who was still chewing a piece of bread and cheese. "Let's go. You can eat later."

Allan swallowed the last bite, hoping he would, indeed, eat later. "Where are we going?"

"I want you to meet someone." She opened the door and went outside, assuming Allan would follow, which he did just a moment later.

"It's early." The sun was barely over the horizon and the village was just beginning to stir. A rooster crowed somewhere in the village and cows lowed on the way to be milked.

She ignored his comment about the time. "We are lucky to still have our chickens and cows. In other villages the Germans have taken those, too, for their own use. Or they have forced the farmers to turn over their eggs and milk, leaving nothing for the villagers."

"Why haven't they done that here?" he asked.

"We're too out of the way and too small. Someday they will realize that that is an advantage to us, especially since we are right on the sea. They will realize how close we are to Spain, and to England. We can only pray that the war will be over before they discover these things about us, because if it isn't, we will all be dead." Annette stopped walking and motioned to Allan for silence. They heard the sound of an automobile moving towards them. Annette took Allan's hand and moved closer to him, and as the automobile came within sight she wrapped her arms around him and kissed him. She had done this before once, when she thought Allan's presence might cause suspicion. But this time the kiss was long and deep, and Allan instinctively responded to the embrace. He wrapped his arms around her as he felt her tongue play on his lips. An open German military vehicle with four uniformed soldiers aboard stopped next to them. Allan continued to kiss Annette. Better the emotion of kissing Annette than the terror he felt at being face to face with Nazi soldiers. The four soldiers were grinning at them when the driver spoke.

"Bit early in the morning, isn't it? Or is this the end of last night?" He laughed at his own feeble humor.

Annette pulled away from Allan and smoothed her dress. She managed to blush and look embarrassed for the soldiers. "It's my husband. He's only here for a few days, and then he has to go back."

"Go back where?" the soldier in the front passenger seat asked.

"Go back to fight, of course. He is with the Vichy Army."

The four soldiers studied Allan, and the driver spoke to him. "Where are you stationed?"

Allan named a city where he knew Vichy forces would be found. One of the soldiers in the back seat looked at his watch and murmured something in German to the driver, who nodded.

The driver put the car in gear. "We have to be back in Ste. Marthe. We don't make it to these coastal villages very often." He looked Annette up and down. "Maybe we should. A pretty girl gets lonely when her man goes off to war." He pushed the accelerator and they disappeared in a cloud of dust.

"I hate them," Annette said.

Without thinking and still playing the role of the lover, Allan put his arm around Annette's waist. "I know. I do, too." There was quiet as they both realized that they were still touching like lovers, now when there was no reason to. The Germans were gone, on their way out of the village. He removed his arm but she did not pull away.

"Allan, we may not live to the end of the war, either of us." She looked up at him, her wide dark eyes brimming with tears. He bent and kissed her cheek where a single tear had traced a path down the side of her face. As he did so, he thought about how Lydia rarely wept. At least now during the war, she never did. She was strong and kept a stiff upper lip as she had been taught to do. He admired Lydia's strength and could not imagine her any other way. They were equal partners and had always been so. But Annette's vulnerability touched him in a way that Lydia's strength did not. He knew Annette was strong; she had to be. She risked her life every day to work with the Resistance movement. She ran errands, delivered messages and traveled from village to village. All these thoughts went through his mind in an instant as he bent to Annette's mouth again and enveloped her in a passionate kiss. Without relinquishing their hold on each other, the two of them moved back away from the road and under the shelter of a willow tree. Annette responded to Allan with all the pent-up emotion of her terror and fear and pushed him back against the trunk of the tree, her body moving against his. He held her close and moved his fingers down the length of her spine. His hands gripped her buttocks and pulled her closer. She made a small sound that resembled a strangled cry, but she pulled away.

"We can't do this now, Allan."

He struggled to catch his breath and bring his body under control. *She* had been the one to pull away. He was the married one, who had never been unfaithful to his wife throughout twelve years of marriage. He had never even been tempted, until now. Now he only wanted to throw Annette on the ground under this tree and take her.

"When?" he asked. He could barely hear his own voice and wondered if she heard him.

But she did. "Tonight." She touched his lips with her finger to quiet him.

"Your father?" he asked.

"He won't mind. I'm not a child. He will understand." She stepped back, straightening her dress again as she did when the Germans had seen them. "We have to live, Allan. It may be our only chance."

They set off along the road, keeping a respectable distance between them as they walked. After they had traveled about half a mile, Annette turned down a path that was barely visible in the overgrowth. They followed the path into the woods for about twenty minutes until they reached an opening. Allan was astonished to see that they had come out at an expanse of garden and wide lawns at the back of a large stone house. The lawns were overgrown now, and the fountain in the midst of the garden was dry, but there were a few spring flowers in bloom, and the house looked in good repair. He wondered if anyone lived there, since the windows on this side were all boarded up and the place was silent.

Annette turned around once to say to Allan, "Follow me." With sure steps she returned to the surrounding woods and skirted the wide lawn. She was not exactly following a path, although she appeared to know exactly where she was going. She let Allan follow, knowing that he would not let her out of his sight. After a few moments, she led him back toward the left side of the house, where the woods grew close to a grape arbor. She turned once to reassure Allan and then continued out of the trees and into the cover of the vines. They followed the garden path through a work area cluttered with pots, trowels and burlap bags of fertilizer, before coming upon a small doorway at the bottom of a series of stone steps. Again Annette turned to Allan, who was right behind her. Silently she turned the knob and pushed the door open into a dark basement. As soon as Allan was inside she closed the door and locked it with the combination lock that hung from the hasp.

As his eyes adjusted to the darkness, he could see that they were in a small room that held the usual contents of a seldom used basement. There were boxes and trunks of various sizes and a wooden rod upon which hung clothing covered in garment bags. It had the smell, too, of an unused basement -- musty, damp and sweet. A mouse scurried across the floor in front of them and he recognized the disgusting sweet smell of a place inhabited by mice. In spite of the little food he had eaten in the last day, or perhaps because of it, Allan felt queasy.

Annette paused only long enough for her eyes to adjust and then walked unerringly across the room and opened another door, also unlocked. They passed through and she closed it behind them and began to ascend a stairway. All Allan could see to indicate the passage was a narrow sliver of light beneath the door at the top of the stairs. He followed her slowly, not wanting to run into her from behind before the door was opened. When she reached the top, she knocked softly on the door and, without waiting for an answer, she soundlessly turned the knob and opened the door, flooding the stairway with light.

Allan followed her into a well-appointed room, furnished in the style of the nineteenth century. But whereas British homes from the Victorian era tended to be dark with heavy layered draperies and overstuffed furniture covered in antimacassars and embroidered pillows, this room was large and spacious, and the uncovered windows looked out onto a portion of the garden that he had not seen from the outside. At first the room appeared to be unoccupied. But then a figure in a chair facing the garden stood, and they saw a petite woman in her early forties, her dark hair pulled neatly up into a bun. She came toward them, smiling, and held out her hands.

"Annette, it's wonderful to see you. Come sit with me. And is this the young man you have been telling me about? L'anglais?"

Allan hardly thought of himself as a young man, especially with Annette, whom he thought must be at least ten years his junior.

"Oui, madame," Annette answered. "This is Allan."

"Bonjour, Allan," the woman said as she held out her hand. He took it, unsure whether to shake it or kiss it in the French manner, but she simply held his hand in both of hers and then released him. "Come and sit. I know we have much to talk about. I'm afraid I cannot offer you anything. I released my one servant for the day. It's better for everyone if you aren't seen here." She led them to a corner of the room where three chairs had been arranged facing each other.

Allan sat and waited for one of the women to speak. He had no idea what role this elegant and apparently wealthy French woman played. Annette looked from one to the other with a smile. She appeared happy to have brought the two of them together. "Madame Grassin is an aristocrat, or at least her family was an aristocratic one once. There is not much left of the family now, and Madame is trying to do what good she can in the last..."

"It's all right, ma cherie," Madame Grassin told her. "I may not live to see the end of this war. But the same is true of both of you. Yes, we must be honest with ourselves about it. But if there is anything I can do to alleviate the suffering of even one person, to help them escape these... these monsters who would kill us all if they could, I want to do it. God knows I have committed enough selfish acts in my time that my only hope is that God will look kindly on my later good deeds and forget the other ones." She laughed and turned to Annette. "Tell Allan what we have been doing."

"Madame has been selling or trading her jewels and other family treasures, one by one so as not to arouse suspicion, in order to help the Jews escape. Mostly we help them cross the mountains into Spain, but of course it takes money. We need to pay off border guards and other officials, buy food and pay for lodging. There is always someone with his hand out."

Annette paused and took a deep breath before she continued. Allan watched Madame Grassin, who waited patiently for Annette to continue. She looked at the younger woman with a fond, maternal look. Annette returned her gaze and then turned to Allan. "Our biggest problem is, therefore, not the money. Madame Grassin's generosity helps us there. She has a number of resources and I won't give you the details now. It is not necessary for you to know; in fact, it could be dangerous." She studied him with her big dark eyes, narrowing them slightly. "If it is ever necessary for you to have that information, I will share it with you. For your own protection, I will not tell you now."

"So what do you need from me?" he asked. "Surely it was a risk even bringing me here today."

"You are right," Annette continued. "But we need your help. We need reliable escorts to accompany individuals across the mountains, especially the families."

"Why are you discussing this with me?" Allan asked. "I am English. I'm not even sure this is something my government would want me to do." He noticed the surprise on the faces of both women. "It's not that I don't want to help. Of course I do. But I'm not sure I am the right person for this particular job. "

"We aren't saying that you should go personally, Allan." Madame Grassin pronounced his name as it would sound in French. "But your expertise would be invaluable in organizing and provisioning the travelers. We have the contacts, of course. But everything must be planned in detail. And the families must be instructed in exactly what they must do. The escorts must be chosen carefully. We know from the past what can happen if there are difficulties between the escort and the persons they are trying to help. There have been tragic situations."

"Additionally," Annette interjected, "we are very interested in finding capable women to serve as escorts."

"I do not know of anyone," Allan answered too quickly. He quickly rejected the thought that it was the kind of work Lydia would want to do. She was so desperate to become more involved in the war effort.

"We didn't expect you to," Madame Grassin said with a soft smile. "The British do not permit women to serve in that capacity. At least not yet."

"What capacity do you mean?" Allan asked. "As spies?"

"Spies, yes, if you want to use that word. Patriots might be another one." Madame Grassin's smile had faded. "Do you have children, Allan?"

"Yes. I have two daughters." He felt the twinge of guilt again for the daughters he rarely saw.

"And where are they?" she asked.

"They are with their grandparents in Wales."

"So they are safe."

"Yes. They are safe."

"You are fortunate, Allan. Your country has been bombed but not invaded. There is a difference. My husband died in the first war, the one that was supposed to end all wars. Are you old enough to remember it?"

"I was a child," Allan answered. "I remember a little bit. Mostly I remember seeing the soldiers come home."

"You are fortunate again." She looked down at her hands. They were small with short fingers, like a child's, and she wore several rings set with large, impressive stones. Allan wondered if she would end up selling those to ensure the safety of someone escaping France, or if they were heirlooms that she would keep. "My husband was killed at Ypres," she said. "He was shot accidentally by one of his own men. Now his son is fighting the Germans. I haven't heard from him in over three months. He could be dead now. So you see..." She looked at Annette and then back at Allan, "I might as well sell my valuables. I may not have any family to pass them on to. And better that the Grassin treasures should go to help someone than remain for the government, or worse, the Germans, to dispose of. At least this way, it is my choice."

Allan was silent as he stared out the window at the broad expanse of lawn rolling down to the edge of the woods. It was beautiful here. He wondered who would live in this house if Madame Grassin's son did not return. It might not continue to be used as a residence after the war at all. It could become a hotel or a museum. He brought his gaze back into the room and saw that both Madame and Annette were looking at him expectantly. "You want me to help you," he stated. "Yes, of course I will, to the extent of my ability and the ability of my government."

"That's all anyone can ask," Annette answered softly.

"What do you want me to do first?" Allan asked.

Madame Grassin removed a large ring from the middle finger of her right hand. "Can you sell this ring for me?"

Allan stared at the ring. It had not looked that significant when it was on Madame Grassin's finger, along with the other gems she was wearing. Now he saw that it was a man's ring. It was set with an enormous ruby and flanked by diamonds of a respectable size themselves. She held out the ring to him and he took it into his hand. He was surprised at the weight of it. He balanced it in his palm and studied the stones as they picked up the flashes of light from the sun through the windows. He glanced at Annette, a question in his eyes.

"We probably can, yes, if that is what you want," she said. Allan knew there were connections, and people with connections, in the Special Branch, who could obtain cash in exchange for something like this. But it might not happen quickly, and he surmised that Madame Grassin wanted cash for this piece as quickly as possible.

The woman seemed to read his mind. "There is a family – the mother and father and a young daughter, whom I would like to help. I believe the money that could be derived from the sale of this ring could pay for what they need to cross the Pyrenees into Spain."

"Yes, I'm sure it could," Allan agreed. He turned the ring over and over in his hand. *Was she thinking of the Picards? But they would not be the only Jewish family with a young daughter.* "I'm sure you want to help this people as quickly as possible. It is growing more dangerous here by the moment for anyone..." He cleared his throat. "Anyone the Germans want to be rid of."

"I realize that," she answered. "I know someone, a jeweler in Toulouse, who would undoubtedly buy it. It is the sort of thing the Germans are interested in, large and impressive looking, and this jeweler has had some dealings with the Germans. They don't suspect his true political beliefs. If you could find some way to get it to him, then the sale could be done relatively quickly."

Allan met Annette's eyes. She was looking at him hopefully. "Do you know the jeweler Madame is talking about?"

"I have not met him," she answered, "but I have heard people in the Resistance talk about him. As far as I know, he is reliable. We can check on it. I know people to ask."

"All right." Allan made his decision. "We will take it for you. I don't know how the arrangements will be made, but I'm sure Annette can help there."

"We need to go now," Annette said, and Allan realized that she had spoken very little during their visit with Madame Grassin. Madame produced a small royal blue velvet bag and handed it to Allan for the ring. He slipped it inside and pulled the drawstring closed. "We'd better go," Annette said again. "I've never seen patrols around here, but there is always a first time."

Allan and Annette stood, and Madame Grassin held out her hands to the two younger people. They each took one and stood in silence for a moment as if they were receiving a blessing. "Bon chance," she whispered, "and God be with you, if there is still a God, and I believe that there is."

Annette released Madame's hand and took Allan's free hand. "Let's go," she said. Without looking back, they quickly retraced their steps through the basement and out through the gardener's door into the grape arbor. "Don't worry about the lock," Annette said. "She will have it secured behind us in a matter of moments."

There was no one in sight and all was still, and they were soon on the forest path and had covered a respectable distance from the house. Annette led Allan through other wooded paths around the edge of the village. As they walked, she listened and scanned any openings in the vegetation for signs of German soldiers. At last they reached the small house she shared with her father. Before crossing the small garden to the door, Annette stopped and motioned to Allan to do the same. "We will wait here for a few minutes," she said to him almost soundlessly.

Allan slowed his breathing and listened to the forest. He could hear nothing but birds and the rhythmic breathing of the two of them. Now and then in the distance they heard the motor of a vehicle. He imagined that he could hear the sea, but he wasn't sure if they were close enough. Then he saw a curtain move aside in the house and then drop back into position. Annette seemed to tense. The movement was repeated. She exhaled and motioned for Allan to follow her. She crossed the last few feet of the garden, where her father had opened the door to admit them. He smiled a welcome. "There have been no problems. Don't worry, Annette. The Germans continue to believe that we are a sleepy little fishing village. At least for one more day they believe it."

"Let's hope they believe it for several more days," Annette said, as she kissed her father's cheek.

"What did Madame have for you this time?" he asked.

"Show him, Allan," Annette answered.

Allan removed the small bag from his pants pocket. It was clear that Annette and her father had done this before. Annette had known exactly what Madame Grassin was going to ask, and undoubtedly Madame Grassin knew as well. It had been a performance to determine if he were willing to become involved in their operation to spirit Jews out of France and to safety. He was a member of British Special

Operations; he was a British intelligence operative. He job was to do whatever might be necessary to help the Allies and defeat the Germans. He had considerable leeway in deciding what constituted legitimate intelligence activity and what did not. He trusted Annette and her father and therefore trusted Madame Grassin, but he was a little annoyed that they had found it necessary to test him like that. Their ploy was not a prerequisite to meeting Madame Grassin; they had simply wanted to see what his reaction would be, and he had evidently passed the test.

He handed the small bag to Monsieur Tunet without a word. The older man opened it and unceremoniously dumped the contents onto the kitchen table. The ring bounced against the wood and rolled to a stop against the sugar bowl. He picked it up and studied it. "This was Jacques' ring. I remember it." He turned it around and looked inside. "He bought it shortly after their son was born. He wanted to pass it to his son, and then to his son's son. He believed he was continuing the Grassin dynasty." He replaced the ring in the bag and handed it to Annette. "Laurent will take it to Toulouse tomorrow. We should have the money in a day or two."

Annette removed a leather cord from her neck, and threaded it through the drawstrings of the jewelry bag. She retied the cord and placed it over her neck, tucking the bag securely into the front of her dress between her breasts. Allan caught himself staring at her and pulled his eyes away before her father noticed, but it was too late. The older man chuckled. "These are strange times, Allan, but still I sleep soundly at night. The joy of an old man is that I know bad times don't last forever, but still you must take your pleasure where you can."

Annette ignored her father's comments but her face showed a slight flush. "I'm going out. We need food. I'll see what I can find in the village. Maybe Francois has some fish. Allan, you can spend the afternoon listening to my father's stories, or you can rest. I would suggest rest. We are going to have a busy night tonight. There are some more people I want you to meet."

Chapter 11

Lydia's Diary – May 5, 1941

With Allan gone again, I spend an increasing amount of time with people with whom I am not comfortable. I am proud of my work with the French Resistance here in London, but I feel friction with a number of the people I work with there. There is Suzanne Valbert, of course, but I can handle her. She is jealous of my position as an art expert and, I believe, as a second competent woman. I think that she loves having the men in awe of her. Not just in awe – they are afraid of her, except for her brother. When I first discovered that they were brother and sister, I thought he was frightened of her, but he isn't. He is wise. He knows how to get around her tantrums. He also knows how to soothe her ruffled feathers, as he did the day we moved the paintings to Swallowfield. As her brother, he knows her better than anyone, and it is clear they have secrets.

Is that what it would be like to have a brother or a sister? As an only child, it is something I will never know. The only person in my life that I have been truly close to, (as an equal, not counting the children) is Allan. And now what is happening to Allan and me? I rarely see him. I know he is unhappy with my work with the French, but we are not together enough to really talk and resolve the issue. The next time he comes home, I must make an effort to really talk to him, like we once did. It's just one more way this war is tearing my family apart.

Enough of that. Dwelling on it will not make it better. Just soldier through one day at a time. Soldier -- I never thought of that expression before. We are all soldiers, in one way or another.

Present Day
London

"It's probably just a coincidence, Nara," Alex said gently. "Just because someone asks questions doesn't mean they are interested in your great-grandparents and their secrets."

Nara, Alex and Lily were having coffee together in a busy shop near the University of London. What was supposed to be Alex's homecoming dinner the night before had turned into a discussion of Lydia Roberts' diaries, and although Nara felt guilty about her obsession with them, she couldn't stop herself, and both Alex and Lily were remarkably patient with her.

"I suppose you are right," she conceded. "A lot of Welsh people were involved in the war."

"Everyone in Britain was involved in the war."

Nara sighed. "You're right. I'm sorry, Alex. I've been up since three this morning," she said. "I can't put the diaries down. I want to know what happens to Lydia."

"Why don't you just go to the end?" Alex asked.

"That wouldn't help. I wouldn't know what came before. And she didn't know she was going to die, did she?"

"Probably not," he admitted.

"And she might have stopped writing in the diaries for some other reason," Lily added. "She might not have written in them up until her death."

"Exactly," Nara said. She stared out the window at a group of students who were running through the rain and laughing, before she turned back to her companions, her decision made. "I think I will take the boxes up to Springfield this week-end. I will feel safer if they are up there."

Alex started to respond to Nara's question when his cell phone rang. He looked at the display and frowned, but did not answer the call.

"Who was that?" Nara asked.

"A student who is doing research here. I told him I would help him." He toyed with his coffee cup, looking down at the cooling brown liquid as if it might hold an omen for his future. "At first I said no, but then Andy talked me into it. You know Andy."

"What is it about, Alex?" Nara knew it was more than a student's request for information.

Lily and Nara sipped their coffee in silence for a moment, until Alex broke the silence. "It's very strange. It's a brother and sister from France. She is a student studying art history. He is sharing a flat with her here and apparently is researching his family history. The strange thing is that he is looking for pieces that he believes were taken from his family during World War II, and he thinks some of them ended up in Wales."

"Why would their belongings from France end up in Wales?" Nara answered. "Oh, wait. I get it. They could have been brought over and hidden? But wouldn't they have been labeled so they could get them back, like Lydia was doing at the French Resistance headquarters?"

"Maybe." Lily dabbed at her lips with a paper napkin. "Or maybe they were stolen."

"Exactly," Alex said. "Or they could have been sold. I think his chances of finding any of their family heirlooms are extremely slim. If they were sold by his family, it was a legitimate sale. There is nothing they can do about it now."

"Do you think it would help if I told him what I have learned?" Nara asked. Her coffee was cold, and she wanted more. She signaled to the waiter for a fresh cup.

"No!" Alex's vehement answer shocked both Nara and Lily, who stared at him before Lily spoke.

"Why not?"

"There's something strange going on with them. Or rather with the brother, Paul. Either he isn't telling the truth, or he has some other ulterior motive. He flies off the handle and either ignores his sister or criticizes her. I don't want him anywhere near you until I learn more."

"I don't think there is much of value in Lydia's boxes," Nara said. "Not to say there isn't historical or sentimental value, but I can't see why anyone else would be interested in their contents."

"Lydia was working with valuable paintings and jewelry from France," Lily said.

"But none of them were hers. She was very clear about that in the diaries. She was adamant about ensuring that everything was labeled with the rightful owners' names."

"Maybe I could get someone at the V&A to go through them with you," Alex said, stirring his fresh cup of coffee and adding sugar. "Then you would have a better idea of what to do with them."

"Right now I want to just read them myself and give Dad a chance to read them," Nara said. She stacked up the coins they had left on the table for a tip, and then spread them out and pushed them under a napkin. "There are his grandmother's, after all. They belong to him more than to me."

Alex yawned. He had intended to be home in bed, but here he sat in Paul and Lisette's small flat with a glass of Scotch in his hand. "What exactly are you looking for?" he asked.

"A painting and a piece of jewelry," Paul answered. "A large ornate piece of jewelry, dating from the sixteenth century." Paul swirled his own Scotch around in the glass. It wasn't the best that money could buy, but he would have that soon enough.

"There is also a ring," Lisette added. "With a family crest and a ruby, I believe."

Paul glowered at her, although Alex had no idea why. He decided to ignore the family squabbles for now. "And the painting?" Alex asked. "Any idea of the artist?"

"Cézanne," Paul answered.

Alex placed his glass on the coaster that Lisette had provided and looked hard at Paul. "Cézanne? Are you sure?"

"Of course I'm sure." Paul stood and drained his glass, before handing it to Lisette for a refill. "Do you think I'm an idiot?"

"Sorry," Alex answered. "I was just surprised. I'm not an expert on modern art. I do know that any number of pieces were lost during the war. I don't doubt you." He took a small sip of his drink. "I'm sure you have proof of the identity of the painting. Do you have photographs of it?"

"Yes, of course." Paul paced back and forth across the room. Lisette handed him a fresh drink. She whispered something to Paul that Alex was unable to hear. "There is a photograph, but I don't have it with me. And it is on the list my father made of all our belongings that disappeared during the war." Paul sat back down on the sofa and faced Alex. "I have evidence that this painting was taken to Wales. And I will find it. It's mine."

"And mine," Lisette said quietly from where she stood behind him. Paul ignored her.

"Have you been to Wales?" Alex asked them.

Lisette began to say something but Paul cut her off. "Not yet. I thought we would do better to begin in London and talk to some experts here. That's why we came to you."

"Modern art is not my area," Alex said. "My specialty is medieval religious art, as I told you before." He took another thoughtful sip of Scotch. "I can help you to a certain point," he said finally. "But when it comes to establishing the authenticity and provenance of this Cézanne -- that is if we are able to locate it -- I will have to defer to other experts."

"Very well." Paul stood and started toward the liquor cabinet again, but Lisette stood in front of it, effectively blocking his way, and he merely set his empty glass on the sideboard and walked to the other end of the room where he turned to face Alex. "The Cézanne is mine, but I don't intend to keep it." Lisette rattled the glasses noisily on the sideboard but said nothing.

"I can't afford to insure such a painting -- a Cézanne that has been lost for over sixty years -- but the income I would derive from the sale would be enough to restore our family to its rightful position." Although he appeared to include his sister this time as part of the family, he did not look at her, nor did she look at him. "I would say $10,000,000 would not be an over-estimation." He glanced out the window at the London night. "I will pay you 10% of the sale price. That's $1,000,000."

Alex was dumbfounded. He knew that lost or stolen paintings were found all the time, and owners and heirs often sold them, just as Paul was planning to do, because they could not afford to keep them. The security and insurance were far too much for most individuals to handle.

"I'm willing to do what I can to help you, Paul." Neither Paul nor Lisette gave away any indication of their feelings, so he continued. "But what if I help you to find this painting, and then you decide not to sell it? I don't work for free. And I will have expenses during the investigation." He would play along with them for now, he thought, and see where it led.

"Of course not," Lisette said quickly. Her brother still stood gazing out the window. Apparently these details were left to his sister. "We will deposit $10,000 in an account for you. When the painting is found, if we decide not to sell, you will receive an additional $10,000."

"There's just one more thing," Paul said suddenly. Both Alex and Lisette turned at looked at him. "Keep this quiet. I don't want our names or the circumstances of our meeting discussed with your co-workers or your girlfriend. Reveal as little as possible. That means don't tell your family, your friends at the V&A, or the women you sleep with. If you reveal any of what we have told you, the deal is off."

"I'll give you a definite answer in the morning," Alex said. He was tempted to accept the offer. He might even learn something that could help Nara in her search for knowledge about her grandparents. He was used to working with the police and Scotland Yard. He knew how to keep what he knew confidential, and he knew when to call in the authorities. The only difference was that he was doing the investigating before the police became involved, instead of after. "You understand that I still have my work for the museum. I can't work for you full time."

"I understand. But I promise you it will be worth your while." Paul had poured himself another drink and took a healthy swallow before continuing. "I'll contact you periodically. I don't want you to contact me," Paul said.

"Oh, Paul, don't be so melodramatic," Lisette said. She was now sitting cross-legged on the sofa watching the negotiations. "We aren't characters in a spy movie."

"Shut up, Lisette," he snarled. "You want this as much as I do."

"That's where you are wrong, Paul," she said softly. "I don't want this at all, but I don't want to see you in prison, either. That's why I'm here -- to save you from yourself."

Paul walked over and stood in front of his sister, towering over her as she sat serenely on the sofa looking up. Alex could see her face but not his, and the sound of the slap of his palm against her cheek sounded like a gunshot.

Lisette's cheek turned bright red and her eyes glistened, but the latent anger in her face betrayed her lack of fear of her brother. "You've had too much to drink," she said. She uncrossed her legs and maneuvered around him as she stood. "I'm going to bed." She ignored Alex and crossed to one of the bedroom doors off the living room. The lock clicked behind her.

"Don't worry about her," Paul said. "The inheritance is mine, as the male heir."

Alex's misgivings grew and he stood. "I'll be in touch," he said as he pulled on his jacket.

"No," Paul corrected him. "I'll be in touch as soon as the money is in the bank."

Nara and Alex spent a wonderful evening together, this time just the two of them without Lily's company, but it did not surprise Nara when Alex changed his mind about accompanying her to Springfield on the week-end. He pleaded fatigue and work that he needed to catch up on after his trip to Los Angeles. She could see from the dark circles under his eyes that he was exhausted. He was quiet and preoccupied through much of the dinner. Nara was disappointed, but at the same time, a part of her relished the thought of the solitary drive. She needed time to sort out her feelings for Alex, as well as her obsession with the boxes and the diaries from Wales. Was she being obsessive? Who wouldn't be eager to learn the true story of Lydia and Allan Roberts? She felt instinctively that something else was going on with Alex, something he was keeping from her. The week-end away and some time alone, as well as time with her father, would help immensely.

Nara drove north from London to Lincolnshire. She had not told her father that she was coming. She had intended to call him, but Alex's mood of the night before had left her feeling depressed, and she wasn't sure her father's level-headed but loving advice was what she needed right now. She adored her father, but at the moment she needed to be alone. It didn't matter if he knew she was coming or not. The bed and breakfast where he lived with his sister Sue was home now. The boxes from Wales were stowed securely in the boot of the car, and Nara did not plan on stopping for more than a few minutes until she reached Springfield. Only Lily and Alex knew where she had gone.

The nearer she came to her destination, however, the more nervous she was about leaving the boxes at the Gate House. Even though Sue had finally installed a modern security system after the break-ins the previous year, there were so many guests who were in and out of the building that Nara wished she had a better place to leave them. Her friend Micki also ran a guest house, and although Micki would be happy to help Nara out, the situation with guests in the house was the same. She intended to keep the diaries with her until she had read them all, but she wanted the boxes stored somewhere that no one would suspect. She kept thinking about whoever it was who had called her great-aunt Rebeca in Wales so soon after she and her father had visited. She certainly was not the only one looking for historical items from World War II, even if she and Lily had found nothing of real value in the boxes.

Nara picked up her cell phone and dialed. "Elaine? Hi, it's Nara." Nara listened to the older woman's voice on the other end and smiled as she drove. Elaine was so much happier than she had been when Nara first met her. She had been married to an abusive husband who had died during the commission of a crime last year. Elaine had her own life for the first time, and was taking her time discovering what she really wanted.

Nara explained about the boxes she had discovered in Wales, and asked Elaine if she could leave them at her house in Lincoln. "There isn't anything valuable in them, at least not that I know of," Nara said, "but I have this feeling that I don't want anyone to know where they are." Nara had no sooner hung up her phone than it rang with an incoming call. This time it was Lily. "Nara, where are you?"

"I've just past Peterborough."

"The strangest thing just happened. Someone broke into our flat. I don't think they took anything, but someone definitely was in here. Everything was pulled out of our desks and the kitchen drawers, and our clothes were all over the place. It was as if someone was looking for something. But as far as I can see all of our jewelry is here. I know mine is, and yours doesn't look disturbed."

"Did you call the police?"

"Yes. They are on their way. I wanted to let you know."

"Good. Thanks. Let me know what the police say."

"It's strange," Lily added. "Maybe someone is looking for the boxes."

"But no one knows about them," Nara said.

"Only you, me and Alex."

"And a few other people," Nara added. "The professor in Bangor knows, and Alex may have told someone at the V&A."

Nara started to tell Lily that she had decided to leave the boxes with Elaine in Lincoln instead of at the Gate House, but she changed her mind. The fewer people who knew the whereabouts of the boxes, the better she would feel. She hung up the phone and quickly called her father to tell him she was on her way to Springfield, but had to go to Lincoln first. She would explain to him about the boxes when she saw him.

Elaine was waiting for Nara when she arrived a short time later. The two of them carried the boxes into her house and stored them in the closet in her spare bedroom. "They will be as safe here as in a bank vault," Elaine assured her. "No one except you and I will know they are here, and I had a security system installed after Dennis died." She looked closely at Nara. "You are sure there is nothing of value in here? It's just old clothes and toys and photographs?"

"Yes, but there may be something I'm not recognizing, or something that holds a clue to what happened to my great-grandparents during the war. And someone broke into our flat after I left today. Lily called to tell me when I was on the road."

Elaine stared at Nara for a long moment. "What did they take?"

"Nothing. That's the strange part. The flat was ransacked but Lily couldn't see that anything was taken."

"You might want to think about storing these in a bank vault," Elaine said. "Or maybe you should go through them again. Do you mind if I take a look?"

"Not at all," Nara answered. "Maybe you will notice something that Lily and I missed. I'm going to talk it over with Dad. I'll tell him they are here, but no one else will know."

"I certainly hope you weren't followed, Nara," Elaine added.

"So do I," Nara said. "So do I."

Nara left Elaine's house and drove around the ring road that took her past the back of Lincoln Cathedral, which dominated the city, and then onto the A15 that would take her to Sleaford and on to Springfield.

The house was quiet when she arrived. It was early afternoon and Nara was hungry for lunch. She hoped there might be something in the kitchen they could eat. She wanted to talk to her father at home today, not out in a restaurant. "I'm becoming paranoid," she said to herself. "The break-in at our flat probably had nothing to do with the boxes."

Nara's father, Jack Blake, was on his way down the stairs when she entered the kitchen. "Great to see you, Nara." He gave her a hug and looked over her shoulder toward the door. "Where are the boxes?"

"I took them to Elaine's," she answered. "Please don't tell anyone where they are, not even Aunt Sue. I have to talk to you about them. But do you think we could find some lunch first?" Her stomach growled audibly.

He laughed. "Of course. Some things never change. Food first." He opened the refrigerator and stared blankly at the contents for a few minutes. "Aw. Here we are." He pulled out a wrapped paper package and placed it on the counter. "Sue bought some sliced beef for sandwiches. How does that sound?"

"Wonderful," Nara answered. "And I assume we have some horseradish?"

"In this house that is a fair assumption," he replied.

Father and daughter busied themselves making sandwiches. They shared an easy companionship. Nara's mother had died when she was only three years old, and she and her father had always been first in each other's lives. At one point they both thought that she would take over his importing business on the Caribbean island of St. Clare where she grew up. But after his bout with cancer and their return to England, they both realized that business was not the right career choice for Nara, at least not the importing business. She had found her niche in the study of art history and hoped to pursue a career in that area. This was one of the reasons she wanted to learn more about her great-grandmother Lydia Roberts, who had been involved in the same type of work before World War II, at a time when a woman with a career, a husband and two children was a highly unusual combination.

At last their plates were filled – Jack added a small mound of Branston's pickle to his sandwich, chuckling at Nara's glare at what she considered an unnecessary treatment of innocent vegetables, and they sat at the kitchen table to enjoy their lunch.

Nara took her first bite and chewed happily, when she realized her father was looking at her intently. "So what is going on with the boxes from Wales, Nara? And why did you take them to Elaine's?"

"Someone broke into our flat this morning." She said around a mouthful of sandwich.

"And you think they were looking for the boxes?"

"I don't know. They didn't take anything, Lily said. But I've been reading Lydia's diaries and, Dad, she didn't die in the Blitz. Allan didn't either."

Jack had begun to take a bite of sandwich but he put it back on his plate. "Of course they did, Nara. That's what Grandmother – my mother – always told us. She was in Wales with her sister, Aunt Rebeca, at their grandparents from 1940 on. They didn't see their parents again."

"That may be," Nara said, "But the diaries go up to late in 1941. I have only started reading them, but the last date is September, 1941, and it is certainly in the same handwriting."

Jack began to eat his sandwich and chewed thoughtfully for a few moments. "That doesn't make any sense. Mom – your grandmother – would have remembered. A child's memory at nine is much clearer than that of a six year old."

"Maybe they didn't go back to Wales."

"Why wouldn't they go back to see their own children?" Jack asked.

"I don't know." Nara had finished her sandwich and was looking around for something to complete the meal. "Maybe Allan died and Lydia stayed on in London."

"Alone? No, Nara, something isn't making sense."

"That's what I'm trying to tell you, Dad. And that's why I took the boxes to Elaine's. I have read far enough in the diaries to know that he was traveling to Spain and maybe even France, at least at the beginning, and she was helping the French Resistance to catalog paintings that had been smuggled out of France."

"Where are the diaries, Nara?" Jack asked.

"In my car," she said.

"I would like to read them."

"Sure," she answered. "But I'm beginning to think the diaries need to be somewhere safe, too. The answer to what happened to Lydia and Allan must be in the diaries. If it isn't there, we may never find out, but it is clear that they did not die in the Blitz."

"All right, I believe you. I'm just having a difficult time adjusting to the information." He picked up a slice of apple that Nara had placed on a plate in front of him. "Could Alex have the diaries scanned for you?"

"I don't know," she said, paying close attention to her slice of apple. "He has been working awfully hard since he returned from Los Angeles. And I don't want anyone to read them before I do."

Jack laughed. "A little possessive, aren't we?" His expression turned serious. "Did you and Alex have a fight?"

"No. No. No," she answered with a broad smile, the smile that usually accompanied any mention of Alex. "He's tired and has been preoccupied lately. He's working with a student who is doing research at the V&A, and he has been extra busy catching up on his own work."

Jack studied his daughter's face but did not pursue the subject of her relationship with Alex. "OK. But I think we need to copy them to be on the safe side. How many are there?"

"Six notebooks. They aren't too big – like school notebooks, covered in cloth, like she wanted to make them look pretty." Nara felt tears in her eyes. This great-grandmother whom she knew nothing about until the last week now had the power to touch Nara's emotions in a way she never expected.

"Let's take them into town and have them copied at the stationer's shop. We can even wait for them if you are worried about letting them out of your sight. We will make two copies, one for you and one for me, and then see where we can store the originals for safekeeping."

Nara jumped up and hugged her father. "Thanks, Dad. You're always there for me."

"I try, Nara. I try," he answered. "You always have the power to drag me into your schemes."

Chapter 12

"The signature of the artist on a painting does not necessarily prove authenticity. A signature can be forged just as well as a painting. The art curator would also do well to remember that painters have been known to copy their own work. Even Michelangelo did. Artists need to make a living and they will sell if they have a buyer. Other times artists will paint numerous copies of the same subject, as Van Gogh did with his sunflowers, just because they are attracted to the subject, or, as in Van Gogh's case, as an obsession."

Lydia Roberts, National Gallery of Art, 1938

Present Day
London

Alex, Paul and Lisette stared at the photograph of a painting entitled "The Willow Tree" by Paul Cézanne. They used the computer to enlarge the signature on the lower right corner to identify the painter. "I was able to find out that a painting by this name was purchased from the artist by a man named Richard Grassin in 1904..." Alex said.

"That was my great-great-grandfather!" Paul shouted.

"<u>Our</u> great-great-grandfather," Lisette added, while Paul ignored her.

"Unfortunately," Alex continued, "that doesn't prove that you own it." Alex leaned in for a closer look. The painting was familiar. "I've seen that painting," he said, as he continued to stare at the computer screen.

Paul ignored Alex's last statement. "Of course I own it," Paul shouted. He jumped from his chair with fists clenched. "My great-grandfather bought the painting from Cézanne. The painting is mine now." Again he ignored his sister. "The painting was taken to Wales and I intend to find it." He slammed his fist on the table causing the computer to shake.

"Please, Paul, sit down," his sister said. She grasped his arm and he turned. For a moment Alex feared that Paul was going to hit her. "Listen to what he says. We will never find it on our own, and you can't attack everyone who tells you something that you don't want to hear."

Alex was beginning to question his decision to help Paul and Lisette. Paul Grassin was too unpredictable, and the way his sister handled him, he wondered sometimes if the man had a clear grip on reality. All this talk of lost treasures could be no more than a figment of his imagination. And Alex wondered what she meant by Paul attacking everyone who tells him something that he doesn't want to hear. Did she mean physically attack? He felt sorry for Lisette, and his concern and sense of fairness made him want to help her, protect her somehow from her brother. And there was the memory of the painting that he was trying to pin down. He knew he had seen it. At the Getty in Los Angeles? It would be easy enough to verify.

Quiet again, Paul sat on the sofa, although he continued to fidget, crossing and uncrossing his legs and biting the skin around his fingernails. "What do we have to do to prove we own the painting?" Lisette asked.

"First we have to find the painting," Alex said. "The entire search is pointless if the painting does not even exist anymore. Or it could have been taken out of the country and be in the hands of a private collector or in a museum. It could be anywhere in the world."

"No. I refuse to believe that." Paul stood and paced the room again, while his sister watched him, her face unreadable.

"It's like looking for a needle in a haystack, Paul," she said. "Where would we start? We can't just say, 'has anybody seen 'The Willow Tree' by Cézanne in the last sixty years and see who answers."

"Actually," Alex said, "we can."

The other two looked at him, and for the moment, Paul was speechless. "How do we do that?" he asked as last.

"We can do a web search, for one thing. We can see if there are any mentions of the painting being up for sale anywhere. If it is in the hands of a private collector, there might be a record of a sale. I assume you have searched museum collections."

"We have tried," Lisette answered. "It's not on the list of any major museums in Europe or the United States. The only mention we have found of the painting was on a list of works 'probably lost during World War II.'"

Alex took a deep breath and faced Paul. He knew what he had to say next would very likely anger the other man. "You are going to have to face two facts. First, you may not find the painting. Your sister is right. It might have been destroyed. The second is this: Your great-great-grandfather, or one of his heirs, may have sold it; in which case it does not belong to your family now. It is the legitimate property of someone else."

Paul did not explode as Alex expected him to, but simply sat with his head down. Lisette watched her brother as if she, too, was waiting for an eruption. "I would like to find the Cézanne because it is worth the most money," he said in a quiet, resigned voice. "But there are other things. There is jewelry that belonged in the family. We will keep searching. All I really need is one good piece."

Taking advantage of Paul's less volatile mood, Alex sat down across from him. "If I may ask..." Paul jerked his head up at Alex's voice. "Why is this so important to you? Is it the money? This is going to cost you a considerable amount to look for the painting, and whatever else you are looking for. And after all these years, it will be very difficult to prove ownership."

Alex was unprepared for Paul's sudden change in mood, and had no time to react before Paul's fist crashed against his jaw. The chair on which Alex was seated tipped to the side and fell, and Alex landed with his head and shoulder against the wood floor, and his legs entangled in the chair legs.

"You commoners don't understand, and you never will," Paul shouted.

"Paul, Paul, you can't do this!" Lisette's voice added to the fray, while Alex lay helpless on the floor. "Paul, this is enough! No one will help us if you react this way. This is what happened last year in Paris. Remember?"

Through the fog of pain Alex wondered what had happened in Paris, and what he had gotten himself into.

"Come," Lisette said, and Alex heard the two of them walk into one of the bedrooms and close the door behind them. He pushed the overturned chair away with his legs and maneuvered himself into a seated position on the floor. His head and shoulder ached fiercely. He gently probed his jaw and his fingers came away with blood from a split lip. He reached the edge of the table and hoisted himself to his feet. He felt weak, but he needed to leave. He needed to go somewhere to think this through, but he couldn't go out on the street with blood dripping from his face, and he wasn't even sure he could walk without appearing to be a drunkard. He collapsed into a nearby easy chair and dabbed at his lip with a handkerchief. Maybe in a few minutes he could make it out of the flat.

The bedroom door opened and Lisette came out. She closed the door softly behind her and came to sit next to Alex. "He'll sleep now," she said.

"What's wrong with him?" Alex asked, his voice unclear with the lip which was swiftly increasing in size.

"Let me get you some ice," Lisette said, and disappeared into the kitchen. She returned a couple of moments later with some ice cubes in a plastic bag along with a kitchen towel. "Here," she said. "Hold this on it." She seemed to be accustomed to tending injuries, and clearly was calm in a crisis, which brought Alex's thoughts back to his question.

"What's wrong with him?" he asked again.

"He was diagnosed with bipolar disorder when he was seventeen. He gets these rages," she said. "I just gave him a tranquilizer, so he should sleep for a while." She placed her hand on Alex's where he held the cloth against his face, and adjusted the placement of the ice.

"But he's obsessed with finding the Cézanne, and whatever else he thinks belongs to your family. Where did this come from? Is there some basis in fact? Or is he delusional?"

"Both," Lisette answered flatly. "Our family was wealthy once, and the Grassins were an aristocratic family even after the Revolution. There is an estate that my father was forced to sell because we couldn't keep it up, and there are stories..." Her voice trailed away.

"What kind of stories?" The ice was numbing the pain in Alex's face, and his curiosity was returning.

"Stories of wealth, of jewels and stories of my great-grandmother giving it all away. She may have had an illness similar to Paul's. I don't know. But what really makes him angry are the stories that she gave the family treasures away to help the Jews. And so Paul hates Jews on top of everything else. He somehow blames them for our family losing their fortune."

"But that doesn't make any sense," Alex replied. "What good would a Cézanne painting do in the hands of a Jew on his way to a concentration camp?"

"That's just the point," Lisette said. "She used the money from the sale of the paintings to finance Jews who were able to escape over the Pyrenees into Spain."

Alex believed Lisette was telling the truth up to a point. She walked a fine line in her attempt to keep her brother from hurting himself or someone else. Was he crazy himself to be involved in this hair-brained scheme? And the more he thought about it, the more he believed he had seen this particular Cézanne just last week at the Getty. A simple phone call would verify it.

He pulled himself to his feet. Lisette's eyes held genuine concern. "I've got to go, Lisette. I have some phone calls to make."

"Are you sure you are all right?" She touched his arm with her fingertips.

"I'm all right. I'll be in touch, Lisette. Your brother is out of his mind, but if the Cézanne exists, I'll find it."

As Alex headed for the nearest Underground stop, he became aware of heads turning in his direction and then politely turning away. Did his face look that bad? He hadn't bothered to check in a mirror before he left the flat. He gingerly pressed his lower lip with his finger. At least the bleeding had stopped. He found a seat on the train and sat with his head down. His swollen lip stung. He would need to put more ice on it when he got home. He hadn't been hit in the face since he was at school in his short career playing soccer, and he had gotten in the way of the ball. Through the physical pain, he doubted the wisdom of continuing to help Paul and Lisette in the search for the painting. But at the same time, he was concerned about Lisette. It wasn't his business, but if he could see it through, it could save Lisette's life. How would he feel if he abandoned them, and then read in the newspapers that Paul had harmed his sister? And then there was Nara. She would want him as far as possible from these people if she knew the truth. But the Grassins and Nara were looking for the same thing in a sense – information about their great-grandparents doing World War II. There might even be a connection. By the time he reached Russell Square, he had made his decision. He would continue looking for the Cézanne for a while longer, but he would keep it from Nara.

It had been a relaxing, fruitful, but all too short week-end. Nara attended classes all day on Monday, and although she did not regret the time she spent driving up to Lincolnshire to visit with her father and her aunt, she now paid the price for neglecting her books for two days. She left her last class intending to go directly back to her flat and put in some catch-up time with her books. When she stopped in the corridor to check her cell phone, she saw a message from Elaine.

"Nara, it's Elaine. Call me as soon as you can. Nothing's wrong; I just need to talk to you about something."

Nara walked down the corridor, pushing the buttons on her cell phone as she walked. "Elaine, it's Nara. What's wrong?"

"What makes you think something is wrong?" Elaine laughed.

"The boxes."

"Yes, the boxes. The boxes are fine, but I have some news for you."

"What news?" Nara walked through the double outer doors and stopped. The drizzle at lunch time had turned into a downpour. She stepped back into the building and moved into a corner, out of the way of the other students who were shuffling books and pushing up umbrellas before venturing out into the rain.

"You said you didn't mind if I looked through them, so..."

"It's okay, Elaine. I'm glad you opened them. You might be able to help me. I don't know if there is anything that is worth anything, or what to do with any of it. Should I have the clothing cleaned, do you think?" Nara put her hand over one ear as a particularly noisy group of students huddled in the doorway before tackling the rain.

"Nara, did you go through everything in the boxes?"

"I think so," Nara replied. "I went through everything quickly, but I think I looked at whatever was there at least once."

"Did you see the painting?"

"I'm sorry, Elaine. Did you say 'painting'?" The building was suddenly quiet as the last group of people left.

"The painting in the bottom of the box of clothing. The doll was sitting right on top of it."

"I love that doll," Nara said. "It looks so well-loved. It's been washed and mended, but I wonder why she had it with her in London when her children were in Wales."

"Listen to me, Nara," Elaine's voice was impatient. "I called about the painting."

"What painting, Elaine?"

A professor walked by and smiled at Nara, and then grimaced as she raised her umbrella and stepped outside. "Bloody rain," she muttered, and forged out into the street with her umbrella pointed forward as if she were entering a jousting tournament.

"What painting?" Nara repeated when the door closed again.

"That's what I'm trying to tell you," Elaine's voice held a clear edge of impatience. "It was in the bottom of the box under the doll. It was wrapped in brown paper about the same color as the box. That's probably how you missed it."

"Well, what is it?"

"It's a landscape – an oil. But Nara, the signature is 'Cézanne'."

"Can't be. It must be a copy."

"Most likely, but you ought to have someone look at it. Maybe Alex knows someone at the museum."

"I'll ask him," Nara said, "but I'm not sure when I can get back up there now. What did you do with the painting?"

"It's back in the box. I thought that was the safest place until I talked to you."

"I'll try to find someone who can tell us if it's genuine. Maybe I can discreetly ask one of my professors. I wonder if Dad could bring it down to London."

"Let me know, Nara. And I'll leave it in the box until I hear from you. A few more days won't make a difference."

"I suppose not. How strange. A Cézanne painting in the bottom of a box of old clothes."

"Stranger things have happened, Nara."

"Right. I know."

As Nara put away her phone, a door closed softly behind her. She turned around and made out a shadow just behind the glass in the first classroom. Was someone listening to her conversation, or was the person hiding in the classroom for their own reasons? Clearly whoever it was did not want to be seen. *But there is no reason to think this has anything to do with me*, she thought. *Just the same, I need to be careful. What if the painting is real? And why is someone always one step behind me and Lydia's boxes? First at the house in Wales, and then at the flat in London?*

Nara stood quietly in the corridor for a few minutes, but the shadowy figure in the classroom was in no hurry to reveal herself. Somehow Nara assumed it was a woman. She pulled out her own umbrella and headed out into the rain and down the street to the Underground. She pulled out a copy of the diaries and started to read.

Lydia's Diary
May 13, 1941

Another dreary, rainy day. (How appropriate, Nara thought – London never changes.) The Scotland Yard inspector stopped by again today, and Allan has been gone for three weeks. Mrs. Dexter was all in a state about it. Apparently the inspector stopped by earlier in the afternoon and scared her to death. Of course it doesn't take much to put Amelia Dexter in a fit.

Mrs. Dexter – Amelia – made a comment that she "doesn't want to harbor criminals in her house on top of everything else." We are not criminals. I know she knows that. Or maybe she doesn't. I don't know what we would do if she asked us to leave. Surely Major Dexter would not allow such a thing to happen. Oh, I wish Allan would come home.

Perhaps I should have a talk with Major Dexter tomorrow. He surely knows where Allan is. The more questions the Scotland Yard inspector asks, the worse it looks for Allan, with him being gone so long. Surely Dexter can see that. Allan did not kill that boy. That is one thing that is sure. But who did? And why?

Present Day
London

Nara had her key in the lock before she realized he was behind her. "Nara?" He was close enough that she could feel his breath on her neck. She jumped and tried to turn around, but he pushed her forward into the flat.

"I didn't mean to frighten you, and I'm sorry I pushed you just now. I lost my footing. My name is Paul Grassin." He spoke with a pronounced French accent and held out his hand, the picture of gentility.

"Who the hell are you?" Nara screamed.

Paul kicked the door closed behind them. "Don't worry. I'm not dangerous." He laughed in a way that might not be dangerous, but was certainly not Nara's definition of normal. He held his hands up in a gesture of submission and innocence. "I just want to talk to you," he said. "We have a family connection, or at least our families were connected back in the '40s, when your thieving great-grandparents took my family fortune away from my great-grandmother."

Nara inhaled and let her breath out slowly. So that was what this was about. Then maybe, just maybe, he wasn't here to do her bodily harm. And the boxes from Wales were safely in Lincolnshire.

As if he read her mind, Paul asked her, "Where are the boxes you picked up in Wales?"

Nara tried not to register surprise that he knew about the boxes and her trip to Wales. "They are not here."

He took a step closer to her. "Why not? Did you have to hide them because they contain something valuable? If there is anything valuable in those boxes, Nara Blake, it's mine." He hissed the last word.

Nara laughed, and her voice was shrill, betraying the fear she felt. "You don't even know what's in them! How can it be yours? But just so you know, all that's in them is old clothes, family photos, a few toys, some notebooks..." As she reeled off the last item, she realized it was the one he would jump onto.

"Notebooks? Like diaries? Lists of stolen goods?"

Nara was beginning to feel more frightened, wondering where this would lead. Lily was due home soon, wasn't she? "Nothing like that. It's mostly about how much she misses her husband and her children. Nothing of real historical interest."

"You might be surprised what is of historical interest, Nara," Paul continued. "Have you finished reading the diaries?"

"Not quite," she answered. Her body tensed as she anticipated his next question.

"May I read them?" Paul's small, intense brown eyes had never left Nara's face although his voice took on a wheedling tone. "It would mean so much to me if you would allow it, Nara. Perhaps we can help each other."

"I don't think so. And I think you should leave." Nara tried to move around him to open the door, either to show him out or to make a run for it herself, but he blocked her way.

"Do you have the diaries with you, Nara?" Paul asked in the same cajoling tone.

She said nothing.

"Couldn't I look at them here and not take them from this room?"

Would he be satisfied with reading one of the notebooks? Nara had read nothing so far that would indicate his family was involved at all. Nara removed the photocopies of the first of Lydia's notebooks from her bag and handed them to Paul. "You copied them," he said in a flat voice.

Paul grabbed her wrist, knocking the papers to the floor. "Copies? I want to see the originals. I demand to see the originals. Where are they?" He looked around the room as if they might be on a shelf in plain sight.

Nara took a deep breath. "The originals are safe. They are in a bank vault. I didn't want to risk them being lost or damaged while I am reading them, so I had them copied and put away safely."

"This is outrageous," Paul screamed. He moved so close Nara could smell his breath. "I want the originals by tomorrow, do you understand?"

"No. You have no right to them. You don't even have a right to the copies. Now leave this flat now." Nara heard footsteps pounding up the stairs. It had to be Lily; she had probably heard the raised voices.

The door flew open and Paul spun around, colliding with Lily as she burst inside. The bags of groceries she was carrying fell from her arms and spilled onto the floor, showering Paul with orange juice.

"Fucking bitches," he said as he left the flat, wiping his face with his jacket sleeves.

"Nara..." Lily began.

"I'm okay," she answered, grabbing a towel to wipe orange juice off her sweater. "But he knows about the boxes."

"Then he was the one who broke into the flat and probably called your aunt's house in Wales. I think we should call the police."

"No," Nara said. "Let me talk to Alex first."

"But he broke into our flat, and he threatened you!" Lily pulled off a length of paper towels to clean up the floor.

"We have no proof it was him, and I don't remember his name."

"Nara..." Lily's eyes were inches from Nara's face as the two of them bent to clean up the spilled groceries.

"I'll talk to Alex," Nara said at last. "Don't say anything. I'll talk to him."

Chapter 13

Lydia's Diary
May 20, 1941

I'm to go back to the office again. I knew this would happen. I was doing something useful with the French Resistance, but it was only temporary. Of course I didn't feel at all comfortable there, especially not with Suzanne. I can only hope that something else will come up. I know that I did an excellent job cataloging the paintings and then finding a place to store them in Swallowfield. I'm sure Special Branch is aware that it was a difficult job under the circumstances.

I would very much like to take a couple of days and go visit the family in Wales. Major Dexter said I could go, and that I might as well take advantage of the opportunity. Does that mean he has another assignment for me when I get back? I really hate to leave when I haven't seen Allan for almost three weeks. This is the longest he has ever been gone.

I'll decide by the end of the day today. That will still give me time to make arrangements to travel to Wales this weekend, if Allan has not returned.

I must get dressed and ready for work now. I can hear Major Dexter's booming voice downstairs. He has probably already had his breakfast. We will see what today brings.

July 15, 1941 -- lunch time

I don't usually write in my diary during the day, but here it is. Major Dexter instructed me – no, ordered me – to take a few days off and go to Wales. He said that Allan will definitely not be home until at least the beginning of next week. I asked him if Allan was all right, and he said yes of course, and told me not to worry. I looked into his eyes and could tell that he was not hiding anything from me. And why should he? If something had happened to Allan there would be no reason to keep it from me. People are losing loved ones all the time. I'm not that special. The only good news in all this is that Dexter hinted that there will be another special assignment for me next week, so I won't be "condemned" to typing lists again. I know some women don't mind that, and it is still part of the war effort, but I need to do more. That's just the way I am and have always been.

I asked Dexter about Scotland Yard and the investigation of the boy who was killed. He said it would be taken care of. I told him I was worried because they were asking questions about Allan. He didn't seem to take my concerns that seriously, but at the same time, he was not forthcoming at all about the entire matter. I suppose it really has nothing to do with me, except for the fact that I visited the boy once, but it still bothers me. And he would neither confirm nor deny whether Allan had actually been there the night the inspector said he was. Must hurry and pack and catch the train to Bangor. I have not had time to notify Mother and Dad that I am coming, so I will just surprise them.

Lydia collapsed into a seat when the train reached Chester. The crowd usually thinned out at that point since fewer people traveled on into Wales. Lydia relaxed and watched the countryside unroll as the land became more mountainous. This was where she grew up, and as much as she loved London and the life she had created there, Wales was home. She spoke a few words to herself in the Welsh tongue for practice. The soft sounds came easily and reminded her of her childhood. She wondered if the girls were learning to speak Welsh, or Cymru in that tongue. They knew only a few words when they lived in London, but their grandparents doubtless were encouraging them to speak it.

She dozed off as the train gathered speed. Occasionally her head would fall against the window and she would jerk awake. She had not slept that well in London. Although she had not needed to gather up her belongings and move to a bomb shelter in some time, the memory of the night their flat was bombed was still fresh in her mind each time she laid her head on her pillow. And there had been so much tension in her life lately – with the stress of living with the Dexters, Allan's frequent absences, her work, the children – she rarely was able to feel relaxed. She woke up and went to the loo to freshen up when she saw that the train was approaching Bangor. She would have to find a way to get up the mountain from there. There might be a bus that could take her to Nevin, and she could walk the rest of the way. Fortunately the sky was clear, so it would be a pleasant walk.

Several passengers left the train at Bangor. There were a few soldiers on leave, some local people returning home and a few well-dressed older professional men, possibly connected with the university. Lydia saw one man who looked somewhat familiar from the time she had spent here when they were storing the paintings from the National Gallery in the slate mines. She hurried her steps and was about to greet him when she saw to her surprise that a bus headed for Nevin was waiting at the curb. She walked quickly and climbed aboard, nodded at a few familiar faces and found a seat to herself just past the middle of the bus. She hoisted her small suitcase into the rack above her seat and settled in, just in time to see the man she recognized embrace a woman with two small children. Lydia smiled; how wonderful it was to see a happy family reunion.

"Lydia Roberts?" She turned to locate the speaker. A woman about her own age stood next to her. Her dark hair was pulled back into a bun and her skin had the blush of someone who spends time outdoors, but not too much. She was a few inches shorter than Lydia and a few pounds heavier.

"Ann Davis!" Lydia exclaimed. "But not Davis now, is it?"

"Do you mind?" The woman indicated the seat next to Lydia.

"Of course! Please join me." Lydia smoothed her own skirt out of the way to clear the other seat.

"It's Ann Morris now. I married David Morris, remember him? Finally."

"Finally?" Lydia asked.

"I worked in Bangor for several years, even took a few courses at the university. I thought I might go on and get a degree and a job, like you did. But I finally gave it up. It was too lonely, and then David asked me to marry him and I said yes." She looked wistfully out of the window. "But I still read a lot, and I encourage my children. Maybe one of them will go on to the university, or maybe go to London and work when the war is over."

"How many children do you have?" Lydia asked.

"Two. A boy and a girl. Little David is seven now and Nora is four." She smiled as she spoke of her children. "They are in school with your girls now." She studied Lydia before speaking again. "You must miss them terribly. But I'm sure your work in London is very important, with the war and all. Sometimes I wish I could do more, but I just stay on the farm."

"And David?"

"He's too old to serve actively, of course. But he works in Cardiff now, in the shipyards. He comes home every few weeks."

"That's about how often I see Allan," Lydia said.

"Really?" Ann blue eyes opened wide. "I thought you worked together."

"No. Not now. Not since the museum moved everything to safer locations."

"So what kind of work are you doing?"

It was the question Lydia always dreaded. "I'm doing similar work to what I was doing at the museum. Mostly cataloging. We are working to keep accurate lists of works of art in this country. Whatever happens, we don't want to lose touch with our heritage."

"Do you think the Germans will invade? Tell me the truth, Lydia. You are in London; you must hear more than we do here."

"I don't know, Ann. My heart says no, especially when I see how hard everyone is working to make certain that they don't. That is one thing I see in London -- how much effort everyone, from the Prime Minister on down to a waitress in a tea shop -- everyone is doing their utmost in whatever capacity they can. But when the bombs fall – I held a baby a few weeks ago whose mother had just been killed in a raid – I don't know. I lose heart."

"But then you get it back again?"

"Yes. I do. I have to. I have to believe we will get through this."

The two women were silent for a few moments. "What happened to the baby?" Ann asked.

"I took her to a hospital. Her relatives were to come for her."

"What about her father?"

"Serving at sea somewhere. I found that out later."

"Poor little mite. She will never know her mother."

"No, she won't." Lydia stared out the window as the bus wound its way up into the Welsh hills. The sun was gone and a light mist was falling. It might not be such a pleasant walk up to the farm after all. Her thoughts slid back to her constant worries these days, as she wondered how well her children would remember her once the war was over. She was not the kind of mother she wanted to be, but who was, ever, what they thought they would be?

Ann put her hand gently on Lydia's arm. "How long will you be home, Lydia?"

"Just a few days. I have to go back on Sunday."

"I know you want to spend as much time as possible with your girls and your parents, but if you have a free hour, I would love to have tea with you."

"Thank you, Ann." Lydia's eyes brimmed with tears that she did not want to show. "I'll try to do that. I really will." She thought about how quickly the hours would pass. Only two full days, and Sunday afternoon she would be back on the train.

"And Lydia..." Ann's voice was a whisper. "It's okay to cry. I do it all the time."

Lydia tried to smile but her lips trembled, and she turned back to the window and let the tears flow.

"David will be here to meet me," Ann said as the bus approached Nevin. "Is your father meeting you?"

"No," Lydia answered. "They don't know I'm coming." Lydia turned back to face her old friend.

Ann looked at Lydia in surprise. "You didn't tell them?"

"There wasn't time. I was only told yesterday that I could have these few days off before I begin a new assignment." As she said the words, Lydia realized she might be giving too much away. Someone who merely typed lists in an office would be unlikely to be given time off before a new assignment, but Ann gave no indication that she found anything unusual in Lydia's statement.

"We would be happy to give you a ride up the hill," Ann said, her bright eyes full of friendship. "I don't know if David will have the children with him or not. He might have left them with his parents, but we can squeeze you in somehow. You'll be soaked if you walk up in this rain."

It was still only drizzling, but Lydia knew that she would be thoroughly wet after the twenty minute walk up to her parents' farm.

"Thank you. I appreciate it," Lydia smiled.

"Oh, there they are!" Ann shouted as the bus showed to its stop in the village of Nevin. "He has the older one with him. He must have left the baby with his mother." She laughed and added, "Well, she won't be the baby for much longer. I was in Bangor to see the doctor." She lowered her voice and spoke confidentially to Lydia. "I'm expecting again. In December."

After a round of hugs and greetings, Lydia's suitcase was stowed away in the boot and she climbed into the back seat of David and Ann's old car. "I just hope it lasts until this blasted war is over. I have enough petrol for our needs since I am technically a farmer -- that is when I'm not working at the shipyards -- and qualify for additional rations, but it's getting to be almost impossible to get parts. If she breaks down many more times, that may be the end of her," David said, although his tone of voice was cheerful enough.

The rain increased as they drove up the side of the mountain, and Lydia was more than grateful for the ride. They pulled up in front of her parents' stone farmhouse just as the downpour intensified. Ann reached around to the back seat and took Lydia's hand. "Please come and see me," she begged. "I want to know about your life."

"I'll do the best I can," Lydia answered as she patted Ann's hand. *Little did Ann know*, she thought, *how she sometimes wished for an unexciting life like Ann's.*

Lydia dashed to the front door, suitcase in hand, not bothering with her umbrella. Her father had opened the door when the car pulled up in front and stood waiting for her. "You're drenched, girl. Have you no more sense than to run through the rain with no umbrella or macintosh? Is that what people do in London? Damn foolish." He took her suitcase from her.

"Thank you, Dad." She stepped inside the front door and removed her wet shoes. Her mother and her two daughters stood in the kitchen doorway, staring at her.

"Mama!" The older one, Catherine, broke the silence.

"You didn't call," Lydia's mother said. "We were about to have our tea. I'll check that we have enough for one more." She turned and retreated into the kitchen.

"It's all right..." she called to the retreating figure, but her stomach had been grumbling for the past half hour and she had been looking forward to a cup of hot tea and a thick slice of bread with butter made on the farm. She turned her attention to her daughters. They were the ones she was really here to see.

"Catherine! Rebeca!" She opened her arms to them. "I know I'm all wet. I'll go change in a minute. But I need kisses from my girls."

A wide smile spread across Catherine's face and she hugged her mother in spite of her wet clothing. "I didn't know you were coming, Mama," she said.

"I didn't either until this morning, darling," Lydia replied. "And I only had time to pack a suitcase and hop on the train." She reached out her hand to Rebeca, who still stood shyly in the kitchen doorway.

"Rebeca, a kiss for Mama?" Rebeca walked slowly toward her mother, her thumb in her mouth. *She looks so small*, Lydia thought, and so helpless.

"She misses you, Lydia," her father said. "More than the other one, maybe, even though she doesn't show it. We do our best and we will as long as we need to, but they need their mother and father."

"I know, Dad." Lydia's eyes brimmed with tears as she held both girls close in spite of her wet clothes. *It's almost better not to come*, she thought. *Maybe Allan has the right idea -- to stay away until this is finally over and we can be a family again.*

"Let me go upstairs and change into some dry clothes before tea," she said softly, breathing in the scent of her daughters' hair and skin as she held them. "Come with me if you want."

The girls each took one of her hands and they went together upstairs to the bedroom the girls' shared. "I'll sleep with you tonight," she said. Catherine smiled, and Rebeca looked up with her big brown eyes.

"Did you bring us presents, Mama?" Rebeca asked.

"Becky," Catherine reprimanded her younger sister. "You're not supposed to ask for gifts, Granny said."

"It's all right," Lydia said. "I do try to bring you presents when I come, and I don't mind your asking." Normally, she would have taught them the same thing as her mother, but when she saw them only every two or three months, she allowed them more privileges. *There would be readjustments for all of them when the war was over*, she thought. *They would have to get used to being a family once again, and the normal rules of behavior, for both children and adults, would have to be put back into place. It would be difficult for all of them.*

Lydia opened her suitcase and the girls stood on either side of her, watching eagerly. Lydia relished the feeling of their small bodies breathing, and the warmth of their skin, on either side of her. She wanted to feel this sensation forever, with Allan here with them of course. She removed two small white paper bags and handed one to each of the girls. Their eyes brightened and she watched how each of them opened the treasure they had just been handed. Catherine opened the paper slowly, savoring the anticipation, and looked inside. "She has a yellow dress," the little girl said in awe, before removing the tiny doll from the wrapping.

Rebeca followed her sister's lead and opened her bag, now that she had an idea what she could expect to find inside. Even though Rebeca was by nature a more serious child, she could not help but show her delight at what she saw. She reached in and carefully removed an identical doll, but while Catherine's was blonde and dressed in yellow, her favorite color, Rebeca's was a brunette, like Rebeca herself, and dressed in dark green. "She's beautiful," the little girl breathed. Then she turned her serious gaze to her mother. "Granny said you can't get toys anymore, that the factories can't make them because they are all making things for the war like airplanes and guns and things."

Lydia cringed at the mention of the war from the mouth of her small child, but she responded with equal seriousness. "I suspect that these were made before the war. I found them in a small shop that was going out of business. These were the only dolls they had left."

"Thank you, Mama," Catherine said, and grinned, showing a gap where her upper baby teeth had been, and hugged her mother around the waist.

"Thank you, Mama," Rebeca parroted her sister, but before she could wrap her arms around her mother in a mirror of Catherine's hug, Lydia's mother spoke from the bedroom doorway.

"Come, girls," she said. "Let your mother unpack. It's time for you to wash and help set the table for tea. Your grandfather is hungry."

And what about me? Lydia thought, as the girls obediently followed their grandmother. *What about what I need? I need my children, for the short time that I can be with them.* "I'll be right down," she said to whichever of them were listening to her as they made their way downstairs. She snapped the suitcase shut – it could wait until later – and noticed that both the dolls lay on her bed. *Maybe it was just as well*, she thought, *their grandmother might take them from them until after dinner, or to put them away so they would not be damaged.* They could play with them here, with her, and when she left at the end of the week-end, it would be out of her hands. She used the old-fashioned basin and pitcher in the bedroom and washed her face and hands and hurried down for tea.

Tea was an uncomfortable affair. Lydia's father led them all in a prayer so long that the girls began to fidget, and Lydia wondered if the food would be cold before they began to eat it. Eventually he completed his litany of all those in need of divine protection, and thanksgiving for their food, their health, and the presence of the mother of the two innocent children at the table. Lydia's mother had made a soup of mutton and vegetables – carrots, onion and leeks, and it had only cooled from the steaming state it possessed when placed on the table, so it was hot and tasty. Lydia spooned it appreciatively into her mouth and helped herself to some of the soft brown bread and fresh cheese. "This is delicious, Mama," Lydia said to her mother after a few minutes. "Thank you."

"I'm glad to hear that you still enjoy our simple food."

"We have enough, thank God, to feed ourselves and the two little ones," added her father as he helped himself to another slice of bread.

"That's an advantage you have here on the farm where you grow almost everything you eat." Lydia realized as soon as the words were out of her mouth that her father would not take them in the way she intended.

"I wouldn't say it is an advantage when we live up here on our own with no one to help us," he said. "We have greater distances to travel and not enough petrol." He held up his hand as if to fend off any response that Lydia might make. "Oh, I know. You are going to say that we receive a greater ration of petrol because of the farm, but it still is not enough. We must take care of ourselves, no one to help us in cold, rain or sickness. Don't tell me we have any advantage living here. The only advantage we have is that we don't have bombs falling on our heads, and that could start any day, too, I've no doubt." He took a noisy slurp of tea. "You live in the city, Lydia. You work with these people who run our government. What do they say? When will the Germans be here on our soil?"

"Please, Tom, the children," Lydia's mother hissed at her husband. "Your talk will frighten them."

He glanced at his two granddaughters who sat quietly eating their soup. "Are you girls frightened of the Germans?"

"Dad, please!" Lydia shouted. "If you are angry at me, say so, and I know you are. But don't take it out on my children!"

"Your children," he repeated with sarcasm. "You go away and leave them here so you can work at your fancy job in London, your husband is heaven knows where, and then you speak of your children? They are more mine than yours." He stood and left the table, going outdoors into the dusk.

Catherine and Rebeca had stopped eating and were staring at the two adults remaining at the table. Finally little Rebeca turned to her grandmother. "Gran?"

"It's all right, dear," she answered soothingly. "Grandpa is just worried about the war, as everyone is."

"Is the war going to come here?" Rebeca asked.

"No." Lydia found her voice. "The war is not going to come here. That is why Daddy and I have to be away in London working. We are working with many other people to make sure that the war does not come here. We want you to grow up and be safe and happy. That is why you need to stay with Granny and Grandpa for a while. We want you safe. We want everyone in Wales and in England, and everywhere, to be safe. We are making this sacrifice now so we can all have safe, happy lives in the future."

"When the war is over, Mama?" Catherine asked. "Will we live in Wales or in London?"

"Where would you prefer to live, Catherine?" Lydia's mother interrupted before Lydia had a chance to speak.

"I would rather live wherever Mama and Daddy are," the little girl said.

"And you, Rebeca?" The older woman turned to the younger of her granddaughters.

"Mom, that's not fair!" Lydia turned on her mother. "It's not fair or right to ask them where they would rather live. Allan and I are their parents. When the war is over and we get back to our normal lives, of course they will both live with us. There is no reason to even talk about it any further."

"Well, you have to think about what is best..."

"Mom, no. This conversation is completely out of line. If I could I would take both of them back to London with me, but you know that is impossible." She stood. "Girls, let's help Grandma with the washing up and then let's go out for a little walk on the hills while it is still light. That is one thing I miss about Wales when I am in London – the hills and the light."

The four of them cleared the table and washed up the dishes. The girls evidently were used to the routine because they both took up dish towels and dried the dishes and put them in their proper places in the cupboards while Lydia washed. Her mother puttered around the kitchen, not really doing anything, but seemingly reluctant to leave her daughter alone with Catherine and Rebeca. When they had finished and hung the damp towels by the stove to dry, Lydia announced, "Let's go for a walk, girls."

"Oh, Lydia, surely it's getting too dark," her mother said.

The sky was rosy in the west, but it was by no means dark. "Oh, it's not nearly dark, Mom," Lydia said. "And we aren't going far. I just want to get out of the house for a bit."

Her mother looked about to say something else, but closed her mouth. The two girls had already obediently put on their jackets and stood unsmiling at the door. It flashed through Lydia's mind that she could invite her mother to come with them, but she rejected the idea. She was the girls' mother, and surely she had a right to a little time alone with them.

They took the path that led up the hill behind the house to the pasture above. Lydia had climbed this hill often as a child, and she knew she could do it no matter how dark it might be. They walked in silence for a few minutes with Lydia in the lead, followed by Catherine and then Rebeca, whose short legs had to work twice as hard. They reached a level area where they could look down at the house, the village and the valley beyond. Lydia yearned to ask the girls if they were happy here, how their grandparents treated them, if they missed her and Allan and thought about them every day, but those questions just didn't seem fair. As young as they were, the girls were old enough to sense the tension between the generations in their family, and their grandmother was already pressuring them to choose life with them in Wales over life with their parents. Lydia didn't want to add to the pressure, she just wanted to enjoy her time with them. She wanted their memories of these visits to be happy ones, or at least memories of a mother who listened to them and wanted to be with them.

"Mama?" It was Catherine who spoke.

"Yes, love?" she answered.

"I like it when you are here." Her small face turned up to Lydia's.

"I like it, too," she answered.

Rebeca moved in close to her sister and her mother. "Can we go to the village and buy cakes tomorrow, Mama? Granny and Grandpa hardly ever let us buy cakes."

Lydia laughed and hugged her younger daughter. Was this her way of expressing the feelings she could not put into words? Could this mother who appeared every month or two give her something her grandparents refused to give? Lydia saw no reason why Rebeca should not have cake from the village tomorrow, if that would bring a smile to her face. "I think that is an excellent plan," she said. "The cakes are much better here than they are in London."

Catherine spoke up. "Mama, remember the cakes we used to buy in the shop near our house when we lived in London? The one with the fat man with white hair that I said looked like a cake with white frosting? And you were always shushing me?"

"I remember that, Catherine!" Lydia said. "You were very small, about four, I think."

"Was I there?" Rebeca asked.

"Yes, I think you were, Rebeca," Lydia said. "But you would have been very young, just about two years old. I believe you had some bites of cake from the man who looked like a cake."

"Can we go back there sometime so I can see him?" Rebeca asked.

"We can certainly try," Lydia answered as she wondered about the man in the bakery. Was he still there? That section of London was relatively unscathed by bombing, but she had no idea if the bakery was still open.

They heard voices down below, and then a sharp whistle. The quick running footsteps grew louder as a sheep dog bounded up the hill. The girls laughed. "Here comes Benny to round us up!" Catherine said.

"Yes, I think we have no choice but to go back down. He'll round us up as if we are sheep and won't take no for an answer."

The black and white dog reached their sides and gave a few short barks as he circled around Lydia and her daughters. "All right. All right, Benny," Lydia said. "We are on our way."

They began the descent with Catherine in the lead this time. As Lydia suspected, the girls knew their way just as she had as a child, and this pleased her. Benny did not leave their sides until they reached the bottom, when another sharp whistle from Lydia's father brought him to his side with one last bark. It was as if he were saying, "Did I do that well?"

"Good job, Benny," the man said, and patted the dog's head. "It's almost dark," he added to Lydia. "Time to go in and get the girls to bed."

Lydia started to open her mouth but Rebeca beat her to it. "Oh, Grandpa, can't we stay up a little later since Mama is here?"

It was too dark to see clearly what emotions were fighting for control in her father's face, but Lydia was sure by his silence that his anger from earlier in the evening had not completely evaporated. And his authority had been questioned by a little girl, even if she was his youngest granddaughter. "We'll ask Granny," he said finally. *Ah*, thought Lydia, *there's the coward's way out if I ever heard one.*

Rebeca ran inside without another word, followed by Catherine. When the door had closed behind them, Lydia and her father stood in the silence. A dog barked in the distance and Benny perked up his ears, but evidently decided it wasn't an important canine message and went back to sniffing around his food bowl looking for anything he might have missed earlier.

"I'm sorry for what I said, Lydia. They are of course your children. Yours and Allan's."

Lydia could see his face in the light from the kitchen door, and knew what it cost him to say those words. She laid her hand on his arm; more affection than that would disturb him, she knew. "Thank you, Papa. These are difficult times."

"Times are always difficult, Lydia," he said. He gave her hand a pat and then moved back slightly. "You are too young to remember the last war. I was too old to go and fight then, and I thought that somehow I had been given a reprieve from war directly touching my family. I was proud of you going off to London, getting an education, even though it's not what I would have expected from a daughter, but there it is. Then this war came along, and I thought you would all come home to Wales and be safe, like last time. And when you and

Allan decided to stay and work for the war effort, I understood, or tried to understand, but it's too close to us now. Not physically. I don't really expect the Germans to care about Wales, except for the shipyards around Cardiff maybe, but that's far from us. I'm terrified that something will happen to you, Lydia. You are my only child."

Lydia had never heard her father speak with such emotion, and it frightened her.

"I'll be all right, Dad. I work in an office," she reassured him. She could never tell him how she hated working in the office at Whitehall, and longed to be more actively involved in the war effort.

"Offices get bombed, Lydia." His voice was barely audible.

"Yes, but most bombing raids are at night, and we're fighting them off, Dad. We will win this."

"I believe we will, Lydia. But please take care."

"I do take care."

Before she could say anything else, Catherine appeared at the kitchen door. She was dressed in her pajamas and hopped back and forth in her bare feet as she stood on the cold stone stoop. "Mama, Mama, come in. Grandma says we may have one story from you before we go to sleep. Come please before Rebeca falls asleep. She is such a baby sometimes."

"I'm coming," Lydia answered. "Coming in now, Dad?"

"In a moment," he answered. He pulled his pipe from his pocket. "Your mother doesn't like for me to smoke inside."

"All right, Dad." Their eyes met briefly, and Lydia knew that that was the closest to a declaration of fatherly love that she was likely to receive from this reticent Welshman.

Lydia's Diary
May 25, 1941 – evening

Everyone is asleep, but I can't relax. I just want to sit here in the dark and listen to the girls sleep. I couldn't write in my diary last night. I was exhausted, emotionally and physically, and the girls were too excited. I sat up with Mom and Dad and talked about inconsequential things for a while, and then we all went to bed.

Tonight I took a chance and turned on my torch so I could write a little bit. It doesn't seem to bother the girls. They didn't even roll over when I clicked it on. I'm sitting on the floor near the window, so I have a bit of moonlight to write by as well.

Today went by too quickly. I took the girls into the village and bought cakes for them as they asked. They saw several of their friends from school and both of them seemed pleased to show off their mother. Their friends probably wondered if they really had a mother. But it hurt to hear them ask, "Where is your father?" Catherine answered them proudly, "He's working in London. He has a very important job." But I'm not sure that made the proper impression on these country girls. There are some, of course, who have older brothers or uncles and a few fathers, who are fighting. But "an important job in London" just doesn't have the same ring to it. I'm so happy that I had the opportunity to come here this week-end. I think I smoothed things out with Dad, or rather he smoothed things out with me. I wonder if men will ever learn to tell their daughters that they love them? Allan does, or did, but will he still when the girls are adults? But maybe it doesn't matter. Maybe what they don't say in words, but show in other ways, is just as important or maybe even more important. I never knew until last night how much my father loves me, and he didn't say the word "love" once.

I saw Ann Davis in town, and we talked for a few minutes outside the bakery. She was with her husband and children and she looked so happy, glowing is more the word. Her world is smaller than mine, but yet so full. I envy her and women like her, sometimes. They are satisfied with less of the world, but their little corner is full to overflowing. She has lived in the same village all her life, married her childhood sweetheart, and has two beautiful children and another one on the way. Her family is everything to her, and she would be miserable in London. I think when she visits other places, even Bangor, small as it is, she only goes so that she can come home again.

Is there something wrong with me that I am not like that?

I wonder how Allan would feel about having another child when the war is over? Or am I too old?

I must be strong tomorrow, and try not to dread taking the train back to London. I will come back as soon as I can. This is so wonderful here but it isn't permanent. But what is permanent now? I will go to chapel with my parents and the girls in the morning and then take the five o'clock train from Bangor. I will get into London late, but that's all right. I can be tired on Monday. That gives me one more full day here. Oh, and I must look for another doll for Rebeca. She wants a baby doll like the one Catherine has. Catherine doesn't play with hers that much anymore, but it's not fair to ask a little girl to give up her doll, even in these times. I don't know if Mom and Dad would buy one for her or not, probably not. They think the girls have too many toys as it is, and I want it to be from me.

Allan, I love you. Where are you? I miss you so.

Why is Dad hammering so early in the morning? Lydia thought in her haze of sleep. She had not slept until almost two, and was just now in the deep, refreshing sleep that she needed. *Wait. It's Sunday. He wouldn't be hammering at all on Sunday, the Lord's Day. What is that noise?*

"I'm coming. Have you no idea of the time?" Lydia heard her father muttering as he went down the stairs. Benny started barking, adding to the commotion. Lydia looked at the girls who still slept peacefully through the noise. Catherine's growing legs stretched out in the small bed against the far wall, and her face was relaxed in sleep even though sunlight was beginning to cast a ray through the window. Rebeca slept in the other narrow bed with Lydia, and she too slept soundly, curled into a ball to keep warm.

The pounding had stopped, and since Lydia was not fully awake, she curled up next to Rebeca to savor her closeness and warmth.

"Lydia. Lydia." There was a soft knock on her bedroom door.

She inhaled Rebeca's fragrance one last time and climbed out of the warm bed. She opened the door a crack to see her father standing there, still in his nightshirt, and an envelope in his hand. "What is it?" she whispered.

"This came for you," he said softly, as he handed her the envelope. "The Wellers' have the only telephone in the village. I hope it's not bad news," he added needlessly.

She took it from him. "I'll be right out." She set the envelope on the bed and stared at it. It could not contain good news, but there were degrees of bad news. She wrapped her robe around her and found her slippers. Her feet were already freezing from contact with the bare floor. She could hear her father still in the hall outside her room, talking softly with her mother now. She had to open the envelope; it wasn't fair to keep them waiting because of her fear. She removed the single sheet of paper and read. It was from Major Dexter in London. Allan was back. "Thank God," she whispered. It was not the worst news. But there was a problem with the situation with Samuel Picard, and so Lydia needed to return to London on the earliest possible train. *They must have arrested Allan*, she thought. Mr. Dexter would not have been able to say it outright since he had to give the phone message to a third party, but what else could it be? The earliest possible train? No! I wanted the latest possible train. She read on. And he had a new assignment for her, and would like to speak to her this evening, if possible. Both of these are of the utmost urgency. The note ended with a post script from

Mr. Weller, who had taken the message. "Happy to see that Allan is all right. Sorry you have to return to London so soon. We will miss seeing you at chapel. The first train is at nine a.m. if you want to try to make it."

Lydia's mind was spinning. Allan was all right. He was in London but was probably being blamed for the death of Samuel Picard. That was ridiculous of course. She had to see him, and she could make the nine a.m. train. Except -- she did not want to say good-bye to her children so soon.

There was a soft knock on the door, and her mother's voice, "Lydia, is everything all right?"

She pulled her thoughts back to the present and opened the door and stepped out into the hall. She ran a hand through her hair, which must be standing on end just as her mother's was.

"Is everything all right?" she said again. "Mr. Weller didn't say anything to your father about what was in the note, as he shouldn't since it was for you."

She took a deep breath. "Everything is all right. That is – Allan is fine and is back in London. But there is some trouble about a French boy studying at Compton School who was killed, and Allan had some contact with him." *Have I said too much*? she thought. She wanted her parents to appreciate the urgency of the situation.

"I have to go back on the earliest train. There is a new assignment for me as well."

"Oh, Lydia, surely it can't be that important," her mother began.

"It is," Lydia said firmly. "Sometimes an assignment in the office can be every bit as important as an assignment on the front lines. We are the ones who keep things organized, after all. Sometimes there are lists of supplies that are requisitioned, special rationing situations and things like that. And I do have top level security clearance so I am trusted with things that other people are not." *Would they believe her*? she wondered. What she just said didn't make sense even to her.

All her mother said was, "What will you tell the girls?"

In the end, Lydia was glad she was able to take the nine a.m. train from Bangor to London. It was definitely less crowded than the late afternoon one would be. And it avoided the long day when they all knew she would be leaving at the end. The girls were sad but like the brave little soldiers that they were, they assured their mother that it was fine. There were no tears, since it all happened too fast. They helped Lydia pack and the girls rode along to the train station, which was excitement for them. Lydia's mother stayed at home, to get the girls' clothes ready for chapel, she said. Once Lydia was settled in her seat on the train, her thoughts turned to events in London. She had not even taken the time to send a message to Mr. Dexter to inform him that she was on her way. She just assumed that he would know that she would be there when called.

It was possible that Allan had been arrested, but Lydia had no doubt that Special Branch would have him free immediately, maybe even by the time she reached London. And maybe now she would hear the full story of why Allan had visited the boy the night before he left for France. As the train moved toward London, she began to feel a twinge of excitement at the prospect of a new assignment. Contrary to what she had told her parents, she believed that it must be something important for Major Dexter to call her back on a Sunday. It wasn't merely typing secret documents. She would love to have more responsibilities with rescuing art work as she had done with the French. She had heard that statues had been transported from Italian churches as well, and although that was not her area of expertise, she was certainly qualified to do the evaluation and cataloging.

Lydia dozed on the train. The lack of sleep the night before along with the tension of the last few days, and now anticipation of what was to come, had exhausted her. She woke with a start from time to time as the wild Welsh countryside gave way to the more manicured landscape of England. Eventually they entered the outskirts of London, and she began to prepare herself to arrive at Euston Station. She combed her hair and reapplied lipstick with the aid of the small gold compact with the key that Allan had given her years ago. She joined the crowd leaving the train, carrying her handbag over her arm and her small suitcase in the other hand, lighter now that she had given the girls their gifts. Since she was seated near the end of the car, she was one of the first off the train. Major Dexter, along with another man she didn't know, stood on the platform scanning the crowds. When he saw her, Dexter said something to the other man and the two of them looked relieved.

Lydia, however, was not relieved. Their presence could only mean that Allan's problems were more serious than she had thought.

Dexter quickly introduced Lydia and his associate, a solicitor for Special Branch by the name of Alistair Adams. He took Lydia's suitcase and they whisked her hurriedly through the station to a car waiting just outside. Dexter sat in the back with Lydia while Adams took the front seat next to the driver. Only when the car moved out into traffic did Major Dexter speak. "I don't want you to worry about Allan, Lydia. We will have him out of the clutches of Scotland Yard before the end of the day, I assure you. They are anxious to arrest someone, and Allan was their obvious choice since they hadn't bothered to look very hard."

"Allan didn't kill him," Lydia said. "He wouldn't."

"We know that," the solicitor answered. "There was no motive, and Scotland Yard knows that. They would let him go sooner or later, but it will be done today, I assure you."

"So why are you here?" Lydia asked Adams. "If you know Allan is innocent, and he will be out today, surely you aren't here just to explain it to me."

"That's right, Lydia." The two men exchanged a glance that seemed to confirm a previous description of Lydia. She said what they expected her to say. "Solicitor Adams wants to ask you a few questions about the boy, since you visited him as well. It may well be that his murder is connected to our activities in France and with the French Resistance. And we want to be several steps ahead of Scotland Yard when they discover that fact."

Solicitor Adams rested his right arm on the seat back and he turned to face Lydia. He was good-looking in a way that did not appeal to Lydia. He was probably about her age, middle thirties, which would explain why he was here in London and not actively serving in the military. His hair was blond and cut very short and his eyes an intense, glacial blue. She could see the thick blond hairs on the back of his hand as it dangled from the seat. "Why did you visit Samuel Picard at his school, Lydia?"

Something about his tone of voice offended her. "Is this an interrogation?"

He laughed a short bark of a laugh, not the kind of laugh she would have expected from him. "Of course not. We are just trying to learn the facts."

"Is Scotland Yard going to interrogate me?"

"Not if we can help it. We protect our own, Lydia."

For the first time since the beginning of the conversation, she trusted him. "I visited him because Allan asked me to. The boy was sent here to school in 1939. The family is Jewish, and they thought he would be safe here and would benefit from an English education. They set up a bank account for him in London to cover his expenses, and a banker oversees it and gives him a certain amount of money each month, I believe. Allan asked me to visit the boy because he met the family in France, and they were worried about him. They wanted to reassure him that they loved him and that he was better off at school in England that in France, where it was growing more dangerous day by day for Jews."

"I see," said Adams, his glacial blue eyes never leaving Lydia's face. "And was your visit a success? Were you able to reassure him?"

"The visit was certainly not a success from my point of view," Lydia said.

"And why was that?"

Lydia glanced at Dexter, who was watching her and listening to the exchange impassively.

"I found him a thoroughly unpleasant young man with no manners whatsoever. But that doesn't mean I am pleased that he is dead. He was only fifteen; children of that age are often unpleasant."

"What exactly did he say or do that you found unpleasant?" Adams asked.

"His only interest in his parents seemed to be that he wanted – no, demanded -- that they send him more money. He said that what they allowed him from the bank was insufficient for his needs. When I tried to explain their circumstances in France, he cut me off. Perhaps he just couldn't face the reality of their situation, but he didn't even seem interested. And he was very rude. He almost seemed to blame me for his lack of money."

The car had pulled up in front of the Dexters' home in Pimlico. "Lydia, we are going to leave you here. I'm sure you want to rest and freshen up after your journey. Amelia can see that you have something to eat if you are hungry. Adams and I are going to see if we can get Allan released. But I will be back in a few hours at the most. I have something else I want to discuss with you. I have an assignment you might be interested in."

"Of course! You said something about it in the phone message this morning."

"Yes, I thought two reasons to take the early train would be better than only one. And I was right," he added.

"What...?" she started to ask.

"The first thing you need to learn is patience. You need to rest and gather your thoughts for a few hours, and we have work to do. I have some people I want you to meet later, and with any luck Allan will be with us."

Major Dexter walked her to the front door and set her suitcase just inside. "Lydia, I'm so glad to see you," his wife Amelia cried when she saw them. "Did you know that Allan...?"

"Amelia," he said warningly, and she closed her mouth.

"Sorry. I forgot. I'm sure you would like some tea, Lydia, and then you can rest. John says it's important."

Lydia looked back out the door and saw Solicitor Adams watching her from the front seat of the car. He seemed to be studying her, looking for something. As Dexter returned to the car, Adams got out and moved to the back seat with the other man. Lydia was sure she heard Adams say, "Yes. I think she will do."

Chapter 14

Lydia's Diary – June 1, 1941

"Loose lips sink ships." Funny expression but so true. Since Allan's arrest I have become more conscious of the necessity of keeping one's private business to oneself. Amelia Dexter seems so well-meaning in her solicitous questions about Allan, about my plans and about the children. But I have the feeling that behind her caring attitude is the desire to know. And the desire to know will lead to her need to pass on the information to her friends, to the cook and the postman who will then pass on the information to their friends, and the friends' cooks and spouses will find out. One never knows what damage could be done.

The murder of a fifteen year old student is a serious incident, and the arrest of an innocent man is even more serious in many ways. An innocent man is in jail, and a black mark placed on his reputation even though he will be found innocent in the end. But the real damage is that a killer is free, and will want to remain free.

Present Day
London

Lisette silently cursed the crowds in the Underground that slowed her journey across London. "I should have taken a taxi," she muttered. She found a seat after King's Cross and tried to call her brother, but her phone had lost the signal as the train traveled underground. When she reached her stop, she was first to exit the car. She ran up the stairs, unwilling to wait for the escalator. She was breathless when she reached the top, but slowed her pace only briefly as she ran down the street to the flat she shared with her brother Paul.

She unlocked the door to find him seated on the sofa with a glass in his hand and a bottle on the table in front of him. "Where have you been?" he asked with a slur of alcohol.

"Doing more for us that you apparently have," she snapped as she hung up her jacket.

"Bitch," he muttered and poured another glass from the bottle.

"What are you drinking?"

"None of your business," he replied as he took a healthy slurp from his glass.

Lisette was not willing to involve herself in another argument about Paul's drinking. She could recite all the rational reasons why it was bad for him physically and every other way. It interacted with his medications; it exacerbated the symptoms of his illness; it was too expensive because he insisted on buying only the best brands of Scotch available and had them delivered to the flat. And he did not think clearly when he drank. How could he make elaborate plans to regain his heritage when he was drunk? She knew her arguments, and she knew his counter-arguments. There was no point in going through it all again.

"I know where the Cézanne is," she said bluntly.

He had the glass to his lips, but he replaced it on the table. "I knew you would come through! Where is it? Can we get our hands on it?"

"I don't know exactly where it is yet, but I will find out. You were right. I overheard Nara Blake talking about it on her mobile phone with someone. But apparently Nara doesn't believe it is authentic."

"It's authentic all right," Paul began.

"Unless she doesn't have the original."

"We have to find out. Where is it? You said you know where it is." His face clouded with anger.

"I don't know exactly where it is, but Nara does."

"Find out fast, Lisette. She must have taken it from the house in Wales. It wasn't in her flat. Where is it?"

"We'll find out, Paul. It shouldn't be difficult. But you have to be patient."

"And the jewelry? What about that?"

Lisette sighed and sat down next to him on the sofa. She was so tired of this, so tired of the arguments, of caring for him during him mood swings, his drinking, his delusional episodes and trips to the hospital. They owed thousands of euros for his hospitalization in private mental institutions in France. His illness was the only reason she tolerated his behavior. Once they either regained the objects that were stolen from them, or Paul accepted the fact that everything was gone, she would leave him to his own devices. His mental instability had worsened after the deaths of both their parents. First their mother succumbed to cancer when they were teenagers, and then their father died just two years ago. Jean-Paul Grassin had died in an auto accident, his sports car wrapped around a tree in the suburbs of Paris. His blood was filled with alcohol and enough prescription drugs to kill five men. Since that time, Paul's behavior had become more and more erratic, and although he and his sister had never been close, she feared losing her last remaining family member. As Paul showed every indication of following his father's path of alcohol and drugs, Lisette left the university just six months before she would have graduated in order to care for him. They had grown up with the stories of the fortune that had disappeared from the hands of their great-grandmother during the 1940s. Their mother, when she was alive, had no interest in searching for these lost treasures. "If Grandmère lost them, she probably gave them away," she maintained. "Or sold them. Give it up and get on with your lives." She had met her husband's grandmother when she was a white-haired, elderly lady in her 80s. "If she knew anything or was interested in recovering them, she would have said so."

Lisette was inclined to agree with her mother's thinking. But now Lisette and Paul were the only family members remaining. She couldn't abandon her brother, even in his obsessions with finding what the family had lost. She would see it through now, and either find what was lost once and for all, or force him to give up the search. They had followed the trail to Wales and just missed the possibility of gaining access to the boxes that had been stored since the 1940s. They had also just missed finding the boxes in Nara Blake's flat. Now they had no idea where they were, but Nara did, and possibly her sister Lily and her fiancé Alex.

"Find out where she is going this week-end," Paul said. He stretched his legs out on the couch, preparing to sleep off the alcohol he had ingested during the afternoon.

"I'll try," Lisette answered. She stood up to allow him to stretch out fully. If he were sleeping for the next few hours, she could have some time to herself, although when he woke up he would want to go out, and Lisette was not in the mood for club hopping and spending money that they didn't have. "Grassins don't work," he said whenever she mentioned that one of them should get a job doing something. They had inherited a small amount of money when their father had died, but Paul's expensive tastes always meant that they lived far beyond their monthly allotment.

Paul Grassin began to prepare himself. He had three days. He kept his Wednesday meeting with Alex Collier at the Victoria and Albert Museum. He spent three hours perusing documents that Alex had found that were related to French art work and World War II. They discussed the likelihood of the Grassins regaining their lost art, and Paul verbally agreed with Alex that the chances were slim. He made every effort to come across as a most rational and pragmatic human being. At the end of their meeting, he reiterated his offer to Alex of a percentage of the profit if they found the missing Cézanne. However, he jovially admitted that the chances were not good.

His anger at Lisette had reached a boiling point, but she was his sister, his only living relative, part of the Grassin family, and he might need her in the future. He decided that it was time to strike out on his own; he would leave Lisette in London to plod along in her college courses. Somehow she was under the delusion that her studies of history would assist them in finding their stolen fortune. Paul no longer had time for the delay. Nara Blake had the boxes from her great-grandparents, and the more Paul thought about the boxes that had lain unopened in the attic of a farmhouse in Wales for sixty years, the more he believed that, at the very least, a genuine Cézanne painting and a piece of jewelry from the sixteenth century were hidden in the boxes. He didn't need to know where Nara was going this week-end; all he had to do was follow her. All he needed to do was to follow Nara, and she would lead him to his family's treasures.

By Friday he was ready. He left a note for Lisette in the morning, and arrived early outside Nara's flat. He guessed she would travel by train, since she and her sister shared a car. He was prepared to follow her throughout the day, so as not to miss her when she left the city. He knew that these days when he behaved with sanity did not indicate that he was, in fact, sane. The truth was that he knew how to manipulate the symptoms of his illness to appear sane when he had a goal in mind. And now he was close -- so close. He was also cleverer than his sister. He followed Nara to the University and trailed her to her classes, keeping himself discreetly out of sight.

At three o'clock in the afternoon Nara left her last class of the day. She hoisted her backpack once again and headed for the nearest Underground stop. Paul easily followed her to King's Cross, where she purchased a ticket for a train headed north. He was unable to hear exactly where she was headed, which forced him to purchase a ticket for Edinburgh, the last destination of the train. Paul chuckled to himself as he purchased a newspaper and boarded the car a few minutes after Nara. Now all he had to do was to wait and follow her when she left the train. It was so much easier without Lisette. He had eluded her, and she would not try to follow him. She never did. When she was fed up with him, as she was right now, she wouldn't trouble herself to try to find out where he was. She would undoubtedly call him; in fact, he was surprised that she had left him no messages yet today. She must be really disgusted with him not to leave any messages all day, but she knew he would contact her when he needed her. And right now, he didn't need her. He was Sherlock Holmes, James Bond, Adolph Hitler – he was brilliant, powerful, and ruthless.

There was one thing he could have done to make his work easier, but his ego had not allowed him to do it. He could have asked Alex Collier if he knew where Nara was going this week-end. But if he suspected that Nara might be in any danger, Alex might not tell him, or worse, he might refuse to help find the painting or maybe go to the police. It was better if Alex didn't know. Paul took enough of a risk when he offered Alex a percentage of the profits when they found the Cézanne. He had no intention of following through on his end of the deal, but that was something he would worry about in the future. He planned on giving Lisette enough of the profits to get her off his back, but the fortune was his. And once he had at least part of it, he would have the resources to find and regain the rest. He reviewed his plans in his mind, as he had done many times before, and his body relaxed and his eyes closed. He woke suddenly as the train jerked to a stop and for a moment he was unsure where he was and what he was doing there. He jumped to his feet as he saw Nara striding purposely across the platform in the direction of the stairs. Where were they? He grabbed his bag and leapt off the train, running to the stairway where he had last seen Nara. He sprinted up the stairs and caught a glimpse of her at the other end of the walkway leading to connecting trains. He slowed to a walk and checked the platform. A train to Springfield and Sleaford would be arriving in ten minutes. Where were they? He was beginning to think he should have researched Nara Blake a little more before setting out, but it was too late now. He slipped behind a post where he could keep an eye on her while they waited for the train. His phone rang, and as he expected, it was Lisette. He answered. "Lisette, don't call again. Everything's fine."

"I'm going back to France, Paul. You're on your own."

"No, Lisette. Wait until I get back to London. I'm going to get the Cézanne; I'm sure of it."

"No, Paul. I can't do this anymore. Either you are faking being ill or faking being sane, but either way, I've had enough. I'm taking the Eurostar tomorrow morning."

"If you are not in the flat when I get back, you'll get nothing from me."

"You've got nothing, Paul. Fifty percent of zero is zero, and you probably wouldn't even give me fifty percent." The voice of the loudspeaker announced the arrival of the train. "Where are you, Paul? Where are you going?"

He closed the connection and hurried to board the train. It was only two cars long, so he watched Nara board the first and he followed onto the second. This was going to be easier than he had dreamed. This time he made sure that he stayed awake. When this train stopped, it would not be for more than a few minutes. He would need to leap off quickly and still stay out of Nara's sight.

He was forced to pay for a taxi to follow her. The town was small, and he would not be able to manage the anonymity that he had in London. There was a very real chance that someone would remember seeing him. He knew he would have to be very careful.

Paul climbed into a taxi and told the driver he was unsure of the address. He said that it was a private residence, and he knew that he would recognize the house when he saw it. He had visited here in the past, he said, but had left the address behind. His phone calls to the friend that he was visiting continued to result in no answer. Paul repeated dialed a random number on his phone and pretended to react to his frustration. "Damn!" he said. "I told her I would be here today." The driver asked him the name of the person he was visiting and he made up a name, which of course the driver did not recognize. All the time Paul kept the car in which Nara was riding in his sight. He just hoped he didn't lose her. He flashed a £50 note to keep the driver cooperative and hoped Nara would reach her destination soon. When he saw where they lived, he would simply ask the driver to go a bit farther and then ask him to stop and let him out. All he needed was to know where she was going, and that was most likely where his family's wealth was. He was so close he could feel it.

He panicked briefly when the taxi was forced to stop at a stoplight and Nara's car pulled ahead, but then relief washed over him when the car ahead pulled into a driveway just past the intersection. "Now I remember!" He slapped his head. "It's just past here."

"There's nothing past here, mate," the driver told him. "Pinchbeck Road goes on out of town here. The next houses you see will be in Sleaford. Well, there are still a few farmhouses, but not for a mile or two. Are you sure you are in the right town?" The man laughed.

"Well, I thought I was," Paul joined him in the laughter. It didn't matter now, however, because now he knew where Nara Blake lived. He punched some numbers on his phone and swore again. "Tell you what, mate. Why don't you take me back into the center of town and drop me off. I'll keep calling. She's bound to answer her phone eventually."

The driver made a quick U-turn and drove back into town on Pinchbeck Road. As they passed the house where he had seen Nara and her father turn in, he noticed a sign reading Gate House Bed & Breakfast. He opened his mouth to ask the driver about, but then decided against it. If anyone should question the driver, he did not want him to remember that he asked about the house. He knew where it was, and that was what mattered.

Paul got out of the taxi at the town center, and gave the driver a healthy, but not too healthy tip for his trouble. "Sorry to put you to all that trouble," he said.

"No trouble," he said, pocketing the money. "Hope you find your girl."

"So do I," Paul answered, as the man drove away.

As soon as the taxi was out of sight, Paul walked into the large hotel facing the square and asked for a room. He was soon settled in comfortable accommodations on the third floor. He considered calling Lisette to tell her that he was fine and not to worry, but then changed his mind. Let her stew. He was a grown man; he had a right to go where he chose. He called down to the front desk and asked about room service; they could send up a hamburger and chips if he wanted. That was fine, he said. It was food. As he ate, he considered what his next move should be. Nara would undoubtedly be home for the entire week-end. But should he try to break into the house to look for the painting? Where would it be? He couldn't book a room at the bed and breakfast because she would recognize him. Now that he was here, he realized that he couldn't even walk around the town without the risk of her seeing him. He needed to minimize the risk, but at the same time he needed to find the boxes. He would have to wait until dark and then go to the house. With the lights on inside, he might be able to learn something just by looking through the windows from a discreet distance.

Nara was forced to wait until after dinner before she had a chance to speak with her father about the painting. Aunt Sue was busy with guests, and finally they were able to excuse themselves and go up to Jack's room to talk. As soon as the door was closed behind them, Jack said, "I have the painting."

"What do you think?" she asked.

"I have no idea," he laughed. "I'm not an artist, or an art historian or any of those things. All I can see is a very nice painting with the signature Cézanne. Whether it is a legitimate copy, a forgery or the real thing, I haven't a clue." He made himself comfortable in his easy chair and sipped his after dinner coffee. "What I don't understand is why you want me to take it to an appraiser here instead of asking Alex?"

"I did ask Alex," Nara said. She made herself comfortable in across-legged position on the floor. "But after our flat was broken into, and those strangers showed up at Aunt Rebeca's house in Wales, we both thought it would be better to keep the painting away from London."

"So you want me to take it to an appraiser and find out if it's genuine? There are appraisers in Lincoln, Nara. Why don't we take it to one of them tomorrow? It's a start."

"All right. It does make me nervous hiding it here, even with the security system."

Paul sat huddled by the garden shed outside the Gate House. His view of Jack Blake's bedroom window was perfect, although he wondered why the man kept his curtains open even at night. Who felt that secure? He watched Jack and Nara as they talked and sipped their coffee. He could tell the conversation was serious, even at some times uncomfortable, as Nara paced and Jack spilled his coffee. But they did no more than talk. He waited at every moment to see his painting – yes, it was his painting -- or at least the boxes that contained the painting along with other things – possibly other items that rightfully belonged to his family. But there was nothing. Eventually the two people in the house settled to a more relaxed conversation, and Paul could see the man in his chair, but Nara had apparently moved to another seat out of sight.

Paul was cold, and a light drizzle had begun; furthermore, the entire situation made him angry. He was a descendant of the Comte de Grassin; his family had been French aristocrats since the time of Louis XIII. They had survived the Revolution, had even come into prominence again during Napoleon's time, and regained their property and wealth during the reign of Napoleon III. It has been his great-grandmother who had decimated their fortune, and she had only been a Grassin through marriage, so she had no right. Her son had died at Ypres in 1915, leaving a young son, their heir to the family fortune. She took him in along with his mother, and the boy grew up at the family estate outside Bordeaux. He was just of an age to fight when the Germans invaded in 1940, and according to the family stories, he had gone off to war and she heard nothing from him. Believing her grandson and only heir to the Grassin fortune to be dead, Mme. Grassin took it upon herself to sell or give away their priceless pieces of art, as well as her own jewelry, to help the French Resistance, and especially to aid French Jews in escaping the Nazis. At the end of the war, little of any value remained in her possession.

Then in 1945, her grandson, Paul's grandfather Jean-Paul Grassin, returned to France after being held as a prisoner of war on the eastern front. His son, Paul's father, had told him the story many times. He had returned to the estate to find his grandmother living on onions and potatoes, and occasionally a pigeon or rabbit that someone killed and prepared for her.

Her cook was still with her, and the two of them lived in the manor house as virtual prisoners of their own making. When her grandson walked in the door in December of 1945, she didn't recognize him. When she finally believed that he was truly her grandson, she took to her bed for several days. Neither of them ever expressed any regret at the loss of their family treasures. Neither, in fact, had Paul's father, who inherited an estate that was too large and expensive to maintain. He sold the estate, completed a law degree, and provided a comfortable, middle-class life for his wife and his children, Paul and Lisette. However, he became increasingly moody after his wife died when the children were in their early teens, and he died in an auto accident just two years later.

Paul inherited his father's emotional instability and moodiness, and his problems manifested themselves as full blown mental illness as he reached his early twenties. He spent some time in a mental institution, but when he showed improvement he was released, and Lisette resolved to help him with the transition to normal life. Lisette believed that it would take only a couple of years to get her brother settled and on an even keel, but although he seemed to function well in society, he refused to consider any type of career or work. His only interest was in regaining the family's lost wealth and prominence as French aristocrats. As he was the only family she had, Lisette devoted herself to helping Paul, even accompanying him to England and Wales when the trail of their lost possessions led them there.

Now, however, Lisette had gone back to France and abandoned him, or so she said. But at the moment Paul didn't care. For the first time since they left France; in fact, for the first time since he had seriously begun his search after his release from the mental institution, Paul believed that the end was in sight. If the painting was not here in Springfield in the bed and breakfast where Nara Blake's father lived, this was where he would find out where it was. He returned to his hotel, with the plan to be on watch early in the morning. He might do well to rent a car at this point so he could follow them more easily.

Chapter 15

Letter from Lydia to her daughters – Written in her diary.

Dear Catherine and Rebeca,

I hope you had a good day with Grandma and Granddad after I left on Sunday. The week-end was too short, and even if I had been able to stay with you all day as I had planned, it would still have been too short.

Rebeca, I am looking for a baby doll for you. I know you are wishing for one. Maybe I will find one for your birthday. Whenever I pass a store that still sells toys, I stop and look. One day I will find the perfect one for you.

Catherine, I am so proud to see all the books that you are reading. It helps you pass the time, and when the war is over and you are back in school in London, you will most likely be ahead of the other children.

I am not sure when I will be able to visit again. I hope to see Daddy tomorrow and will give him a big hug from the two of you.

(I can't send this. I feel as if they will read between the lines and know that Allan is somehow not with me.)

Present Day
London

Lisette did not returned to France. Her devotion to her brother had begun to border on the obsessive, and she feared that it could be the family mental illness that she also might have inherited, although it was the first time she had felt this way.

She was alone in the flat for the first time, and in spite of the tension that was always present with Paul, she still felt uneasy. He was undoubtedly following Nara Blake and the trail to his supposed inheritance. But his volatile temper and lack of good judgment would land him in trouble, possibly with the police, Lisette had no doubt. She could take the Eurostar in the morning, as she told Paul she intended to do. But tonight, she just couldn't stay in the flat and do nothing. She knew very few people in London. She had briefly met Nara's sister Lily, but did not have her phone number, and could think of no reason to contact her. The other person she knew was Alex Collier.

Twenty minutes later Lisette was on her way to the White Hart pub in Kensington. Alex was at a table with two men when she walked in, but he saw her immediately and stood with a smile. He stood and met her halfway to the door and asked, "Are you okay? You sounded a little upset on the phone."

"I'm fine," she answered. "But Paul has disappeared, and I'm going back to France. I felt a little at loose ends tonight."

"Paul has disappeared?" He sounded truly shocked. "We need to talk. Just a minute."

He moved to the table where he had been sitting with two men about his age. They were both dressed in dark pants and wore wool sweaters and glasses. They could not have looked more like academics if they had been cast in the parts in a movie, Lisette thought. They turned and looked at Lisette, with the appropriate amount of approval and sympathy on their faces, and Alex led her to an empty table nearby. "Would you like something to drink?" he asked.

"Yes. A glass of Beaujolais, if they have it," she said.

He returned a moment later with the requested drink. She sipped it and set it on the table, revealing nothing of her opinion of its quality. "Thank you."

"Now tell me," Alex began. "What happened to Paul?"

"He is trying to find the Cézanne," she said.

"He is?" Alex asked. "Does he have an idea where it is?"

"He thinks he does. He thinks your girlfriend Nara has it."

"He thinks a Cézanne painting is in one of the boxes Nara picked up in Wales?" Alex nearly choked on his beer with the surprise.

"He may be right, Alex," Lisette said.

Alex studied her face but said nothing.

Alex sighed. "It's doubtful, Lisette." He was thoughtful for a moment. "Lydia Roberts was an art expert. She would not have stored a valuable painting in a box with a bunch of old clothes."

"She might have, if she was in a hurry and intended to return in a short time to repack the boxes and put the painting in a safer place," Lisette replied. She debated telling Alex that she had overheard Nara's conversation about the painting, but he knew that would upset him and he would rush to protect Nara.

"So where do you think Paul has gone?" Alex asked. His blue eyes bore into Lisette's. *He is attractive*, she thought, *in an academic sort of way*. His intelligence and lack of self-consciousness gave him a sexiness that was quite different from the men to whom Lisette was usually attracted. Maybe when Paul was settled, she would have time for romance in her life.

"I think most likely he went to Wales," she lied. She took another small sip of her wine. "But it could be anywhere. He will contact me eventually. He always does."

"He's done this before? Gone off like this?"

"Oh, yes. Many times. I just wait, and he calls. And then he comes back." She twirled her glass in her fingers before she continued. "I haven't mentioned this to Paul, because I know how upset he gets, but I think it is very likely that our great-grandmother sold the painting. She did that with a lot of things. She sold so many pieces of art and jewelry during the war."

"That still doesn't explain why he thinks that a painting by Cézanne would be in a box of old clothes belonging to Lydia Roberts. She was supposed to have died in the Blitz along with her husband."

"Can we get our hands on the diaries?" Lisette asked.

"Not likely," Alex answered. "Do you think Nara is going to let those out of her hands?" *No way would I let you and Paul read those diaries*, Alex thought.

"It might be easier to get our hands on the painting," she laughed. She looked at her empty wine glass and Alex rose to get her another.

Lisette sat quietly for a moment, idly twirling her wine glass with the fingers of her left hand. Finally she said, "I want out of this. But at the same time, Paul may be right."

"Let me do some checking," Alex said. "Give me a couple of days. If I don't come up with anything concrete, you can take the Eurostar on Sunday."

Paul slept later than he had intended, and only had time to dress quickly and grab a cup of bad coffee from the hotel restaurant. He wanted to go home to France; the coffee was so much better there. He had noticed the night before that there was a restaurant just across the street from the bed and breakfast where Nara lived, so he parked there in his rental car, relieved to see that all the cars that had been parked at the bed and breakfast the night before were still there. Nara and her father had not gone anywhere yet. He had been there less than ten minutes, drinking his coffee from the paper cup and grimacing with each taste, when Nara and Jack Blake emerged from the house. Jack strode purposely toward his car while Nara followed, fumbling with her shoulder bag, and then with a manila folder containing papers. Both were much too small to contain the Cézanne. Paul was confused now; when he was confused he missed the company of Lisette. She was always able to help him see clearly, but he was on his own now, and he had to make a decision immediately. He could either follow Nara and her father, and hope that they weren't going out for a shopping trip, or try to get into the house and look for the painting there. He decided that there were still too many people in the Gate House, and with guests eating breakfast and preparing to check out, it would be much too busy to try to slip in and look around. Therefore, he would follow Nara and her father, wherever they might go.

They had no reason to think that they were being followed, so he easily slipped behind them, and was able to maintain a reasonable distance between the two cars. After about forty-five minutes of leisurely driving, it was clear that they were approaching the city of Lincoln. Paul had no idea what size this city was, but it might be large enough for an art appraiser or auction house. But where was the painting? It was more difficult following them once they entered the city. He could see that the cathedral and castle were perched on a hill in the highest section of the city, and he hoped that was not the area for which they were headed. It would be too easy to lose them in narrow streets that had been laid out in the days of William the Conqueror. The only advantage was that they had no idea they were being followed. They did, indeed, begin climbing the hill after following a ring road around to the opposite side of the city from which they approached. Traffic was becoming quite heavy, and Paul was having difficulty maintaining his distance and still keeping the car in sight. Twice he was sure that he had lost them. The third time it happened, he was almost upon them when he saw that they had parked the car. Nara was standing next to the car waiting for her father to be able to safely step out on the street side. The combination of the coffee, the driving and his nervousness at handling the situation without Lisette were taking their toll on Paul. His hands shook on the steering wheel as the traffic came to a standstill with his car next to Nara's father. Paul didn't think Nara could see his face from where she was standing, and she would not be looking for him. Her father took the opportunity to slip out of the car and joined his daughter. The traffic moved on, and Paul, biting his lips to stop the trembling, pulled into a parking space just ahead on the opposite side of the street. He watched in the rear view mirror as they knocked on the door of a residence where they were immediately admitted.

Paul emerged from his car to stretch his legs. He could not sit in the cramped vehicle for another minute. He wondered if he dared to cross the street and see if he could learn what Nara and Jack were doing and whom they were visiting. There was a break in traffic and he crossed without giving himself time to think. He kept one eye on the door and walked casually toward the car. The manila folder that Nara had been carrying lay on the back seat. He quickly tried the back door handle. It was locked. He could pick a simple car lock, but did he have time? Nara and her father could emerge at any moment, or they could be enjoying a leisurely cup of tea. The street was busy, and if he spent too much time here a neighbor or bystander might notice him. He tried the driver's door handle and it opened. Evidently while Nara was standing and waiting for her father to get out of the car, she had forgotten to lock her door. Paul moved quickly. It was a simple matter to reach back and unlock the back door, and then to open the door and take the manila folder. He closed it and walked briskly down the street as if he had business at one of the local shops.

A short ways up the street there was a bus stop and a bench occupied by a very large woman. Paul normally was scornful of people who allowed their weight to get out of hand, but this time he was grateful. He would be hidden from Nara's view if she came out of the house and looked this way. Sitting down on the bench on the far side of the woman, he opened the folder.

At first he was not sure what he was looking at. The folder contained a thick stack of papers, photocopies of fine handwritten lines. As he flipped through the pages he noticed the dates – 1941 and 1942. He had not found his painting, but these pages might hold valuable clues to its whereabouts. He recognized the diaries of Nara's great-grandmother. It was she and her husband who had been involved in spiriting works of art out of France. These were photocopies, it was true, but they could still provide him with information. Paul patted the folder appreciatively. The bus came and the large woman left her seat next to him and climbed laboriously onto the bus. He was visible now, but for the moment Paul didn't care.

He flipped through the pages, more slowly now, looking for names he might recognize. There were constant references to the woman's husband who was working with the French Resistance, but nothing about what he was doing. Apparently she didn't know. There was a French boy who was killed in England. What was that all about? The name – Picard. That name sounded familiar – he knew it did. Wait. That was the name of the Jewish family his great-grandparents had been so close to. There were even stories that they had helped them escape from France. Then it served him right if he was killed! None of it made sense, and Paul wanted answers now. He wished once again that Lisette were still with him. She would be able to read the diary entries while he took a nap or got drunk or something. He took out his phone and started to call her when he remembered that she was on her way back to France. She could be in Paris by now. And he would not give in and call her. He had to show her that he was sane and could do this on his own. He looked further on into the diary. The next entry he read described how the woman had worked with the French Resistance in London.

As he began to read, two teenage boys came and sat on the bench next to Paul. He looked at them briefly as they laughed and shared music back and forth on their iPods. He had never been that exuberant and fun-loving at any time in his childhood or adolescence. He still considered that kind of behavior a waste of time. He stood and crossed the street and returned to his car. He sat in the driver's seat for a few moments, clutching the diaries to his chest. He didn't have the Cézanne, but he had something. He would find the painting, and the diaries might hold a clue to its whereabouts. Paul laid the folder securely on the seat next to him and maneuvered out into the traffic.

When he returned to his hotel room, it became clear to Paul that he did not have the patience to read the diaries. He was not good at that sort of thing. He wanted results, and he did not read English that well. But here he was alone in a small town in northern England and he had no choice. Maybe some exercise would help calm him down, or alternatively, a good meal, if such a thing were to be found in this country. It might be possible in London, maybe, but not here. Oh, how he wanted to be back in France. Maybe he should give up, too, and go back to France, find Lisette, and figure out what their next step would be. But she might not be willing to help him now, and he couldn't force her. He could wheedle and cry and plead, but he could not force her. She was his sister and their personalities were similar enough that he knew what she would and would not do. Any other person, especially a woman, he could threaten, but he could not threaten Lisette. He lay on his bed in his hotel room and wished he had a woman, any woman. Then he remembered that he had not taken his medicine that day. Maybe that was contributing to his restlessness. He jumped up and found the pills in his bag, took two for good measure and then lay back down on the bed.

He awoke hours later, and at first had no idea where he was. He called out for Lisette, but the sound of his call echoing in the room reminded him that he was alone. He pulled himself groggily to his feet and went to look out of the window. There was still daylight, but the street below had the look of late afternoon. The iron gate of a nearby electronics store rattled closed. He was ravenously hungry. There must be a decent restaurant in this town. He would pay whatever it cost for a first class meal and a bottle of wine. He felt relaxed now. He picked up the folder with the copy of the diaries. After he ate he could read this. It would be a simple matter to skim through and look for references to his family or the writer's connections with France, and he would only need to read those sections carefully. He laughed softly to himself. Nara would not even realize that her papers had been stolen, but would simply believe that she had mislaid them. She obviously had the original someplace, maybe even another copy. She would not be unduly distressed.

Paul showered and dressed in a clean shirt and trousers. Most of the wrinkles had disappeared from his clothing after hanging in the closet all day. He put on a tie and left the room. The desk clerk told him about several restaurants in town that he might enjoy. One was quite close to the bed and breakfast where Nara lived, and he eliminated that one. He retrieved his rental car from the car park and headed out of town in the opposite direction to a place called Le Jour. He doubted that the French name really implied any higher quality, but he did not believe her could stomach British pub food or the ubiquitous chicken tikka masala.

The dinner – a filet mignon with roasted potatoes – was passable, and the wine adequate, and Paul felt better for having eaten. He flirted with the waitress, a plump, short, British version of Lisette. He even went so far as to ask her what time she got off work, but when she said it wasn't until eleven, he regretfully drove back to the hotel alone.

The sleep, food and wine, and perhaps a little fresh air, had helped to focus Paul's mind. He stretched out on the bed with three pillows propped behind his back and began to read Lydia Roberts' diaries. Unlike Nara, the fate of Lydia and Allan was the least of his concerns. But to his disappointment, there was no mention of the Cézanne painting. However, in his unstable mind, the antique jeweled necklace that Lydia mentioned was clearly the property of the Grassin family and might be worth as much as the painting. He dismissed the idea that the Picard family had given the necklace to Allan and Lydia Roberts. The Picard family was gone – except for the old woman near Bordeaux, and she would never know. The intentions of the family meant nothing to him.

Lydia had been clear in her diary that she intended to store a necklace in the box that she sent to Wales, the box that Nara had in her possession now, and that he had been trying to access for the past two weeks. Paul thought carefully. The copy of the diary that he had stolen was presumably not the only copy. Also, there was a good chance Nara had read the entire diary and knew about the necklace. He had to get his hands on the box before she found the necklace. He did not believe that his great-grandmother would ever have given away such a treasure, and even if she had, that proved she had not been in her right mind. Paul was intimately familiar with the comings and goings of his rational mind, and believed his forebear might have suffered from some similar mental malady. She had to have – to give away their heritage.

Chapter 16

Lydia's Diary – June 10, 1941
Sunday evening

I don't know why I'm back in London. Allan is in jail and they won't let me see him. And Major Dexter won't tell me what my new assignment is going to be. I'm stuck here in the house listening to Amelia Dexter complain. The bombing has eased off over the summer, so her focus of complaint has shifted somewhat. I am trying not to worry about Allan. Dexter keeps assuring me that MI6 will persuade Scotland Yard to release him very soon, but I won't feel at ease until I see him free. I cannot imagine how they can think that he murdered that boy! There is absolutely no reason he would do such a thing. Scotland Yard needs to put their inspectors to work finding out who really did such a horrible thing. It could even have been one of the other students. If he treats his classmates the way he treated me when I visited him, one of them could have easily shoved him out the window. Why don't they work on that instead of focusing on Allan? I must talk with Dexter about it, although he will probably tell me that they are already investigating that line of thinking.

Nevertheless, I have been promised that I will be able to visit Allan tomorrow morning, and I will definitely mention the idea to him.

I am exhausted, but I know I won't be able to sleep. This morning I was snug in the bedroom with my girls, and now I am back in a house where I do not feel welcome – no, that's not the right word – I am welcome. But I'm not accepted for who I am. Come to think of it, the only people who really accept me for who I am are my daughters, and that's only because I am their mother. I feel as if I have to do something. If Dexter doesn't come through with a challenging assignment where I can use my talents and abilities, I may consider going back to Wales. At least on the farm I could keep busy.

Everything does seem to be coming to a head now. Dexter wants to see me at nine o'clock tomorrow morning. I'm not sure if he wants to talk to me about Allan, or my new assignment or both. I spent most of the evening with Amelia. She was quite upset about Allan's arrest, and for some reason thinks her husband could be in danger of being arrested as well. The idea is totally ridiculous, but somehow I ended up trying to reassure her, when it is my husband who is being held. I am sure that she has no more knowledge about the matter than I do, but I cannot help but pick up on her nervousness. Dexter finally arrived home about ten p.m. and simply told me that he wanted to see me at nine a.m. in his office at Whitehall. Then he disappeared into his office, and we could hear him on the telephone. It was a good opportunity for me to say good night, but I still cannot sleep, although I know I must.

Pentonville Prison, North London

"I'd like to talk with my wife," Allan said, for what he thought must be the hundredth time. He was in a cell alone, and he supposed it was reasonably comfortable as jail cells went, but after just two nights and no news about when he would be released, he was becoming increasingly restless and frustrated. The solicitor sent by MI6 had visited him for a short time Sunday morning, but had been unable to tell him anything other than they were doing their best to straighten out the confusion. He had also promised Allan that he would be able to see Lydia, but gave no indication of when.

He brushed his teeth and washed up as best he could in the basin provided, and then sat on the bed and waited. He understood now how prisoners reacted the way they did to their confinement. He could see himself shaking the bars at his door and screaming for his lawyer, his wife, his freedom. He could also imagine how he could lie down on his meager bed and turn off his thoughts and become nobody, just allow his mind to drift into the past, the future or nothing at all. He stood and paced to the opening that passed for a window. He could see the blue sky with a scattering of clouds. Perhaps it would not be a rainy London day.

"Mr. Roberts." Allan jumped at the sound of the voice, and the barred door opened behind him. "I've brought your breakfast, mate. And the tea is still hot. I made sure of that, as you're not one of our ordinary prisoners." The guard set the tray on the small table in the corner. He might be fifty or sixty years old; it was hard to tell. His hair may have been brown at one time, but the transition to gray had turned it into a color that resembled dust. He must have shaved once in a while, but not in the last few days. One side of his face appeared sunken due to the lack of teeth on that side, giving him a lopsided look. Nevertheless, the man was congenial enough. Allan wondered if he was as friendly to other prisoners who were not visited by solicitors from MI6; he doubted it.

"Thank you," Allan answered. "Do you know..." he began.

The guard returned to the door and only turned around when he was on the other side. Whatever sympathy he might have for Allan Roberts, he still followed the rules. "I don't know anything, mate. I only do what I'm told. I'm told to bring you breakfast. If I'm told to let you out and meet your lovely wife in Brighton, I'll do that. But right now all I know is the breakfast, and now I've got to get it to the other blokes, and if I stand here talking, their tea will be stone cold." He walked away.

Allan sat at the table and faced his breakfast. He was not hungry, but it would give him something to do, and, he supposed, keep up his strength for whatever was to come. The tea was still hot, a bit too sweet for his taste, but drinkable. The two slices of white toast were cold, and slathered with something that definitely was not butter, but retained an oily texture. He ate the two slices quickly and ignored the residue they left in his mouth, and followed it by a quick swallow of tea. He tried to drink the rest of the tea slowly to make it last, but he was too thirsty. He drank the entire cup down. Maybe later the guard might bring him another cup. Even when he was hiding out in Spain working with the Resistance, he had never felt that he didn't have enough to eat or drink.

He stood and craned his neck to look out the window again. The same blue sky taunted him with its beauty and allure of freedom. But he was probably being too impatient. Major Dexter would surely pull all strings possible to have him released. Surely MI6 outranked Scotland Yard, and Dexter knew he was innocent. They knew he had returned to London late that Friday night after he had visited the boy, and he had been on his way to Spain Saturday morning.

The boy was decidedly unpleasant; Lydia was right about that, and his demand for money was bizarre. There was a good chance he was involved in something – gambling, women, buying and selling on the black market. Any of these activities might appeal to an adolescent boy without parental supervision. And the majority of the students at his prep school were from wealthy, aristocratic families. He may very well have gotten himself involved in something unsavory or even illegal in his desire to keep up with and impress his wealthier classmates. Allan sat down on his chair and picked up one of the books he had been brought yesterday, although the last thing he felt like doing was trying to become engrossed in a novel. *The story I am living right now is fiction enough,* he thought.

He had also asked for, and received, a small notebook and a pencil. He had intended to spend some time writing down the events of the evening of his visit to the boy, and had made several false starts, only to tear the sheets into tiny pieces and stuff them into his pockets. How much did Scotland Yard really know of the activities of MI6? He needed Dexter, or a solicitor, to advise him, and neither had been available for more than a few minutes yesterday. He could try to write a letter to Lydia, but Dexter had promised him that he would bring her to visit him, so what was the point? It was not as if he were on death row; he could be released at any moment. He thought then that instead he could write an account of his arrest and confinement here. Even though he believed that his treatment was somewhat better than that of an ordinary prisoner, the experience of his seventy-two hours of incarceration must be valuable on some level. He picked up the pencil and began with his arrival at Waterloo Station on Saturday evening. He had expected to take a taxi to the Dexters' home in Pimlico, and to find Lydia there waiting for him. Instead he had been met by two officers of Scotland Yard and taken to jail.

Lydia was seated outside John Dexter's office in Whitehall at ten minutes before nine o'clock. Butterflies danced in her stomach. She had been unable to eat any breakfast, having managed only a couple of bites of toast and half of a cup of tea, which had somehow served to upset her stomach even more, in spite of Amelia Dexter's assurances of its calming qualities. Lydia escaped the house as soon as possible and walked briskly from Pimlico to Whitehall. The exercise had momentarily soothed her, but now that she was seated outside Dexter's office, all the nervousness and fear for Allan returned full force. She could hear Major Dexter's voice as well as another voice inside the office. Sometimes one or the other voice was raised, but she was still unable to understand any of the words. The voices did not sound angry, only assertive. Lydia wondered if any of their conversation concerned her or Allan. It was human nature, she believed, to think that any conversation that one could not understand, either due to language difference or lack of sound clarity, related to the person listening, but she also knew it probably wasn't true.

The voices moved nearer to the door, and Lydia could comprehend a few words, but not enough to gain any meaning from the conversation. The door opened and Major John Dexter, along with Captain Roland and another man that Lydia did not recognize, emerged from the office. None of them noticed her at first, and their conversation was too general to mean anything to Lydia. Dexter noticed Lydia seated outside his office and paused mid-sentence.

"Lydia!" Did his voice sound artificially hearty, she wondered? "Come in! Come in! Let me just get rid of these jokers who have been taking up my time."

Captain Roland nodded to her, with only the slightest indication that they had met previously. The other man, who was taller than either Dexter or Roland, studied her intently. His look seemed to bore into her and she felt sure that he knew who she was, even though they had not been introduced.

"Come, Lydia." Dexter stood aside to allow her to precede him into the office. "I'll speak with you later, Jeffries. You, too, Roland," he added to the two men as they left the office.

Lydia took a seat in front of Major Dexter's desk, a seat she had occupied many times since she began working for the MI6. She had always believed him to be fair and honest, and that was what she expected from him today. "Lydia, there is someone I want you to meet. She should be here in about fifteen minutes. I wanted to have a few moments to speak with you myself, and answer any general questions you might have." Lydia was a bit surprised by his business-like attitude. Although he was her superior, he had always shown her great kindness, to the extent of inviting her and Allan to live in their home after their flat was destroyed.

A buzzer sounded on his desk and his secretary's voice asked, "Shall I bring the tea now, Mr. Dexter?"

"Wait a few minutes, Joan," he answered. "Bring it in when Miss Latham arrives."

He turned his attention back to Lydia. "I was very impressed with the work you did with the French Resistance. And Captain Roland was just filling me in on some details I was unaware of."

"Thank you, Major Dexter," she answered formally.

"This is war time," he continued, "and we make decisions quickly based on the information that we have. Here at the MI6 we also choose people for jobs based on their ability and dedication, and other factors are secondary."

"Other factors?" Lydia was unsure where this conversation was going, although clearly it related to her new assignment.

"Lydia." Dexter kept his eyes on Lydia's face and seemed to be studying her for her reaction to his words. "You have proved your dedication and ability to the British war effort beyond a shadow of a doubt. Now..." He lined up his collection of pencils in precise parallel formation on his desk. "Churchill has begun allowing women to be parachuted into France to work with the Resistance behind the lines. It's dangerous work, but all of us are in danger now as you well know. And you have been specifically recommended for this particular job by another agent."

Lydia's mind brimmed with questions. "What is the job?" she asked. "And who recommended me, or am I allowed to ask that?"

"You can ask whatever you like," he answered with the hint of a smile. "But I can't answer every question. You know that. First of all, you asked about the 'other factors' that might or might not be considered in our choices. You are a married woman with children. Ordinarily – or I should say before this war – we would not have considered a married woman, let alone one with two children, for a sensitive job, but times have changed, and times are desperate." He paused and studied her face, looking for the questions he knew were there, but she said nothing.

"You won't be going alone. There will be other women and men who will be parachuted in at the same time. Your job will be to escort a group of Jewish children out of France and into Spain, before the Nazis get their hands on them."

"That answers two of my questions," Lydia replied softly, as she tried to absorb what she was being told.

"You asked who recommended you. And that leads us, a little prematurely, to the second reason for you being here this morning."

"Allan recommended me?"

"Yes. Unhesitatingly, and knowing full well the dangers of the job."

Lydia sat stunned. This was what she had wanted to do for so long. It was more than she had dreamed of; it was also more dangerous than she had imagined. Parachuting into France? Just the thought of parachuting out of an airplane was terrifying, but into France? Into a land controlled by Germany? "I don't know how to parachute," was all she could think of to say.

"You'll learn, and as I said, you won't be alone." He gazed around the office as if looking for an object that could help him to find the words he wanted to use next. "Allan knows how important it is to rescue as many children as we can," he said finally, as he met Lydia's eyes with something like sadness. "As a mother, we know you will do everything you can to help rescue these children."

"Of course," she answered, "but..."

"But what, Lydia?"

"Is Allan going, too? And where is he, and when can I see him?"

There were voices in the reception area outside the door, and then a short, sharp knock. Major Dexter looked up. "Just one moment," he called out toward the closed door.

"Allan will not be going," he said succinctly. "That would be too risky for both of you. I am sure you can understand that. And you will see him today." He pressed his telephone buzzer and spoke to his secretary. "You can send Miss Latham in now."

A tall dark-haired woman with hazel eyes and lanky limbs opened the door. "Good morning." She smiled at both of them. "I'm Ellen Latham." She held out her hand to Lydia. "You must be Lydia Roberts. I'm looking forward to working with you."

Lydia stood and grasped the other woman's hand. "Pleased to meet you." Before Lydia could add any other pleasantry, Major Dexter spoke.

"I know I'm the odd man out here, but I'm John Dexter, your boss, as it were."

Ellen laughed, and her face lit up with joy and a sense of fun that was clear to Lydia. Then in an instant it transformed into seriousness. But it was more than just a sense of the gravity of their task, there was a deep sadness as well. "How could I forget," she said. "But after all, Lydia and I will be working together. And in that sense, she is more important than you are."

John Dexter met her look. He seemed about to press his point, but didn't. "You are, of course, right," he said. "As long as both of you are following my orders."

"I think we are both well-trained enough to know that," Lydia answered.

Ellen Latham flashed her smile again. "We will make a good pair." All at once she turned business-like. "John, can we use your office? I would like to brief Lydia on some of the things we will be doing, and I know this office is secure."

Once again he seemed about to object, but acquiesced. "Certainly. I need to meet with General Davis anyway, so I'll be off to the War Cabinet Rooms for about an hour."

As he walked out the door, Lydia was on the verge of saying, "But you promised I would see Allan today," but she stopped herself just in time. He had promised. That should be all the reassurance she needed. She did not need to continue to pester him like a child asking for ice cream.

Chapter 17

Lydia's Diary - July 3, 1941

We leave for the coast in four days, and then we will be flown across to southern France at night to parachute in. I have made two jumps, and we will have one or two more practice jumps before we go across. I feel more or less confident that I can jump successfully in the calm, daylight conditions we have jumped in so far, but night jumping makes me nervous. There is no question that it is dangerous. Everyone says just follow the routine we have learned, and to remember that there will be French partisans there to help us when we land. What they don't say is that there are Germans there, too, but we all try not to think about that. Will they shoot me on sight if they see me floating down in the night sky? I suppose I won't even know if that happens. Do the Germans know that women are coming into France from Britain? I suppose it wouldn't make any difference. I know what to do; I just have to do it.

Before I received this assignment, and before Allan was in prison, I worried so much about the future and about the children. I don't have time for that anymore. I think of Catherine and Rebeca and I know they are safe, and then I go back to reviewing the procedures for jumping out of an airplane over France, contacting the Resistance, and following orders. I have also been trying to think in French, and Ellen and I and the others speech French to each other as much as possible so we will be comfortable and fluent when we arrive. It will also be an advantage should we be captured by the Germans, as they will be less likely to suspect we are British.

I can't think about Allan's situation too much either, because it only terrifies me. I can't believe we are in this predicament! Who would have thought before the war that Allan would be in prison, and I would be a spy (might as well use the word!), and the children would be far away from us with Mom and Dad. Life is certainly strange.

All I know is – once this is over, I want the truth to come out. I want our children to know the work we are doing, and that we are doing it for them. I want the truth about the murder of that young boy, and Allan's innocence to come out. I want my family and this country to know the truth. It's no good otherwise.

I need to go to sleep now, but I am too keyed up. I thought that writing all of this down would relax me, but it has only made me more wide awake. They told us in training that we need to cultivate the ability to fall asleep instantly, because we never know when we might have to grab a few winks in an unexpected or awkward situation. I guess tonight will be good practice for that.

London
1941

Allan was not released that week, nor even yet the next week. Although Lydia wanted to be involved in the day-to-day efforts to bring about his release, and which Dexter and the Special Branch solicitor assured her were taking place, Lydia was involved in her own training and had little time to worry, let alone visit him frequently. On her occasional visits, he assured her that his greatest desire, since he could not be involved in his own work, was to see her doing an important job. He had moved past his initial fear and restlessness and had immersed himself in serious study of French history and culture. He counted on being released at any moment and going back to his espionage work for the British government. He was even more eager to get to France now that Lydia was training to go. Neither of them spoke of the danger. As news of German atrocities trickled into Britain, they both determined to be part of stopping them. They consciously did not speak of their own children, but like the proverbial elephant in the room, they were in their parents' thoughts constantly.

Their conversations were sprinkled with the phrase, "After the war..."

"After the war we will go on a second honeymoon..."

"After the war, we will have a house again with a garden..."

But Allan was still in prison. Although the police could find no motive, the fact that he had been with the boy just hours before his death seemed to pin their suspicions on him. At Lydia's insistence, Allan asked the solicitor about the possibility that one of the other students had pushed the boy out the window, or if one of them might have seen something, but every time he mentioned it he was met with such stony silence that he felt sure he had touched a nerve, and that something was being covered up.

Several times he was on the verge of mentioning his suspicions to Lydia, but restrained himself before he spoke. It wasn't fair for him to burden her with that worry when she was learning to parachute out of an airplane over enemy territory. He spoke several times to Dexter and Adams, the solicitor, but neither of them was able to help. The weeks went by, and it was time for Lydia to leave for France. Allan still sat in prison, accused of a crime he didn't commit.

Pentonville Prison

"John, I didn't kill him. This is the most sophisticated intelligence organization in the world, possibly with the exception of the Americans or the Russians. We should be able to find out who did it. And since when did Scotland Yard, or a local police force for that matter, outrank Special Operations? I thought it was the other way around."

John Dexter sighed and rubbed his forehead. He seemed to be more tired the last few weeks than he had ever been. "Normally, Allan, that is true. But things aren't normal right now."

"Then what? Someone is pulling rank? Who?"

John stared at him. "Think about it. Think about the way things work in this country."

Allan thought. "Someone in Parliament. Someone with money. Someone with a title." He met John Dexter's gaze. "Someone with a title and money. The son of someone with a title and money. They know who did it, but he is the son of someone with a title and money, and so I am the fall guy?" Allan leapt to his feet in the small visitor's room. "That's not right! I could hang for murder!"

"Sit down, Allan. It won't come to that. They will hold you for a while to make it look good, and then release you for lack of evidence."

"Does Lydia know about this?"

"About why you are still in custody? No. And she is being kept too busy right now to think about it too much. You were right, Allan. She is going to do a fantastic job. You can be proud of her."

"I am proud of her. But that's changing the subject. I want you to get me out of here."

"I will, Allan." Dexter sighed and rubbed his hand across his chin. "I've got the best people working on your release."

A guard walked by Allan's cell and looked in. "Time's almost up, gov'ner," he said. "You can come back tomorrow. This bloke ain't goin' nowhere."

Allan bit his lips to control the emotion he felt. He was desperately lonely, and now that he was confined here, he could think of nothing but his girls and Lydia. "Bring me more books: history, law, French and English. Anything to keep my mind busy."

"Of course, Allan," Dexter replied. "If I don't come tomorrow, I'll send them with Adams."

The guard was at the cell door again, and Dexter left without a word.

"The date has been moved up, Lydia. We're leaving London on Friday." Ellen burst into the small room at Whitehall where Lydia sat reviewing her notes and going over procedures for the umpteenth time. She wasn't worried about her French. She had spent two summers in France during her university years, as well as several visits since that time, both for pleasure and in connection to her job at the National Gallery, and she prided herself on her near-native fluency. She had an ear for languages, since she had been brought up speaking both Welsh and English.

Now she looked up from her papers at the excited woman who had burst in upon her solitude. "Friday? That can't be," she answered.

"Oh, yes, it's true. There will be time for one or two more practice jumps, but we will fly in on Sunday."

Lydia sat open-mouthed. "Why?" she blurted finally. "We weren't supposed to go until the beginning of next week!"

"Everything's changed," Ellen answered. She paced around the room, barely able to contain her excitement and energy. "The weather for one thing. There are storms brewing over the Atlantic. We will be much better off if we get into France ahead of them. And the Germans are... well... doing what they do. They have intensified their activities in southern France. More Jews are being deported, and the Resistance needs help disrupting transport – trains and so on." Ellen's usual precise speech and clear articulation evaporated when she was under stress.

"I hope I have time to see Allan before we go." The enormity of what they were about to do hit Lydia with a force that was physical.

"Oh, yes." Ellen stared at her for a long minute, and her gaze wavered between sympathy and hard, cold disapproval. "Don't misunderstand me, Lydia. But it is times like this when I am happy that I am not married."

Lydia felt as if she had been slapped. She started to speak but the words refused to come.

Ellen broke the tension. "I'm sorry. I get so excited about what we are doing sometimes that I forget about other people's feelings. And it's even worse because I know we have to trust each other. Forget that I said what I said. You are making a bigger sacrifice than I am, risking your life when you have a husband and children, and I know you are worried about your husband. We have to support each other, Lydia. Can we start again?"

"Of course," Lydia answered. Her normal reaction would be to justify herself to Ellen, to tell her about her qualifications, her experience, how she lived and worked alone while Allan was traveling, how her children were in the capable hands of her parents in Wales, but she didn't. She couldn't. None of that mattered. She had been chosen for this task just as Ellen had been, and while Ellen was more flamboyant and out-spoken, that did not mean that she was better at what she did. They both knew that parachuting into German-occupied France was a one-way journey. The only way out, until the war ended, was across the Pyrenees into Spain and Portugal. They would probably not work together once they arrived, as they would be absorbed into the Resistance. And they might not survive to come home. They *had* to support each other now. "Where will we leave from?" she asked. "Dover?"

"No. Hastings. It's further south. But don't mention it to anyone. Not even Allan."

"Of course not," Lydia replied, once again feeling as if Ellen was acting as her superior. She and Allan were both accustomed to keeping certain aspects of their work in confidence, even from each other.

"We have a meeting this afternoon at 1 p.m." Ellen added. "With Dexter and Roland."

"Roland? What does he have to do with this?"

"He works with the French Resistance, Lydia," Ellen said. She was pacing around the room but paused in her path to give Lydia a hard look.

"I know. I've worked with him before."

"Ah," Ellen said. "He's quite attractive, even to a married woman, I see."

Lydia decided to let the remark pass. She was trying to think of a way to change the direction of the conversation when there was a tap on the door, and Major Dexter and Captain Roland walked in. Dexter's brow was furrowed with the gravity of their task, but Roland flashed Lydia a brilliant smile when he saw her.

"Lydia! It's wonderful to see you! When John told me you were joining us, I couldn't have imagined a better person for the job."

Lydia smiled in spite of herself and relaxed, basking just a little in Roland's praise.

"Thank you, Captain Roland," she said.

John Dexter did not bother with greetings or small talk. Lydia had always seen him as a serious, business-like man, but he was beyond that now. He was completely focused. "We are meeting at 1300 hours today, but I just wanted to see you two informally beforehand. There will be two other agents, and General Collings from RAF will be joining us this afternoon." He looked from one woman to the other before he spoke again. "As you know, the Prime Minister has just authorized the acceptance of women agents in the Special Branch. You two are the first. There will be more who will be flown in on a regular basis. I know both of you well, and I have every confidence that you can do the work we are assigning you to do. At the same time, the two of you are very different, and your tasks are different." Lydia could feel Ellen's eyes on her, although she kept her attention on Dexter's face.

Dexter's eyes flickered from one woman to the other before he continued. "You'll find out more details this afternoon," he said. "Lydia, may I see you for a moment?" He motioned for her to follow him out into the corridor.

"I know you are concerned about Allan's situation, and you would like to see him before you go."

"Yes, Major Dexter," she said. "Yes to both."

He began to walk down the hallway and Lydia fell into step next to him. "I'll make arrangements for you to visit him sometime tomorrow, Lydia. I'll let you know what time." He stopped and faced her. Behind them Captain Roland and Ellen emerged laughing from the room and turned in the opposite direction. "As to the other part – we will get him released, and I'll make every effort to get a message to you when that happens. Ordinarily Special Branch outranks any police force including Scotland Yard, but someone is pulling strings, probably covering something up, and even our men can't find out who it is. It's someone high up in the government, a peer of the realm, if you will. We are guessing the father of another student who knows something, and we can't get past it, Lydia. That's the way this country is. And unfortunately we don't have the manpower to conduct our own investigation, because we are fighting a war, which some people seem to forget." His voice was bitter, and Lydia noticed a gray cast to his complexion that she had not been aware of before. "Eventually either the local police or Scotland Yard will investigate to the point where they will have to let Allan go. They have no evidence to even think of putting him on trial." He touched her arm briefly and dropped his hand quickly to his side. "Both of you just have to be patient. And it will be more difficult for Allan than for you in the present situation. You, at least, have something to do." He smiled quickly. "Go have some lunch and I'll see you at 1300."

Lydia's Diary

I'm too nervous to eat lunch. I know I should but I can't. Maybe Ellen is nervous, too. Maybe that is why she acts the way she does. I know when it comes down to it she will look out for me and back me up, but she has a very superior attitude, and seems to take pleasure in making me feel uncomfortable. And she seems to know all the sensitive spots in my life – Allan, my children – even Capt. Roland.

But this is ridiculous. I am worrying about all these petty school girl conflicts, when I might be dead in a week. At the same time, Ellen and I, and the rest of the agents who go to France, may be instrumental in bringing this war to an end sooner rather than later.

And if I die, maybe Allan will be in a better situation to care for the children than I would be, and all because he is in prison. How strange and ironic life is! Allan may survive this war to care for our family, and all because he is in prison for a crime he didn't commit!

I wonder what it will be like in France? I suppose what happens will just be a matter of luck. If I am really lucky, I won't see a German soldier at all! And if I'm really unlucky – I don't know – there are so many "worsts" that could happen, I can't even list them. So what really happens will probably be something in between. And someday – I want my children to know the truth, that we didn't abandon them. Their father and I have worked throughout this war because we love them.

I just realized that I will not be able to take my diary with me to France, so I will have to pack it away with my belongings. I wonder if the Dexters would be kind enough to hold onto my things for me, or maybe they could ship them back to my parents in Wales.

Unless a miracle happens, it looks like Allan will not be released until after I have gone, so it would be better to send my things on to Wales. Someday – I want my girls to read my diary, or, if I survive the war, I want to share my experience with them. I want them to understand why both their mother and father had to spend so much time away from them. It will be good for them to know that sometimes there are issues in the world that are much bigger than an individual person, or even a family. My parents don't understand that, but we always hope that the next generation will understand more. But I have to think that both Allan and I will survive, and we will have a normal family life with our girls again. I have to go to France believing that.

John Dexter began the afternoon meeting with introductions between the two women and two men who would be flown across the Channel to parachute into France together. The two men, who were in military uniforms, wore short haircuts and serious demeanors, were demolitions experts. They, along with Ellen, were to be part of a contingent of French Resistance workers who were to use explosives to disrupt trains traveling from France to Germany.

"We are concentrating on the tracks. Our goal is not to kill so much as to disrupt the German operations. Railroad tracks, as you well know, are crucial to the movement of weapons, armaments, supplies and troops from Germany to the western occupied countries, principally France.

"Going the other direction, they use the trains to transport people, meaning primarily Jews, to forced labor camps and worse. This traffic is increasing week to week, which is why we moved up your departure." He paused to glance around the room at the attentive faces. Only Lydia looked confused, because he had specifically said that the sabotage of the railroads would involve only the other three. He smiled slightly in her direction, as if to reassure her that he had not forgotten her. "Of less importance than the human cargo, but still vitally important, is the cargo of art objects that the Germans are stealing – there is no other word for it – from the countries they occupy."

At this Lydia looked up.

Dexter continued, "The Germans are transporting carload after carload of paintings from museums and private collections, as well as silver, jewelry, family heirlooms including furniture, china, anything of any value. We also want to disrupt or stop as much of this theft as possible."

One of the men looked up. "So you are saying we are to blow up the railroad tracks, bring the Nazi rail traffic to a standstill."

"We hope you can do that, at least in the area of southern France where you will be working. The Resistance workers there will work with you and show you exactly which sections of track are the most vulnerable, and will create the most havoc for the Nazis.

"I don't need to remind any of you of the danger you will face. The Germans are not going to take any disruption of their plans easily. And if any of you are caught, you know the consequences. You will be given all the usual supplies and necessities that agents are normally given."

"Meaning cyanide pills," said the dark-haired agent, who sat doodling on his note pad.

"Meaning cyanide pills," repeated Dexter, who then turned to Lydia.

"Lydia, you will be working on a different assignment," he began, when there was a knock on the door. "Come in," he called.

Suzanne Valbert from the French Resistance headquarters stepped into the room. "Hello," she said to the room in general, and her eyes settled on Lydia.

"I think you have all met Mlle. Valbert," Dexter said. He turned to her. "You arrived at just the right time," he added. "I was just about to explain Lydia's assignment."

Ellen interrupted. "Wait. I don't mean to question your decisions, but is Lydia ready for a solo operation?"

Captain Roland spoke for the first time. "Just because Lydia is not working with the three of you does not mean she is working alone. Lydia's operation will be to accompany a group of Jewish children out of France into Spain. A dangerous journey, but one their parents are willing to risk, considering the alternative could be transport to Germany and almost certain death."

"Lydia," Suzanne spoke in a softer, more compassionate voice than Lydia had ever heard her use when she worked with her in Pimlico.

"I will be traveling with you as far as Hastings, Lydia," Suzanne continued, "so I can give you the detailed instructions for contacting our counterparts in France. I also want to talk with you privately after this meeting. You will definitely not be alone in this operation, Lydia. We have several French operatives who will be helping you all along the way." Suzanne settled in a chair and looked to John Dexter to continue the meeting. His voice droned on with the usual directives and warnings for agents being sent into enemy territory, and Lydia did her best to listen and take notes, although the note-taking was habit as much as anything, a habit left over from her school days. She was usually able to remember information just through the act of writing down the words, and rarely looked at her notes after she took them. She wanted this meeting to be over, because the discussions that related to what she was really concerned about, her own assignment and her husband's fate, would be discussed later, out of earshot of individuals who had no need to know the details.

As Dexter was closing the meeting, a clerk came to the door and summoned him to the telephone. "Urgent," he said, "from the solicitor Adams."

With a start Lydia realized that this was the solicitor who was working on Allan's case, and she wondered if the urgent call had anything to do with him. Maybe he was being released?

Dexter left the room, and the rest of the group drifted out, except for Suzanne, who deftly cornered Lydia and began an earnest conversation about French impressionists, which effectively excluded the rest of the group. Lydia saw Ellen give her a sideways glance but she continued out of the room.

As soon as the door closed behind them, Suzanne removed a small package from her bag. It was about two inches by two inches, roughly square, and wrapped in brown packing paper. "Put this away, Lydia. It is a gift for you and Allan, from the family of one of the girls you are to escort out of France."

"I can't possibly... I'm not doing this for payment." Lydia was horrified.

"Of course you are not," Suzanne replied. She closed her hands around Lydia's as she placed the package firmly in the other woman's hands. "This is from a French woman who knows and trusts Allan." She dropped her hands to her sides before continuing. "She has sold many of her jewels to finance our operations, especially the protection of the children."

"But why is she giving this to me instead of selling it?" Lydia was shocked.

"It is her choice. As you can see, she has ultimate trust and faith in Allan, and in you." As Lydia still hesitated, and held the package gingerly in her hands, Suzanne continued,

"Just put it away for now. Take it out when the war is over and you will know what to do with it."

Suzanne reached into her bag and pulled out a large brown envelope. "This is for you, too. It was given to my brother Henri by the same woman. He was supposed to sell it for her. There is a letter inside explaining it all. It is very valuable. Someday you will know what to do with it."

Lydia hesitated. "What is it?"

"A painting. Very valuable. Just put it away. It will keep until after the war."

It was only hours later, when Lydia had finally returned to her room at the Dexters' home, that Lydia had the time and privacy to open the small package. The brown paper wrapping contained tissue paper wrapping, and within that rested a gold necklace, from which hung a heavy pendant set with jewels. Lydia let the chain dangle from her finger and watched the jewels catch the light from her small bedside lamp. She identified diamonds, sapphires, and rubies, set in a circular design. "This is worth a fortune," Lydia breathed. "And how old is it? Sixteenth century? Earlier?" Lydia caressed the pendant, knowing as she did so that she was not just holding a valuable antique, but a priceless family heirloom. She re-wrapped the necklace in the brown paper and tucked it in a corner of the box that the Dexters would ship to Wales for her. Tomorrow she would repack the box and find a more secure spot for this valuable piece. She had a good idea of where she would place it.

The painting was securely wrapped in brown paper, and there was no time to open it. Lydia placed it securely on the bottom of the box, where it could lie flat. "Not the best storage for a painting, but it's the best I can do at the moment."

Lydia's Diary
Midnight

I have time for one more entry before I close up my boxes and send them. I still need to pack a small bag to carry to Hastings with me, but I won't need much.

I'm really more concerned about seeing Allan, and making sure that this box is sealed and ready to go. I suppose the necklace will be safe enough in the box. No one will know it is there. I hate to just chuck it in with my clothes and the other odds and ends, but I'm sure it will be fine. It will be well hidden from anyone who just opens the box and looks inside. Oh, and I need to save room for the doll I bought for Rebeca. I'll see them again in a couple of months. I have to believe that. All of them – Rebeca, Catherine, Allan, my parents – I'll see all of them in a couple of months.

In the meantime – I have to save somebody else's children. Dexter told me that they chose me for this assignment because I am flexible, intelligent and compassionate, and I don't give up. He says I'm resourceful and focused. I hope so.

Funny thing is that I'm not nervous, at least not about what I will do once I get there. Once I have a task – and someone or something to take care of – whether it is children or works of art – Dexter is right – I am focused.

Allan had been awake for a couple of hours already. He had not slept at all well. Lydia had visited him yesterday morning, and was now, he knew, in Hastings, preparing for her jump in to France. Allan felt an overwhelming sense of sadness when he thought of her and the children. It had been all right as long as he was occupied himself traveling back and forth across the Channel. Now there was too much time to think, and in his heart he was terrified for Lydia. In his mind, he knew she would carry out her mission successfully, and he was infinitely proud of his wife. But in his heart, he was terrified. He was not sure if the terror was for her, or for the two of them. He tried to wrap himself in the thin blanket and only succeeded in exposing his feet to the cold.

"Roberts, warden wants to see you."

"Now? What time is it?"

"You on a schedule, Roberts?" the guard said. "Got other appointments scheduled today?"

"I'm coming." Allan rolled out of his bunk, cringing slightly as his feet hit the cold cement floor. He used the bucket that served as his toilet, and pulled on his pants. He shivered as he buttoned his prison issue shirt and tied his shoes. No matter how long he was here, and he expected each day that it would be his last as a prisoner, he believed he would never get used to the cold. He followed the guard out of the cell and down the hallway, between rows of cells of sleeping men. A snore or a sleepy snort was the only sound at this hour. Although light bulbs illumined the darkness, the air had the feel of early morning. Allan knew it would be light soon. He followed the guard, who he knew as Sandy, down the length of the hall and through a door which Sandy unlocked with a key from the bunch he carried at his waist. After locking the door behind them, Sandy turned to the left.

"I thought we were going to the warden's office," Allan said as he hesitated.

"We are," Sandy answered. "The other way is blocked by some building equipment. There was bomb damage here last week."

Allan had no choice but to follow Sandy down the alternate corridor. As he walked he tried to remember bombings in this part of London, but he could not say for sure when, or if, there had been any.

The hallway opened onto an outdoor ledge that had once been a balcony that ran along the eastern side of the building and toward the old section that had been built at the beginning of the century. A frigid breeze took Allan's breath away as he glanced to the east where the sun was, indeed, beginning to brighten the sky over east London. Sandy paused and looked back, his eyes flickering briefly past Allan. "Almost morning," he commented.

Before Allan could wonder why Sandy was suddenly willing to stop and exchange pleasantries, Allan felt himself lurch forward. He tried to catch himself on the railing but the metal crumbled and pulled out of its rusted anchor in the stone below. He pitched forward and landed on the walkway two stories below. His limbs moved slightly as blood began to seep from his head. A figure in dark gray workman's clothes emerged from the shadows and stood over Allan, and then struck the back of his head with a hammer. He pushed the now motionless body into a drainage ditch that led to the canal at Camden and began to wash down the area with buckets of water, as if it were his usual morning routine. Sandy turned and retraced his steps to the warden's office, where he would report that Allan Roberts had fallen off the balcony and into the ditch as he tried to escape.

Chapter 18

Lydia's Diary – July 5, 1941

Dear Mother and Dad,

I am working on a new assignment that may take me out of London. (Should I tell them that?)

I am going to be extremely busy in the next few weeks, but I will write when I can. (I'll never hear the end of it if I say that.)

I am preparing a box to send to you and the girls. (Better) Allan is in London now, and we have some time together. (What a liar I have become!)

I finally found a doll for Rebeca, but I will save it for her birthday.

(Can't write this letter now. I'm too restless, too upset. I just want Allan free.)

Why is there always something that we "just want." If only this, if only that and I would be happy. But there is always something else. If only this war were over, I would never complain again about slow buses, the cost of food and school tuition, or my parents. If only...

Present Day
Springfield

It was late – nearly eleven – but thanks to a good dinner and several hours sleep, Paul was wide awake and alert. It was a perfect time to visit the Gate House bed and breakfast. He had no illusions that he would find the painting in a house full of sleeping people, but he could survey the building from the outside and look for weak spots in the locks on the doors and windows. He knew how to pick an unsophisticated lock, although he was no expert. He had learned his skill from another mental patient while he was in an institution near Paris. The two of them would break into the cabinet of controlled substances during the night and take a few pills. Paul hadn't cared much about the pills – the attendants gave him enough of those without stealing more – but he loved the excitement of the act of theft. The knowledge had proved useful to him a number of times.

Paul left the hotel with a nod to the desk clerk who sat engrossed in an old movie on the television set behind the front desk. The air had grown chilly and a fine mist was falling. He cleared the moisture off the car windows and drove through the quiet streets until he was within a few blocks of the Gate House. He parked the car, making sure he was in a legal parking space and would not return to find that the car had been towed. It was an easy matter then to walk down the dark street and around the corner to his destination. The street lights provided enough illumination for him to see where he was going, but when he reached the Gate House he moved off into the garden. As he rounded the back of the house, he moved in closer to the back wall of the building. The ground floor was dark, and a small, solitary light shone from the second story. Probably someone reading late, he thought. As he paused to consider his next action he heard a voice from the car park on the other side of the building, and the sound of a car door closing, and then opening. Paul froze and waited for the car to leave, or for the person to go back inside the house. Instead, he heard a female voice. "Damn! Where is it?"

She's looking for the copies of the diaries, Paul thought, *and she has no idea when or where they disappeared*, *because she has been so preoccupied with the painting. My painting!* A surge of anger coursed through Paul's body, like an ocean wave engulfing a drowning victim. Paul had not felt this kind of anger for a long time. Lisette usually had the capability to ward it off with calm words, a distraction, or a regular dose of medication. But Lisette wasn't with him now, and Paul possessed no inner resources to stop the wave, even if he wanted to. He circled around the other cars until he was behind Nara, who was bent over inside the back seat, searching underneath the front passenger seat. "Looking for something?" he said.

When she started to rise, it was a simple movement for Paul to shove her forward with his knee until she lay sprawled across the floor behind the seats. Her face scraped along the rough carpet and she burst out with, "Ouch!"

"Shut up!" he ordered.

"Who...?"

"Shut up!" he shouted, and she was silent, although she tried to rise from the floor. Paul grabbed the back of her shirt and pulled her out. "Need help?" he asked, his lips almost touching her ear, so she could feel his warm breath against her neck. He tightened his grip and put his finger around her throat. "Where is my painting?"

"What?"

"My painting!" As he spoke, he slammed her head against the door frame of the car and her head slumped forward. "Shit!" Paul said. "I hit her too hard." He knew he would get no answers now, and his only desire was to get away. The house remained quiet, and he wondered if he had killed her. He lifted her unconscious body into the back seat, surprised at how light she was. She moaned softly as he pushed her across the seat and she landed sprawled with her head hanging down off the edge of the seat. He closed the door. No one would miss her until morning, and she could be dead by then. Paul padded around the house and back to his parked car, avoiding the brightness of the street lights. He sat in the car for a few moments and then returned through the deserted streets to the hotel. The clerk sat nodding at the desk, and Paul tiptoed past him and climbed the stairs to his room. He had been gone less than an hour, but his energy had evaporated. He kicked off his shoes and fell on the bed into an exhausted sleep.

"Come on, sweetie, wake up." Jack Blake tried in vain to rouse his daughter, who lay sprawled across the back seat of her car. "Nara, what happened?" He touched her face and in the darkness he felt the wetness of her blood. "Nara!" He realized that she needed more than her father's touch, and reluctant though he was to leave her, he ran back into the house to the kitchen phone and dialed 999. Once he was assured that help was on the way, he wasted a few seconds in indecision, and decided he needed to wake his sister Sue. Sue was a nurse. She would know what to do.

He ran quickly up the stairs to her bedroom and knocked softly on the door, and then he knocked a little louder. He heard rustling sounds within and opened the door a crack. "Sue," he hissed. "Hurry. Something happened to Nara. She's unconscious. I called 999 but she needs help now."

"My God!" He could hear Sue pulling on clothing and she was at the door in seconds. "Where is she?"

"In her car." Jack was already half way down the stairs.

"Her car?!" Sue continued without breaking stride. "What was she doing in her car? Was she in an accident?"

"I don't think so." Jack lowered his voice to a whisper when they reached the ground floor. There were several people sleeping in the rooms reserved for bed and breakfast guests, and he did not want to add to their vacation stories, although they would hear soon enough. A siren sounded in the distance, and Jack ran out the door, followed by Sue.

"She's in the back seat," Jack said as they reached the car. Nara moaned when Sue touched her cheek.

"Nara, can you hear me?" She moaned again and moved her head, and then collapsed again against the seat. "I don't want to move her. Not with a head wound," Sue said.

The sound of the siren grew closer. "Say something to her," Sue added.

"Nara." Jack gently touched her shoulder. "Help is on the way, Nara." She didn't move, and her breathing was shallow. Jack turned to Sue. "She didn't do this to herself, Sue. Someone attacked her."

The ambulance pulled into the car park with a screech of tires.

"I don't know, Jack. Maybe we'll know more when we find out the extent of her injuries."

Nara groaned again as the paramedics lifted her out of the back seat and transferred her to a stretcher, but she did not open her eyes. They attached monitors and checked vital signs. She had no other visible injuries besides the blow to the head.

"She's stable," the paramedic said. "You can follow us to the hospital."

As they got into Sue's car for the drive to the hospital, Jack said, "I'm calling the police. She didn't do this to herself."

Sgt. Coley was waiting in the emergency room lobby when Jack and his sister returned from their conversation with the doctor. Coley stood when Jack and Sue came out into the room. He was tall and thin with rangy limbs and pale blond hair that betrayed his Nordic background. He had known Sue for years, since before her divorce. Springfield was a small town, and "real" crimes were relatively rare. Strangely, Sue's bed and breakfast had seemed to be a magnet for wrongdoings of various kinds in the few years since she had become the owner.

"Is she all right?" he asked, although the worry on their faces told him that she was not.

"We don't know yet." Jack's voice shook and he swallowed to bring it under control. "She has a concussion and she is still unconscious. The cut on her forehead required seven stitches. They are taking her up for a CT scan now, and then we will see how bad... if there…" Jack's voice was thick with emotion, and he stopped speaking.

Sue took over for him, adopting her clear nurse's voice, although she was clearly upset as well. "She was hit, or shoved, hard and has a head injury – certainly a concussion but they don't know how severe yet. The CT scan will tell us if there is any damage to her brain, or any bleeding."

"She's not conscious." Coley's words were a statement rather than a question.

"No," Jack answered, cleared his throat and repeated, "No."

A woman with a crying toddler walked into the waiting room and began talking with the nurse on duty. Coley glanced at them and guided Jack and Sue to a quiet corner of the waiting room where there were chairs available. After the three sat and adjusted the chairs, Grant took out his notebook. "Tell me what happened." He wrote the date on the page, and then chewed thoughtfully on the end of his pen while he waited for them to speak.

Jack spoke first. "Nara went out to her car about eleven o'clock to look for something she had left in there earlier today. It was a copy of the diary of her great-grandmother," he added, knowing that would be Coley's next question. "I was waiting for her in my bedroom, and I heard the car door open and close. Then when some time had passed – about twenty minutes I think – I went out to see what was keeping her. She only had to pick up a manila folder from the back seat. It should only have taken a moment."

"And when you went out to look for her?" Coley asked as he wrote.

"I didn't see her at first," Jack said. "Everything was quiet. I walked to the car, and saw her lying on the back seat. I opened the door and saw that her head was bleeding and she was unconscious. I called 999 immediately, and then, although I hated to leave Nara alone even for a moment, I ran in to get Sue. Sue is a nurse, as you know."

"Yes. I know," Coley murmured as he jotted down the information. "And when you got here to the hospital you called the police. Why?"

Jack looked at him blankly and Sue blurted, "Surely you can see...?"

"I just want to report all the information accurately, Sue."

Jack cleared the roughness out of his throat again and continued, "It's obvious she didn't hit herself, and then crawl into the back seat of the car and close the door. Someone did this to her."

Coley closed his notebook. "I'll get someone over to look at the car as soon as possible. It should be fairly easy to determine if someone else was there. And the medical report should give us some clues as well. Is the car locked?"

"I don't think so," Jack answered. He fumbled in his pocket and pulled out a key ring. "I have an extra key to her car." He pulled it off the ring and handed it to the officer.

Coley stood to leave. "No. Don't get up," he said as Jack began to rise. But Jack's attention was on the doctor who was striding toward them.

"She's still stable," he said without preamble. "The good news is that her concussion is not that severe. She needs rest to allow her body to heal itself. We don't know when she will regain consciousness. It could be in a couple of hours, or longer."

"How much longer?" Jack asked.

"There's no way to say," the doctor answered. "Hours, days... "

"Can we see her?" Sue asked.

"Of course. Come with me."

"Someone will be in touch with you later today," Sgt. Coley said to Jack, and then turned to the doctor. "I would like to see the medical report of her injuries if you don't mind."

"Certainly. I'll show it to you and Sue also," he added, nodding to Jack. "I will tell you all one thing that is clear. Someone hit her. Hard. My guess is that whoever it was slammed her against the door frame of the car, and then pushed her inside."

"A burglar?" Sgt. Coley mused, and then straightened his shoulders and put away his notebook. "Someone will be in touch later today after we check out the car."

Alex rolled over in his bed and reached out to touch a cold pillow next to his. Where was Nara? At the same time he became conscious that his cell phone was ringing. *What time is it?* he thought. He picked up his phone and saw that it was 4 a.m., and that the person calling him was Jack Blake, Nara's father.

"Yes?" he answered groggily as he struggled to sit up, and then gave up and lay back down and stared at the ceiling in the dark.

"Alex. I know it's early." Jack's voice was groggy, too, but with a tiredness that was different. "Nara has been in an accident. Well, we think someone attacked her."

Alex sat up straight, sleep disappearing. "What?"

Jack continued, "She is in the hospital -- unconscious. They think she will be all right, but they don't know when she will regain consciousness." He voice broke with the last words.

"My God!" Alex exclaimed. "What happened?"

"We don't know exactly. It looks like someone grabbed her when she went out to get something out of her car last night." Alex was trying to convince his brain to wake up enough to take in the information when Jack continued.

"Yes. Right." Alex was out of bed now looking for his clothes. "I'll be there as soon as I can."

"Thank you, Alex." Jack hung up the phone.

Alex sat down again on the bed, trying to make some kind of sense of all this. Could the attack on Nara have anything to do with the World War II diaries, or the Cézanne painting which wasn't authentic anyway, but only a copy? He had to go to Springfield.

Alex checked the time again. 4:15 a.m. He could be on the road in less than an hour and be in Springfield by 9:00. The drive would give him some time to think, and try to figure out how much of this mess was his fault, and how much of it he could rectify.

After a quick shower, Alex drank a cup of tea, scalding his tongue on the hot liquid but forcing it down. He choked and went into a coughing spasm that forced him to bend double, a horrible suspicion forming in his head. Did Paul Grassin have anything to do with this?

Professor Mark Jones leafed again through the files on his desk. He had sent copies off to Ms. Blake at the address she had given him in Lincolnshire as well as the London address. He thought she would be pleasantly surprised at his findings. He had not, and would not, tell her about the other inquiries he had received about paintings hidden in Wales, and oblique references to Ms. Blake's ancestors. Nor would he tell her that he had not made the decision to share the information with her until after the second inquiry. He knew he had behaved rudely on both occasions. He had no real reason for his attitude with Nara and her father. Somehow he had been put off when he found out that Nara was inquiring for personal reasons, not purely academic ones. But he had gone ahead and pursued the investigation anyway, and come up with some amazing information. Ms. Nara Blake was descended from a truly remarkable woman who deserved recognition alongside any other World War II hero. He wondered why she had not received this recognition. Was it because she was a woman? Because she had died before actually completing her assignment? It didn't matter, as far as Jones was concerned. The woman, Lydia Roberts, had saved the lives of a group of French Jewish children, at the cost of her own.

Now he had a phone call to make. His French was poor, but he had been assured that the woman he was calling would have a translator present. He asked for an international line and waited; when he heard the tone indicating that the university was allowing him to make a call outside of the UK, he dialed the number.

"Allo?" a voice answered.

"Mme. Colline?" he asked. "Je suis Prof. Jones en Wales."

"Ah, le professeur Jones. Enchantée, monsieur. Mon amie est ici. Un moment, s'il vous plait."

He heard soft French voices in the background as he waited. At last the phone was picked up and a younger female voice with only a trace of a French accent asked, "Professor Jones?"

"Yes, I am Professor Jones. Thank you for speaking with me."

"It is my pleasure, Professor," she answered. "I am Diane Montal. I am a neighbor of Mme. Colline and I am happy to translate for you. She has told me a little of the story, and why you are calling. Of course I have heard the story of her escape from France with the other children during World War II many times. It is part of our history. But, please. I am doing all the talking, and you are the one who is calling with questions. What would you like me to ask her?"

Jones cleared his throat. "I would like to know about Lydia Roberts. I believe she was the woman who led the group out of France."

Diane spoke for some time. Now and then she asked Jones to hold on while Mme. Colline added information and clarified some of the events. He took careful notes, and by the end of the conversation, he was sure of one thing. Nara Blake and her family needed to meet this woman.

"I am going to pass on this information to Nara Blake, Lydia Roberts' great-granddaughter. She came to me asking for help in finding out about her family, and I think she should meet Mme. Colline if that is possible."

"I will speak with Madame about it. I am sure she would be delighted if they would visit." Diane paused again to convey the request to her companion. "Yes. She regrets that she does very little traveling these days, but if any of Lydia's family members could visit, she would be happy to tell the story to them in person."

Professor Jones hung up the phone. He sat for some time staring at his desk, the telephone, the notes he had made while listening as well as the doodles that his notes had become. He picked up the phone and dialed Nara's cell phone number. There was no answer, and he left a message for her to call him as soon as possible.

Chapter 19

Present Day
Springfield, Lincolnshire

The pills that Paul had taken the night before made his sleep a deep one, but it was less than refreshing. The light and noise outside his window finally brought him to full awareness, and he sat up on the edge of his bed and rested his head in his hands. His stomach growled, and he stood to head for the bathroom and shower. He nearly fell back again on the bed, but managed to clear the dizziness after a few deep breaths. The events of the day before were returning to him in fragments, light as scraps of paper. He couldn't seem to hold on to a thought longer than a few seconds. He knew he had read those diaries and they made him angry. Why? Did he hit someone? That girl. Nara? There was no way anyone would connect him with that little incident, but maybe he should get back to London anyway. He couldn't risk breaking into the house -- or could he? He still hadn't found the Cézanne, and there was the necklace mentioned in the diary, too.

After a shower Paul began to feel a renewal of energy. He would go down to the restaurant for coffee and something to eat, and maybe then just take a drive past the Gate House and see if there was any way he could get inside. He checked his pants pocket for his cell phone, even though he did not intend to return any calls; in particular he did not intend to speak to Lisette. The phone was nowhere to be found. He checked his clothing and bag again, and then the floor underneath the furniture. Nothing. With a burst of clarity, he realized that he must have dropped it the night before at the Gate House, and it could connect him with the attack on Nara. Would she even remember what happened? Might she think she had merely fallen? Not likely, he thought. He had to get away from this town. His cell phone was lost and he had a rental car. The cell phone alone meant nothing. It was registered to him in France. But he had registered at the hotel using his credit card, and he had a rental car in his name. There was nothing to be done about the hotel, but he needed to remove the car from this town as quickly as possible. It would take some time to track down his phone with the French company. He would simply return the car and take the train back to London and disappear for a while.

    He smiled pleasantly at the desk clerk as he checked out, and was relieved to see his car parked on the side street just where he had left it, without so much as a parking ticket. He took the road that led out of town, past the Woodlands Hotel on the right, through the stop light and toward the Gate House. He slowed slightly when he reached it just so he could check out the activity, or lack of it, around the building. He quickly moved his foot from the brake to the accelerator when he saw to his horror that half the car park was cordoned off with police "crime scene" tape. A panda car was parked next to it, with a lone policeman standing guard. Briefly he thought of stopping to ask what had happened, as if he were a neighbor whiling away his time with idle curiosity, but he might be remembered and reported. He drove on past, wondering how seriously the girl was injured. Was she dead? If that were the case, they would really be on his trail. It would be best to return the car and take the train back to London. Then he could figure things out.

Nara heard her father's voice. She tried to open her eyes but her lids were too heavy. At the same time, the light in the room was so bright she didn't believe that she could open her eyes. A woman spoke very near to her, but she didn't recognize the voice. The woman touched her arm and said something about Nara having good color, whatever that meant. Nara felt the urge to giggle. She knew her skin was dark, and she knew it was good, but what did "good color" mean? She smiled to herself. She felt the woman pat her shoulder, and wondered if she knew that Nara thought her statement was funny. She tried again to open her eyes, and succeeded just a little bit, but the lights were so bright it was painful. "It's too bright, Dad," she said, or tried to say. There seemed to be an echo in the room as well.

She heard another voice. Alex? What was he doing here? She tried again to open her eyes and this time she managed to allow a sliver of light between her lids, but the light was still so bright that she couldn't see who was in the room. It occurred to her that she was in hospital, and she wondered why. It must be serious because she couldn't move, and if her dad and Alex were both here. She desperately wanted to know what was going on. She could give in to sleep again, but her natural curiosity was outweighing the sleepiness. If she could just make her voice heard, someone would come and talk to her. She tried again. "Dad?" There was that echo again. "Dad?"

"Nara?" He heard her! Suddenly both her dad and Alex were standing over her. She could feel the presence of them both as well as see them, large shadows in the light. "Nara?" her father asked again. "Can you hear me?"

"Yes," she answered, and tried to nod her head. Her voice sounded feeble and unclear to her, but Alex and her dad were both joyful. She must be very sick. Her dad leaned over and kissed her gently on the cheek.

"We are so glad you're back, love," he whispered.

Where have I been? she wondered.

"I'll let the nurse know." She heard Alex's voice. It was nice to hear Alex's voice, and to know that he was concerned about her. It seemed as if it was a long time since she had heard his voice.

A nurse bustled in a few moments later and began to fiddle with dials and IV lines. She asked Nara her name and she answered. It didn't sound clear to her but the nurse seemed satisfied. She asked her a few other questions that Nara could not answer. How was she to know what day it was, or what had happened to her? The nurse checked a few more things and then said to her dad and Alex, "I'll let the doctor know. Her vital signs are all good. She'll start coming around little by little now." The nurse patted her hand and left the room.

Once again Nara fought the sleepiness she could so easily succumb to and opened her eyes again. The light did not seem nearly as bright and painful. "Dad?" Her voice sounded clearer, too. "Dad? What happened to me?"

He was instantly at her side, and took her hand in his. "Someone hit you, Nara, when you went out to the car to find your copy of Lydia's diary. Do you remember anything of what happened?"

She tried hard to smile, but it felt as if one side of her mouth went up and one side went down. "I remember the diary," she said softly. "I don't remember anything else."

"That's okay," he said. "You may remember more as time goes on. We are just happy to see you awake."

"Am I going to be okay?" she asked.

"Yes. I'm sure you will be. You had a bad bump on the head, but the doctor said it was just a matter of regaining consciousness in order to see how badly your memory was affected. But it looks like you will be fine."

She thought of something else. "Alex is here?"

"Yes, he is," her father answered. "I called him, and he came immediately."

"Good," she whispered. Her eyelids were drooping again. Maybe now she could sleep for a while, but suddenly Alex was at her side, and her father moved away.

"I'm sleepy, Alex. I can't help it." It seemed funny now, that Alex was here and she could not keep from falling asleep.

"I know, dear." Now she felt both of his warm, strong hands enclosing one of hers. "I just want you to know that I am here, and I love you."

The words relaxed and healed something inside Nara, and she gave in to sleep.

Alex turned to Nara's father. "We need to find out who did this to her, now that we know she is going to be well."

"We don't know that for sure yet, Alex," Jack answered. "But yes, maybe she will remember more the next time she wakes up. The police are investigating, of course."

"They haven't discovered anything yet?"

"Not yet, at least nothing definitive."

Alex stretched his arms over his head. "Maybe I'll go over to the Gate House and have a look around."

Before the other man could say anything, there was a knock at the door, and Sergeant Coley walked in. "Good morning," he said to the two men. "I knew you would be here, Jack, so I stopped over, and the nurse on duty told me that Nara was awake. That's good news."

"Yes," Jack answered. "But she has gone back to sleep now. She doesn't remember anything of the attack, but she remembers the diaries she was reading, and seems coherent but tired."

"That's normal," the officer answered. "She may remember more when she wakes again, and I will want to talk with her at some point. " He nodded at Alex, with whom he had a passing acquaintance from previous cases. "The real reason I am here is to tell you we found a cell phone a few hours ago. It was in the street just around the corner from the Gate House. It is a French phone. We have contacted the French police and should have the name of the owner by the end of the day. It also looks as if we may be able to lift some fingerprints from it."

"French?" Alex asked.

"Yes. We should have a name in a few hours. We asked the neighbors on the street where it was found, but none of them had visitors from France, so..."

Alex stood and walked to the window and turned around to face the other two men. "I might be able to save you some time," he said. "Paul Grassin."

"Who is he?" Jack Blake asked.

"He's a graduate student who was doing some research at the V&A. He was very interested in what Nara was doing – finding out about her great-grandmother. He thought..." Alex paused and looked at his shoes, studying them as if they were experiencing some sort of metamorphosis.

"He thought what?" Coley asked.

"He thought there was something in one of her boxes that belonged to him or his family."

"What did he think was in the box?" Jack asked.

"A painting," Alex answered. "A painting by Cézanne."

Jack Blake stared at Alex. "How did he know?"

Alex shook his head. "Family stories. But it's a copy. I did some research," he added.

"What's the name again?" the officer added.

"Paul Grassin," Alex spelled the last name for him. "He and... He and his sister have a flat in London." Alex was aware that Jack was watching his face closely as he spoke.

"You know the address?" Coley asked, with pen poised above his notebook.

Alex gave him the address in the Bloomsbury section of London.

"Thanks. We'll contact Scotland Yard, and Interpol, too, if we get prints off the phone. See what they have on him." The officer flipped his notebook shut.

"He's a little crazy," Alex said, whether to himself or the police officer he wasn't sure, nor did it matter.

"Aren't they all?" Coley said as he prepared to leave. He glanced at Nara who seemed to be sleeping peacefully.

"No," added Alex. "He's been hospitalized for mental illness. He's got real problems."

The officer left the hospital room and Jack Blake turned to Alex, the man he expected to someday become his son-in-law. "Alex, did you have any idea this... person had the capacity to attack Nara?"

"Of course not, Jack," Alex answered, then lowered his voice after he saw Nara move in her sleep. "Of course not. Paul is obsessed, obsessed with regaining his family possessions, but I never thought... I'm sure he had never even met Nara."

Jack picked up his paper cup of cold coffee and stared into its depths frowning, as if he could read portents in the muddy liquid. "You're certain that the Cézanne is a copy? We found it, you know. I was planning to take it somewhere to have it appraised, but then this happened." He nodded toward Nara.

"I'm certain. The original is in the Getty Museum near Los Angeles, but there were a number of copies made."

"It doesn't matter to Nara, you know."

Alex was about to respond when Jack's cell phone rang. He stood and stepped out into the hallway to take the call. Alex looked across the room at Nara, so vulnerable and small, with a white bandage covering the gash across her forehead. He stepped to the bed and took her hand. She opened her eyes and smiled at him. She was about to speak when Jack came back into the room.

"That was Elaine on the phone," Jack said. "She thinks there is something hidden inside the doll in one of the boxes from Wales. She says there is stitching over it, as if it were mended, but she can feel something hard inside of it. She wants to open it up and see what it is. She says she can do it along the stitching and sew it up again. I told her to go ahead. Is that all right with you?"

"Of course," Nara agreed. "I wonder what it is?"

"Didn't Lydia mention a necklace in her diary? Something she intended to put in a box to go to Wales?"

"That's right! I wonder... Elaine will call as soon as she finds whatever it is, I'm sure."

The words were barely out of her mouth when Jack's phone rang again. He answered, "Yes, Elaine?"

"You won't believe this, Jack. There was the most unbelievable necklace hidden inside the doll. It's silver and encrusted with jewels. I think they are real, but I'm no expert. Diamonds, sapphires, topaz, I think. It looks ancient. And to think I've had it in my house all this time." She laughed nervously. "Do you think this is what the guy was after when he attacked Nara?"

"I don't think so," Jack replied. "I doubt that he knew about it, and the boxes weren't in the car. But he could have been after the Cézanne."

"But wait, Jack. The guy who attacked her must have taken the diary from the car. Maybe that's why she couldn't find it. If he read it, he would know about the necklace."

"Hold on, Elaine. Let me talk to Nara for a minute." He dropped his hand holding the phone to his side as he spoke to his daughter. "Nara, Elaine found the necklace Lydia wrote about. It was hidden inside the doll." Nara's mouth dropped open in amazed delight. "But I have a question for you. Do you remember if the car was locked when you went out there that night?"

Nara wrinkled her brow in thought, or wrinkled it as much as she could with the gauze bandage still covering it. "I don't remember," she said finally. "I think it was locked, but

I really don't remember anything about what happened in much detail. Sorry."

"Don't be sorry, Nara. It doesn't matter now." He spoke into the phone again. "Elaine, why don't you hide the necklace somewhere else in your house? In the sugar bowl or somewhere. The police have a line on a suspect, but I don't see how he could connect anything with you."

"All right, Jack. Give Nara my love. I'll talk to you tomorrow."

Nara was sitting up in her bed eating soup a few hours later when her sister Lily peeked into the room. "You're up! You're eating!"

"I feel much better. But I tried to get out of bed to go to the bathroom and almost fell on my face."

"What are you eating?" Lily peered at Nara's tray, which contained a bowl of broth, which Nara was dutifully spooning into her mouth, and several other dishes that were either colorless and unappetizing or unnaturally bright colored and unappetizing.

"Liquids and mush," she answered. "They said I have to start with liquids and soft things since I haven't eaten for two days, but I'm starved! After I eat this and show them I'm not going to throw up – I'm going to ask for pizza."

"If they won't bring it to you, and they probably won't, I'll go out and get one for you. What kind do you want?"

"Oh, God, anything! No! Black olives, mushrooms, green peppers, and with a thin crust!"

"Eat that applesauce down and I'll go get it for you." Lily's face turned serious. "Now listen to me while you eat, since you are clearly so darn healthy now."

Nara looked up. "What?" She caught her sister's mood immediately.

"You don't remember anything of what happened to you?"

"No." Nara was emphatic. "I remember going out to the car to look for the copy of the diary that I left in there, and then I woke up in this room with Dad and Alex standing over me." She smiled at the thought.

"Nara," Lily said, trying to keep her sister's attention on the conversation. "I'm going to London tomorrow. I have an appointment to talk with a historian at Special Branch, or whatever it is called now. Prof. Thomas at the university got me the appointment. We need to find out what Allan and Lydia Roberts were really doing, and when and how they died. I think there are documents from World War II that will give us that information. And it may clear up some other questions, too, such as why someone seems to be one step behind you wherever you are with Lydia's boxes. And it might explain why someone was in the car park when you went to look for the copies and almost killed you."

"Good idea," Nara said, "but be careful. If someone is after me, they may be after you, too."

"I'm not sure someone is after either of us so much as they want something we have, or they think we have."

"Such as the Cézanne painting."

"Such as the Cézanne. But did your dad or Alex tell you about the Cézanne?"

"No. What about it?"

"It's not real. It's a copy."

"What?" Nara bumped her tray with her knees and nearly spilled her bright orange dessert. "Who says? How do they know?"

Lily reached out and straightened the cutlery that had gone sliding along with the dessert. "Alex found out. He found out that the original is in a museum in California, and there is no doubt it is the original.

"Alex just found out a few days ago. And remember, he didn't know that Elaine had found the painting. It was just something that student of his was asking about. So there was no reason for him to tell you."

There was a light knock at the door and Jack Blake walked into the room, carrying a huge bouquet of red roses. "I almost brought you a pizza instead," he said as he leaned over to kiss her, "but I wasn't sure you were up to eating something like that yet."

Both girls groaned, and then laughed. "What's wrong?" he said.

"Nara is dying for pizza. Look at the stuff they gave her to eat," Lily said.

"Can you eat pizza? It won't upset your stomach or anything?" he asked, giving Nara his concerned father look.

"This stuff is upsetting my stomach," she answered.

"I'll go get it for you." He started to hand the roses to Lily, but she stopped him.

"I'll go. You just got here, Jack. And I said I would get it for her." She grabbed her purse and was out the door. "I'll be back in half an hour."

Chapter 20

On the train to London

The train to London was behind schedule, and Lily was happy that she had allowed plenty of time before her appointment at SIS at one p.m. She had hoped to stop by the flat and drop off her bag before the appointment, but it would be cutting the time too close, and she did not want to risk being late. She was really quite excited about visiting the intelligence agency of the United Kingdom. She only wished that Nara were able to come with her. But they both believed that the sooner they learned Lydia's and Allan's true stories, the better off they would be. Knowing the true story might help them understand Aunt Rebeca's feelings, and her seeming resentment toward her parents, and might also help them understand why someone had almost killed Nara, because there was no doubt in Lily's mind that there was a connection.

She glanced at her own reflection as she passed a plate glass window near the entrance to the SIS headquarters in Vauxhall Street. She looked like a student. Somehow she wished she had a more sophisticated look, maybe more of a Mata Hari look. She laughed to herself at her fantasy. She was a student – jeans, backpack, frizzy ponytail and all. She entered the building and gave her name to the uniformed officer on duty, who then submitted her backpack and its contents to x-ray and careful scrutiny. She passed through the metal detector and was directed to Room 204. She took the elevator and gave her name to a receptionist.

"Go right in." The woman smiled. "Capt. Ivers is waiting for you."

A handsome, dark-haired man in his mid-thirties rose from his desk and came to greet Lily. "Good afternoon, Miss Carrington. Please have a seat." After she had settled herself in one of the two chairs opposite his desk, he sat and continued. "I was a little surprised to find out that you are not actually a descendant of the Roberts family, but then when I was told what had happened to your sister – half-sister – I understand why you came in her stead."

"Yes," Lily answered, "and besides the fact that Nara, my sister, wants to know about her ancestors, there is a good possibility that the person who attacked her is after something he thinks she has, something that was the property of his family prior to World War II."

"I hope this helps." He picked up a folder filled with papers from his desk. "It makes for quite interesting reading. I found it fascinating, and, according to the evidence here, there are still some loose ends. Shall I summarize it for you?"

"Please," Lily said. His words filled her with excitement. She was about to learn the real story of Lydia and Allan, and she wished once again that Nara were here with her to hear the truth about her forebears. What was it Lydia had said in the diary? "If we survive the war, I will tell our children the truth." They had not survived the war, and only one of their children was still alive, but their grandchildren and their great-granddaughter Nara would know the truth at last.

"Lydia was recruited to serve as a spy and parachuted into France, where her assignment was to escort some Jewish children out of France over the Pyrenees into Spain. She began the trip with two members of the French Resistance, and three children. They were close to the border when a German patrol spotted them. The patrol began firing, and they tried to hurry to safety, protecting the children, of course. Lydia was at the end of the group, and was killed by two bullets in the back of her head and neck. They retrieved her body the next day and buried her in the mountains near the border." He looked up at Lily, who sat still and wide-eyed. "It says here that a letter was sent to her parents in Wales, explaining that she died a heroic death. They were notified."

"Then I wonder why the children were told they died in the Blitz?" Lily asked.

"Maybe the grandparents were ashamed that their daughter was a spy," he said. "A common enough attitude."

"And Allan?" Lily asked. "What happened to him?"

He shuffled the papers to find what he was looking for. "His story is a little more complicated. And there are still unanswered questions." His eyes showed a confused hesitancy when they met Lily's. "Would you like something to drink?"

Lily sensed that he wanted something, and was delaying talking about Allan because... why? "Tea would be nice," she said. He pressed a buzzer on his desk and asked the secretary to bring tea. Lily sat quietly while they waited for their tea. Ivers seemed distinctly uncomfortable when he began to talk about Allan. Did that mean he really was guilty of killing the boy at the school? But why would that be so disturbing? It was almost seventy years ago. Why would it matter now?

Once the tea was served and both of them added their preferred amounts of milk and sugar, Capt. Ivers had no alternative but to continue. He took a long drink of tea before he spoke, without referring to the papers in front of him. "It seems that Allan Roberts died, most probably was killed, while in prison, before his innocence could be proven. It was wartime, and Special Branch had all they could do to handle the agents' activities as they related directly to winning the war against Hitler. And since Allan was dead, and very shortly afterward, Lydia, the investigation was delayed, and then just never happened." He took another sip of tea. "There was some evidence that there was pressure from someone high up in the government not to pursue the inquiry." He stopped and looked at Lily, who sat across from him in shocked silence.

"And I assume some notification of his death was sent to his family?" she asked finally.

"Yes, of course. But it was quite brief. It said simply that he had died suddenly at Pentonville Prison. Allan was an only child, and his parents both died shortly after the war ended. Of course Lydia's family was notified, and it may be then that her parents cooked up the story about them dying in the Blitz. It made a simpler, cleaner story to tell the children."

"You said that Allan most probably was killed?" Lily asked. "What happened?"

"We don't know for sure, but he fell, or was pushed, off a walkway next to the canal. His body washed up downstream a couple of days later. No one at the prison ever admitted knowing anything or seeing anything, and all the guards had alibis." He closed the folder and set it aside. "You have to remember that, with the war going on, and with bombs falling on London, it just wasn't possible to pursue an investigation such as would be done today. Things were constantly changing depending on the situation. That prison was evacuated just a few months later and all the inmates were moved to another facility outside of London."

Lily sat, her mind in a tumult, and wondered how Nara would accept the facts of her great-grandparents' deaths. Lydia, clearly, was a brave, heroic woman, and Allan was as well, but he had died a horrible, ignominious death. "If his body was found, where is he buried?"

Capt. Ivers shuffled through some more papers. "His parents lived in Cardiff in Wales. It wasn't possible to transport his body back there, so he was buried in New Southgate Cemetery north of London. Or it was north of

London at the time, now it is part of the city; you can easily reach it on the Tube."

Lily could think of no more questions, and had a strong need now to be by herself to think over what she had learned, maybe go for a long walk in the streets of London. "Can I have a copy of the documents to give to my sister?"

"Of course," Capt. Ivers answered. "These are yours, or hers." He held out the file he had referred to throughout their conversation.

Moments later Lily was on the street. Some of what she had heard was expected, but why had Allan Roberts been killed? And who had covered up the investigation? And did it matter now, so many years later?

Lily was still mulling over the events of the past few days, as well as what she had just learned from Captain Ivers at SIS. What happened to Lydia made sense, and it was certainly gratifying to learn that she had died trying to save a group of children. She could even understand why Lydia's parents had not told the children the truth. Grief-stricken as they must have been, it must have seemed strangely ironic that she had left her own children in order to save someone else's, at such a risk to her own life. But what about Allan? It seemed that someone had framed him for murder, and then killed him, or had him killed. Captain Ivers had said that someone high up in the government had blocked the investigation of what really happened to the boy. But why? And who? Could there have been another student, the son of a government official or even a titled peer, who was responsible? And all these years later, was there any way to learn the truth? Even so, the person responsible could still be alive. He would have been a teenager during the 1940s. Lily felt completely out of her depth. She wanted to learn the truth, for Nara's sake, but she had no way to go about it. Would there be any record of it at the school, and would they reveal the information? It might be worth a visit.

Lily was pondering all these ideas when she arrived at her flat. She dropped her backpack down inside the door and closed it behind her. She needed a shower, she needed sleep, and she needed to contact the school and find out if she could visit and look at their lists of students from the 1940s. But would that even do any good? She walked toward her bedroom, deciding that a shower needed to be the first priority, when she heard a sound behind her. The front door opened with a small click and a young man walked into the flat. "You need to double lock your door. You know how easy it was to break in?" He waved a credit card in her face.

"Who are you?" she asked.

"I'm Paul Grassin, and you and your sister have gotten in my way once too often. Now give me the Cézanne painting and the necklace."

Lily stared at him. "You are wasting your time. I don't know anything about any necklace, and the Cézanne is a copy. It's not worth anything."

"You are lying," he said, and walked toward her menacingly.

Lily looked around for something with which to defend herself, and settled for a large glass vase from a side table. "Get out," she said. "There's nothing here." Lily knew in a flash that this must be the man who had nearly killed Nara.

"I've read the diaries," he added. "I know about the necklace. Now quit lying and tell me where it is. Where are the boxes you two brought back from Wales?"

"Then you know more than I do," she said. "I haven't finished reading them. I've been too busy worrying about my sister's life."

She could see that her statement shocked him, and that he knew nothing about Nara's condition. For all he knew she could be dead and he could be a murderer. Maybe she could keep him off balance until she figured out her next move. "You may have killed her, you know," she said. "She's been in a coma and we don't know if she's going to make it."

Lily's voice broke as she realized how true that was for a time. A light and movement outside in the street caught her eye, and she noticed a police car pull up across the street and stop. It was in her line of vision but not Paul's. She faked throwing the vase toward Paul to get his attention and put him off guard, but then stepped toward the window and threw the heavy vase through the window glass as hard as she could. The window and vase shattered, sending shards of glass raining down on the street below. She saw one of the policemen get out of the car, and almost an instant later there was pounding on the door to the flat. "Police! Open up!" Without waiting, one of them kicked open the door and two plainclothes officers and one in uniform, all with guns drawn, entered the flat. "Hands in the air!"

In her fright, Lily started to raise her hands, but then realized that their eyes were all on Paul. He had no time to resist, and was in handcuffs before he could react. All the while he screamed, "What are you doing? Have you no respect for an aristocrat? I'll have your jobs for this!"

"What is your name?" one of the policemen asked.

"Paul Grassin. But what..."

"Then you are under arrest for attempted murder, and maybe a few other things once we hear from Interpol."

Once Paul was subdued, the other officer approached Lily. "Are you all right, miss?"

"Yes," she said, "just frightened. I'm all right."

"We will need a statement from you," she said.

Lily began to shake as she realized that it was all over. The man who tried to kill Nara, and could have tried to kill her, was in police custody. "Is there someone we can call to be with you?"

"No," Lily answered. "I'm all right now."

As Paul was taken out of the building in handcuffs, Lily heard a shriek from below in the street. Still shaking, she leaned against the window sill and looked down. Lisette Grassin stood on the sidewalk, her usual elegance lost in a torrent of screams and tears. She was dressed in a pair of jeans and a wrinkled man's shirt, and her hair looked as if she had just lifted it from her pillow. When she saw her brother, she began to shriek. "Please! You can't take him away. He is ill! Can't you see that?"

"Are you his sister?" the police sergeant asked.

"Yes! Please! He needs help!" Lisette sniffed and wiped her face with her hand, which served to smear the tears and remnants of makeup until she resembled an unkempt child.

"I think we have some questions for you, miss," the sergeant said. "You can come along with us, too." Lisette started to move toward the police car where her brother now sat, handcuffed, in the back seat.

"No," another officer ordered. "Separate cars."

"Can't I just talk to him for a moment?" she shrieked again.

"All right," the sergeant said. "Just for a moment." He instructed the driver of the car where Paul was being held to roll down the back window.

As soon as Lisette saw her brother's face, she collapsed on the ground in another torrent of tears and screams. "Paul, I'll always be there for you. Don't worry. Wherever they take you, I will be there to help you. I'm still here. I didn't go back to Paris. You are my only family, Paul!"

Paul's eyes were cold as he watched his sister, who seemed to have lost all control of her emotions and any sense of her whereabouts. The police sergeant put his hand on her shoulder and she jerked away. Paul gave her a last haughty look and said simply, "Bitch," before he sat back in the seat. "Let's go," he said to the driver, as if he were riding in a limousine.

Chapter 21

On the Eurostar to Paris, Jack Blake and his daughter Nara had some leisure to go over all that had happened, and all that they had learned in the past few weeks. "I almost feel let down now that we know what happened to Lydia," Nara commented.

"But we still don't know what happen to Allan," Jack said. "Or we know what happened, but not why."

"I know. The historian at SIS said there was nothing in the records to indicate that Allan was guilty of the murder of the boy. Special Branch was working to get him released when he was killed. But there was information indicating that someone was trying to cover up the murder. If that's the case, and since it was so long ago, we may never find out what really happened, and someone, literally, got away with murder."

"And other than the fact that the boy was obviously a jerk, why would someone kill him?"

"It could have been an accident."

"It could have been, but why blame Allan?"

"Because he was there? He was the last person to see the boy alive."

"Alex is hoping to find something out. He and Lily are going to the school today. Those schools are very proud of their history. Even with a black spot like a murder on their record, there may be some information that would help, and by now, everyone involved could be dead."

"Not necessarily. Mme. Colline is still alive."

Jack and Nara changed trains in Paris and traveled south to Bordeaux, where they rented a car and drove to the village of St. Etienne, where Mme. Colline lived. The village was no longer the sleepy fishing village it had been in the 1940s, but was now a popular beach destination for both French and Spanish vacationers, and was quickly being discovered by the rest of Europe. Jack and Nara checked into a small hotel, and were barely in the room when Nara's cell phone rang.

"Bonsoir!" a female voice said. "Is this Nara? This is Diane Contal, Mme. Colline's friend. She wanted me to find out if you had arrived safely, and to welcome you to St. Etienne."

"We have just arrived at our hotel. We are to see you and Mme. at ten tomorrow morning, right?"

"Yes. She regrets that she cannot see you this evening, as she is most anxious to meet you. But she knows that you will be tired, and she goes to bed very early these days."

"That's fine," Nara answered. "We will have a leisurely dinner and walk around the town, and see you tomorrow."

"I will meet you at your hotel," Diane added. "It's easier than giving directions."

"Tomorrow then," Nara said and hung up the phone. "We are almost there," she said as she turned to her father.

He smiled at her. "Let's go have some dinner. I'm famished."

Promptly at ten the next morning, Nara and Jack met Diane Contal in front of their hotel. "It is only a few blocks from here, but it is easier to accompany you than give directions. It's a beautiful morning, don't you agree?"

It was a beautiful morning. The sun was shining and the slight breeze carried the scent of the sea.

They walked down the main street and turned into a residential street at the first corner. This street ended in a small park, which they crossed and followed a walkway through a stand of trees before reaching another street lined with houses built early in the twentieth century. Diane led them to one that was set off by a thick border of red roses along the front of the building. She used a key to open the front door and led them into the dim interior. "She is probably in the room at the back," she told them.

They found Mme. Colline seated in a chair looking out over her back garden, where more roses in a variety of colors bloomed profusely. A pot of coffee and an assortment of small cakes waited on the table. Madame Colline stood and reached for the hands of Jack and Nara, as Diane made the introductions. She was of average height, with a slim elegance. Her hair was still mostly dark with only a few strands of gray. She looked much younger than seventy-five.

"Parlez-vous francais?" she asked, looking from one face to the other.

"Sadly, no," Jack answered. "We will have to rely on Diane's translations."

After they were all seated and held cups of coffee in their hands, Mme. Colline began to speak. Although her visitors could not understand her words, the enthusiasm and emotion were evident in her voice. Her memory of the woman who saved her life so many years ago was still fresh and could still evoke strong feelings in her.

Diane Contal listened carefully and translated her words into English.

"I'll summarize what she said," she began. "She says that she remembers when she first met Lydia as if it were yesterday. Madame is seventy-five years old now. She was ten years old when they left France in 1943. There were three children, Jewish children, two girls and a boy. Madame was the youngest. As the war dragged on, more and more Jews were being sent to labor camps in Germany. At least they were told they were labor camps. When they began to talk about sending the children away, everyone knew that it would not be to labor camps. And they knew that the rumors they had been hearing about the Germans' "final solution" of eliminating all Jews in Europe must be true. Why else would they take the children away?

"Several families in the village decided to entrust their children to members of the French Resistance, who would take them over the mountains into Spain and then to Portugal. By that time there were a number of British spies who had parachuted into France and were helping the Resistance. Most of them were involved in various types of sabotage – blowing up railroad tracks, bridges – that sort of thing. But there were also a few who helped escort people out of France. It was risky and difficult, crossing the Pyrenees, but sometimes it was the best choice.

"She remembers Lydia as tall and beautiful. She spoke French perfectly, and she was very kind. She asked each child his or her name, and took each one of them by the hand. She told them that she had children at home, but for now, they were her children."

Diane paused to listen to Mme. Colline again. The younger woman nodded, repeating "oui" now and then throughout the narrative. Both Nara and Jack were riveted to Madame Colline's expressive face as the spoke. She stopped and took a sip of coffee, and gave Jack and Nara a warm smile while motioning for Diane to continue.

"She was telling me about the night they left their village. There were three adults: Lydia, and two Frenchmen. They all had knapsacks and wore layers of clothing. She remembers saying good-bye to her parents. Her brother had been sent to England at the beginning of the war, so they believed that both of their children would now be safe. She only found out later that her brother had died a few weeks before she left the village. She remembers her mother kissing her and trying hard not to cry, even as she told her that she would see her in a few days. She never knew if her parents really thought that they might follow her over the mountains to safety, or if they only told her that so she wouldn't cry. They walked up in the mountains from the village on a well-known trail. She remembers that Lydia was a very good hiker, very strong. And she was very good with the children. She encouraged them to think of it as a game, and carried their packs for them sometimes when they were tired. They hiked at night, which was the reason there were three adults with only three children. And she remembers that there were people along the way who sheltered them during the day, and they had a chance to sleep. By the third night they were well up into the mountains, but there was news that a German squadron was patrolling the area, so the adults were very nervous." Diane paused. "Excuse me a moment. I need to ask her a question." She spoke rapidly in French to Madame Colline, and listened with care to her response; then she nodded and turned her attention back to Jack and Nara.

"I have heard this story many times, but I wanted to be sure of the next part," she apologized. She lowered her head and waited a few seconds before beginning, as if preparing herself for what she had to say. "They were very close to the border with Spain, where the children and Lydia would be handed off to the Spanish. Everyone was trying to hurry as much as possible, and she remembers the adults kept looking around into the woods. Then they heard a shot from a short way down the mountain. It was so close that they all began to run. There was another shot and Lydia crumpled to the ground. She had been shot in the back. Madame remembers her telling them to run, run, that she would hide and get help later, that she would be all right. The other woman gathered the children and ran with them to the border. There was another shot. One of the men who was with them reached safety just behind the children, and she saw him shake his head sadly. The next day a couple of the Spanish Resistance workers slipped across the border and brought her body to the camp. She was buried there, on the border of France and Spain."

The four people sat in silence, and a clock chimed somewhere in another part of the house. Jack touched his daughter's hand, and Nara realized that her eyes were brimming tears. "She died for them," Nara whispered.

There was a soft interchange between the two French women and Diane added, "She says to tell you that she owes her life to Lydia and she thinks of her every day."

Nara wiped away her tears with a few careful dabs with her napkin. "Merci," her father said, and added, "That's about the only French word I know, but it means a great deal to us to know what happened to Lydia."

Madame Colline seemed to think of something and spoke rapidly to Diane.

"Oh, yes. She wanted me to tell you this. She remembers that her mother sent a necklace to Lydia's husband at the beginning of the war. It was sent to thank him for helping the family. It was very beautiful, and very old, a precious family heirloom. She knows it has been a long time, but she hopes that you are able to find it, because it belongs to you now."

Nara smiled. "Please tell her that yes, we found it. It was sewn inside a doll that Lydia intended to give to her daughter one day. It's beautiful."

Madame spoke again, and Diane translated. "She says that it is very valuable, but she hopes that you don't sell it because it has been passed down hand to hand for several centuries, and it is meant for you now."

As they rose to leave, Madame Colline embraced both Nara and Jack. "I'll walk you back to your hotel," Diane told them.

Madame Colline spoke again, and Diane translated. "She says that you are welcome to visit any time. You are her only family. She has no children, you see."

Alex and Lily met Professor Mark Jones at the Compton train station as they had arranged. Nara had asked them to visit the school where the boy had been killed in order to talk to the headmaster, in the hope that the school might have some information on the murder that had happened so long ago. Professor Jones brought documents from his files at the University of Bangor, as well as his notes from his conversation with Mme. Colline. They hoped that, along with the information Lily had obtained from SIS, they might be able to put together the pieces of what had really happened to Allan Roberts, and why he had been blamed for Samuel Picard's death.

Headmaster Royce greeted the three of them cordially and motioned them to comfortable chairs in his office. He indicated for them to help themselves to the tea that was laid out on a small table in front of them. As they poured cups for themselves, he began to explain what he had learned.

"I went through the archives and located the school's report of the incident after your call last week." He nodded at Alex. "The stories about a boy being murdered are part of the folklore of the school, although the administration went to great pains to hide the location of the actual murder, and to keep the identity of the victim, and the circumstances surrounding his death, a secret.

"I think the headmaster and his administrators at the time had a fairly good idea who was guilty, but they were powerless to do anything without proof. His report of the incident was kept in the archives. It was labeled as 'secret/confidential' and no one but the succeeding headmasters was allowed to read it." He paused at looked at the three people in front of him. "I understand that there is some family relationship between one of you, and Allan Roberts, who was accused of the crime?"

"My half-sister," Lily answered.

At the same time, Alex said, "My fiancée." Lily looked at him in surprise, when he continued, "She is in France with her father right now, meeting the woman that Lydia Roberts, Allan's wife, saved from the Nazis."

"Quite a remarkable family," the headmaster remarked. He folded his hands on the desk in front of him. "It was an unusual event, and an unusual time in our history – the history of our country and of our school. The boy who was killed seems to have been universally disliked. There was some prejudice against him because he was a Jew, but that is not enough to kill a person, at least not on British soil, and be able to get away with it. But he was a braggart and a show-off. He had been caught cheating by one of the teachers, but was allowed to remain in the school because of his special circumstances. There was nowhere else for him to go. We knew the situation in France at that time, and his parents were there.

"When the boys were questioned later, they admitted that Samuel gambled and often owed other students money. Not something the school approved of then or now, but boy will do what boys will do, and when the fathers of several of your students are peers of the realm, it is often difficult to reprimand them as we would like to. And it was much more difficult then than now."

He sighed and looked around his office. The sunlight streamed in the windows and boys could be heard shouting as a group of them played soccer in a field a short distance away. On the walls of his office hung photographs of teachers and students going back more than a hundred years. "We have a strong sense of history and tradition here, as you can imagine. Many students who attend here are fourth and fifth generation students. Samuel was a newcomer. It's difficult for outsiders even now, although we do more to encourage diversity among our student body today."

"Why was he even admitted?" Lily asked.

"He was probably admitted because he was a Jew and more or less a refugee from France. And he was very intelligent. His grades are testimony to that."

Professor Jones had been taking notes as the headmaster spoke, and now asked, "Is there any indication that the administration at the time knew who the real murderer was?"

"Oh, yes," he answered. "They knew." He straightened the papers in front of him and then met their eyes again. "Some of the boys hinted at the boy's identity when they were questioned, and they were able to eliminate some of them, of course." He looked down again, as if deciding what, or how much to tell them. "Of course there was no proof. And it was wartime. Even though we tried our best to continue with our academics here during the war, it was not business as usual. Older boys left to join the military as soon as they could. Many of our graduates died before they reached their twentieth birthdays. All of our younger professors were gone, and a number of them died as well. We did not want a murderer in our midst, but then Allan Roberts died, and the boy who was under suspicion left the school as well."

"He left?" Lily asked. "Why?"

"To join up, of course," he answered. "But he didn't last long. He was wounded and home again in a few months. He lost a leg."

"Then you know who he is," Lily said.

"Yes." The man looked out the window at the boys who were gathering up their things and moving off to the building after their soccer game. The new modern gym was in sharp contrast to the ivy-covered buildings that had comprised the campus in its early days. He turned back to them, his eyes dark with sadness. "The man is eighty-three years old now and in poor health. And of course nothing was ever proven. In my opinion..." He gazed out the window again, as it the landscape would convey upon him the wisdom to deliver the right information in the right manner. He cleared his throat.

"In my opinion, it's better to let it go. This man has carried the guilt of what he did for sixty years. He lost a leg because he left school and joined up, probably to avoid questioning. And unless he confessed, you would have the devil's own job proving it, and still nothing would come of it. They aren't going to lock him up now. You said that Special Branch had already cleared Allan Roberts' name, and that is what is important."

"Can you tell us his name?" Lily asked softly.

"Certainly," he answered. "I intend to give you a copy of this report."

"No," Alex interjected.

"No?" Lily said, and the other two looked at him.

"No," he repeated. "What's the point? The man has suffered, physically and emotionally, I would imagine, for over sixty years. Would we go and confront him with our suspicions now? It wouldn't do Allan Roberts any good. If Nara or her father wants to know the man's name, they can ask for it. But I think they will agree that the best course of action is to let it go."

"I agree with you, Alex," Professor Jones added as he replaced his empty cup on the table. "When we walked in the door here, I was eager to know names, to put all the pieces together and bring the guilty party to justice. True – Allan Roberts died needlessly, but his name has been cleared, and to my mind, he was every bit as much a hero as his wife."

Lily looked from one man to the other. "All right. I suppose you are right. I admit I am curious, but at the same time, it is Nara's call." She turned to Headmaster Royce. "Thank you so much for seeing us."

Royce closed the folder and stood it on his desk to tap the papers into even alignment. "The information will be here if you, or the immediate family, ever want to know more. The school has changed considerably since the 1940s. I don't know who had the more difficult job, the administration during the war years, or us today."

Chapter 22

Nara and Alex had been driving since early in the morning, and had long ago left the traffic and frenetic pace of London behind. Now the mountains of Snowdonia National Park in northwest Wales rose above them. The two of them were silent as they let go of their city tension and gave in to the beauty around them.

"I can't think of any more beautiful place for a honeymoon," Nara said, looking straight ahead as Alex drove.

"You mean you don't want to go back to St. Clare? To the tropics?" Alex said quietly, his eyes on the road as it began to climb up into the mountains.

"I don't think so," she answered. "England is home now. All the people I love most are here. I want to move forward in my life, not backward."

Alex slowed the car and they waited and watched a herd of sheep cross the narrow road, followed by two sheep dogs intent on the work, and a sheep herder who gave them a wave as the group passed the car.

When they moved forward again, and Alex glanced at Nara, tears were rolling down her cheeks. "What's wrong, Nara?"

She turned and smiled at him through her tears. "Nothing really. It's just so beautiful here, and I feel such a strong connection to Lydia here in the place where she grew up. St. Clare is beautiful in one way, and Lincolnshire in another, but Wales has a wild richness that is – magnetic. And coming here and reading the diaries has put together some more of the pieces of my own life. Maybe one of these days I'll find out who I really am."

Alex took one hand off the wheel and reached for Nara's hand. "Can I be your partner in this search, Nara?" he said.

"I think I'm willing to give it a try," she said, tightening her grip on his hand momentarily, "but now we need to deal with my Aunt Rebeca." Nara removed her hand to fish for a tissue to wipe her eyes. "Are you ready for this?"

"I'm ready," Alex said. "Do you have the directions?"

"Straight through the village and then left," she said. "Drive all the way to the end. You can't miss it."

Moments later they pulled up in front of the stone house where Nara and Lily had taken possession of the boxes from Lydia Roberts just a few weeks before. As before, Barney the sheep dog was there to greet them, and Rebeca's son Evan stood quietly at the dog's side.

"Hi, Evan," Nara said as she climbed out of the car. "I'm your cousin Nara. Do you remember me?"

Evan smiled shyly, putting his hand on the dog's collar. "I'll tell Mom you are here." He started to walk toward the house, and then turned back. "Are you afraid of dogs?"

Both Nara and Alex said they were not, and Evan released Barney, who bounded over to the two visitors, wagging his tail and emitting short barks.

Evan stood at the door smiling at the scene. "That means he likes you."

A moment later Rebeca returned to the door with her son. "Come in. Tea is ready," she said. She looked nervous and not much friendlier than she had the last time Nara had visited. She had hoped that her aunt would be more open now that Nara's father Jack, Rebeca's nephew, had told her the whole story of what happened to her parents in the war.

Nothing had changed in the rustic house, except that Evan seemed more at ease than he had on the previous visit. He helped his mother serve the tea and slices of fresh bread and butter to go with it. When they had all been served and adjusted their tea with milk and sugar, Rebeca was the first to speak. "So it turned out there was a treasure in those boxes all these years," she said.

"Yes, there was," Nara answered. "And the diaries led us to the truth about what happened to your parents. Your mother especially was a real hero."

"Yes, she was," Rebeca said. She sipped her tea and seemed to struggle find her next words. "I have to tell you I have spent some sleepless nights since Jack told me about what happened to them. Here all these years I blamed them, Mother especially, for leaving us and then getting themselves killed. And then after I talked with Jack, and read the copy of the diaries he sent me, I see that she really loved us. She did what she thought was best. I hope somehow she knows and can forgive me."

Nara reached out her hand to Rebeca, but then pulled it back. She wasn't sure her aunt was ready for that kind of contact. "She was your mother, Aunt Rebeca. Mothers always forgive."

"And now we have something for you, Mrs. Williams," Alex said softly. "I know that Jack told you about the painting and the necklace that were found in the boxes. Since you, Jack and his sister Sue are the heirs, those things belong to you."

"Jack told me about those things," Rebeca said, her demeanor a practical one once again. "And I agree with him about the necklace, since it was such a personal gift, that we should keep it in the family, possibly lending it to museums if someone wishes to exhibit it. They could pay us a little money for the privilege." She smiled wryly, her mind always on ways to bring in a little extra cash to keep food on the table. "And he said the painting is a copy, so it isn't worth much, if anything."

"That's not quite true," Nara said, smiling at her aunt.

"What isn't?" she asked. She automatically touched Evan's hand. The young man was adding a large pat of butter to what must be his third slice of bread. "That's enough, Evan," she said quietly.

Alex wiped the butter off his fingers with a napkin. "It's true that the painting was a copy, but Cézanne often made several copies of the same painting himself, sometimes with slight changes, sometimes almost identical. I took the painting to some art experts in London, and we are quite certain that the painting that Lydia hid in the box is a copy that the artist made himself of 'The Willow Trees.' If you, along with Jack and Sue, were to sell it, it would probably be worth around £8,000,000."

Rebeca spilled her tea as she set the cup on the saucer. "£8,000,000? Whatever would I do with a third of £8,000,000?" she said.

"You could ensure that Evan is always well-cared for, for one thing," Nara said, hoping Rebeca did not take offence at her words.

"Yes, I could," she answered, her eyes focused off in the distance. "I could do that. And what do Jack and Sue think?"

"They believe it should be sold," Nara answered. "No one can afford to insure something like that. What are they going to do? Hang it in one of the guest bedrooms? Or store it away in a back vault where no one can enjoy it?"

Rebeca laughed along with Nara and Alex, and Evan looked up, not quite sure what the joke was, but happy to hear his mother laughing. "This will make a huge difference in our lives – mine and Evan's," Rebeca said.

After saying their goodbyes, Nara and Alex left the village and drove down the mountain toward Bangor. Neither spoke; they were content to admire the ever-changing light on the mountains, and think their own thoughts. Nara spoke first. "I think that Lydia would be happy at the way things turned out."

"I think so, too," Alex replied. "And I think Allan would too. They accomplished their goal. They helped ensure a future for their children, all the way down to their great-granddaughter." He smiled over at Nara.

"I wonder if we will be able to do the same?" Nara asked wistfully.

"Maybe," Alex answered, negotiating another hairpin turn. "If we can be as devoted to the truth as they were."

"That's it, isn't it, Alex? The truth. That's all that really matters."

The road wound down towards Bangor, and the sunlight played hide and seek with the clouds over the green hills. Blue lakes sparkled in the valleys, and the white dots on the hillside moved, showing that they were not rocks, but sheep. And the truth was what was real.

ABOUT THE AUTHOR

Kathleen Heady is a native of rural Illinois, but has lived and traveled, including numerous trips to Great Britain. Her articles on travel and education have appeared in in several publications such as *The International Educator*, *The Tico Times* (the English language newspaper in Costa Rica), and the *Philadelphia Inquirer*. Her first novel, *The Gate House,* was a finalist for an EPIC award in 2011. She currently lives in Pennsylvania with her husband and two cats.

Made in the USA
Lexington, KY
14 May 2013